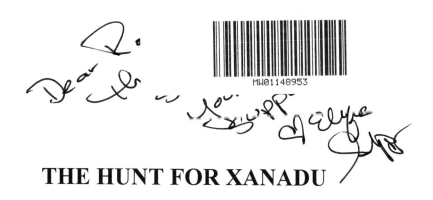

THE HUNT FOR XANADU

By Elyse Salpeter

ELYSE SALPETER

This book is a work of fiction. The names, characters, places and incidents are products of the author's imagination. While certain places are real, the incidences regarding them are works of the author.

Dedication

This book is dedicated to those in the social media and indie world who have been an incredible source of inspiration for me. I want to thank the members of WLC, #artknb, Team P, along with all my Facebook and Twitter friends. They've been an incredible resource, a shoulder to cry on, and simply, great friends.

I also want to thank my editor, Denise Vitola, who always helps me make my novels the best they can be. Frank Tuttle, for his physics knowledge and for overall being a great support and friend, Andrew Meyer for talking to me at length about Tibet and government, and Dean Mead for allowing me to pepper him with questions on Buddhism. I apologize to all of you in advance because I know all the great information I received I twisted around to suit the needs of the book, but your help was invaluable and I appreciate all of you so very much.

Table of Contents

THE HUNT FOR XANADU
By Elyse Salpeter

Prologue

Impermanent are all created things; Strive on with awareness. –
Siddhartha Gautama

India, 537 BC

From her perch atop the hill, Tanha watched the lone, starving man meditate under the Bodhi tree. How many men had attempted to go against her father and failed? More than she could count.

She turned to her sisters. The strand of exquisite black and pink pearls woven in her hair dazzled radiantly in the sunlight. "It's time to meet the rich, coddled fool. They say he was quite breathtaking once."

"He might have been once, but he's not much to look at now," Raga said. She crinkled her nose in distaste and her teardrop-shaped ruby bindi nearly disappeared into the folds of her brow.

Her sister, Arati, huffed and tossed back her black mane. "If that peasant girl hadn't fed him, he'd be dead by now. I have better things to do than Father's silly little errands."

Tanha ignored the banter of her sisters and studied Siddhartha. Before her was a man who wanted nothing more than for human suffering to end. Was that so bad?

She frowned as that strange thought tickled her brain. She wanted to let the idea linger awhile longer, but she was distracted by what was to come. It was what she had been born to do. "Come, sisters. It's time to destroy yet another man's soul."

As they glided down to Siddhartha, their exotic scents permeated the air. He stirred and his chest expanded with a deep, barely controlled breath. Raga alighted next to him and traced her long, painted red fingernails up and down his arm. He flinched at her sensual touch, but kept his eyes closed and continued to meditate.

"Losing your touch, sister?" Arati teased. She stepped before Siddhartha and removed her clothing piece by piece, until her exquisite body was on display. Then, she began to sing, a seductive tune so hauntingly beautiful the man had no choice but to respond. He opened his eyes wide and watched her dancing provocatively in time to her alluring melody. His eyes misted, but then he swallowed hard and shook his head. With extreme effort, he closed his eyes and pulled his desires back under control.

Surprised at his resistance, both girls turned to Tanha.

With a knowing grin, Tanha brazenly straddled his lap. She leaned towards him and unable to stop himself, his breath quickened. She let her long black hair flow around her body and envelop them both. "Siddhartha, don't fight me," she purred. "Leave this silly quest and I'll grant you with carnal pleasures beyond imagination. I am Tanha, Daughter of Desire, and can fulfill your every wish." She ran her lips up and down his jawline.

Siddhartha moaned and squeezed his eyes shut, but his hands found her hips and held her there.

"That's right. Don't resist me. You can't. No man can." Tanha placed her mouth on his. His body responded and he returned her kiss. Then to her astonishment, he pulled back.

"You test me terribly, temptress, but I will not be swayed. I must not yield to you." He stared at her longingly and Tanha leaned towards him again.

Siddhartha shook his head. "No, I won't let you do this to me. To humanity. You and your sisters should return to Mara where you belong." His gaze lingered on her a moment longer, his expression suddenly curious. "Unless that is, you wish to join me?"

Tanha's eyes widened in bewilderment. "Join you? Why would I do that?"

Siddhartha stared at her and then smiled sadly. "Then you must leave, mistress. There is nothing for you here right now." With that, he closed his eyes and ignored her, falling deep into a trance.

Stunned, Tanha stared at the man who had the will to go against her. Was that even possible? A strange, uneasy feeling crept into her gut. "This is not over. I will be back," she whispered, and with a puff, she and her sisters vanished, to let her father fight his own battles.

As Tanha watched from her decadent palace in the depths of the hell realm, no matter what Mara sent, be it demons, monsters or torrential storms, Siddhartha could not be swayed. To her utter amazement she watched his mind grow clear. He reached the state of perfect enlightenment and became a Buddha.

Finally, she could put a word to how she felt about it.

Envy.

Chapter 1

Present Day

Hidden in the security camera's blind spot, she sucked in her gut, closed her eyes and listened intently. *"Come on, already,"* she thought, drumming her fingertips rapidly against the brick wall. She heard the dogs panting now. This sound had replaced the earlier frenzy of them tearing into the drugged, raw hamburger she had thrown over the fence just twenty minutes before. She'd crushed thirty-six Acepromozin tablets into the ground meat, reckoning it would be enough to knock out the four guard dogs, if not kill them outright.

She glanced at her watch and waited. *This is taking so long.* Five more minutes passed, with nothing sounding except the soft, rotating click of the camera. Abruptly, she yanked down the protective goggles resting on her head and placed them over her eyes. The clicking now echoed loudly, indicating the camera was once more faced in her direction. Brazenly she stood, aimed her laser gun and pointed it directly into the lens. The high tech, silicon-based CCD camera had an impressive wavelength sensitivity. The laser's high-powered emitter instantly saturated the pixels of the camera's CCD sensor and burned the chip out instantly.

Ricardo Perez thought he protected himself with the best of everything. He'd under-estimated meeting an assassin so invested in seeing him dead.

Hooking the laser into her belt loop, she flung her knapsack over her shoulders and scaled the wall in a practiced leap. She balanced delicately on the edge to prevent being punctured by the barbed wire and slipped on a pair of leather gloves, grabbed the wire cutters hanging from her backpack and snipped her way through. In less than twenty seconds, she was inside the backyard of the compound. Three of the dogs lay unconscious in the grass nearby, but their twitching feet told her they were still alive. *Where is the other one?*

A deep, menacing growl came from behind her and she whirled to face the remaining Doberman. She had just enough time to register the bits of bloody hamburger still clinging to its snout before it lunged. Her instincts kicked in and she did the only thing she could remember. She punched the animal savagely in its throat like she'd been taught, and it fell to the ground, dead.

Breathing hard, she turned back to the house where Ricardo had hoped to escape from her. Her body shook and she took a deep breath, trying to keep her anger in check. This man couldn't expect to destroy her family and get away with it. He was going to pay.

She moved past the koi pond, stopping only to disable the second security camera with her laser.

She passed the kidney-shaped pool and skirted around the cabana, her eyes never leaving the house. Shadows moved behind the curtained windows on the second floor. At the sound of a sliding door opening, she dove behind a hedge. A well-muscled guard moved onto the balcony and lit a cigarillo. Its smell traveled to her in the gentle breeze. She held back a cough and brushed a wayward blond strand out of her face.

The guard scanned the perimeters, then took out his cell phone and sat back on a lounge chair to make a call. Sweet nothings floated down to her and she took that moment to leap across the hedge and race to the side of the house, hiding herself in the back door portico. She edged around the building until she located the final camera attached to the roof above a spare bedroom. Too far for her laser's range.

She waited until the camera scanned another part of the property and then got to work. She pulled out a long rope from her backpack which she attached to a grappling hook. With a precision borne from hours upon hours of practice, she tossed up the hook and snagged the end over the bedroom's balcony railing. With a jerk, the rope pulled taut and the hook locked in place. Fifteen seconds later she was standing on the terrace.

The clicking camera indicated it was again in range. She leaned around the corner of the wall, aimed her laser and disabled it.

She left her bag and goggles on the terrace and moved to the sliding door leading into the bedroom. It was locked, which wasn't a surprise. The girl leaned her head against the glass, her breath fogging the window, and noticed there was no security bar holding it shut. *That was a mistake, Ricardo.* She removed a set of lock picks from her pack and sixty seconds later broke in.

The house was quiet. With infinite care, she made her way across the room to the bedroom door. She cracked it open, pulling her pistol and stun gun from their holsters. She already knew the layout of the house from her research. There were four bedrooms and two bathrooms on the second floor with a wide hallway opening over the front foyer downstairs. The plush, cream-colored wall-to-wall carpeting, that stretched through every room, was an added benefit. Now she wouldn't have to worry about her footsteps making any noise. The lighting was good, too. An enormous, glittering chandelier hung from the foyer ceiling and lit the entire area with a yellow glow. She peered into Ricardo's bedroom and heard him speak to one of his guards. The sound of his voice made goosebumps on her arms.

"Pablo, go get us a couple of beers."

The guard came out of the bedroom and as he passed her room, she jumped on him and released the stun gun. He barely had time to cry out before she hit him violently in the side of his head with the butt of her gun, silencing him. He fell unconscious to the floor. With great effort, she dragged him by his feet into the bedroom. Thankfully, he wasn't as large as the first guard she had seen or it would have been much harder. In less than a minute, he was trussed up like a Thanksgiving turkey.

She moved quickly down the hall towards Ricardo's room, her pistol in one hand, the stun gun in the other. She peeked inside. Ricardo had moved to the balcony.

What happened next came down fast.

"The dogs are too quiet," the remaining bodyguard said. A whistle sounded and when none of the Dobermans responded, she could distinctly hear him click his gun's safety. "The cameras are dark, too. Ricardo, stay here."

The guard moved across the room and out into the hallway, shocked to see her simply standing there. With a startled shout, he fired at her, but she feinted to the right and fired back. Her heel slipped slightly on the carpet and messed up her aim. She hit him in his hip, rather than his chest. *Dammit to hell.*

The guard fell to the floor with a yell, but fired again, the bullet ricocheting off the wall behind her. She took that moment to pounce upon him, kneeing him fiercely in his groin. He tried to hit her with the butt of his gun and she delivered a brutal elbow strike to his cheek, shattering it. He shrieked, bringing his gun up again. She shoved the stun gun in his side and fired the full voltage.

A bullet whisked by her head, shattering the picture frame on the wall next to her. She flinched and glimpsed Ricardo shooting wildly from behind the door. Their gazes met and fear filled his eyes. With a squeal, he ran back into his bedroom and disappeared from view.

Her adrenaline pumped through her veins and his fear spurred her on. *Run and hide, you coward.* With a savage smile, she raced after him.

The hunt was on.

Chapter 2

STALKED

The West Village Starbucks was crowded that February morning, filled with professors and students from NYU grabbing their caffeine fixes before heading to class. Her backpack loaded with textbooks, Kelsey Porter weaved her way delicately through the swarm. Wearing dark blue jeans, black calf-high leather boots and a black leather jacket, she blended in like any other New Yorker in the coffee shop. Well, mostly she did.

She knew she was attractive. Beautiful, actually. She had high cheekbones and a heart shaped face and her skin was like porcelain. But it was her deep blue eyes she thought were her best feature. Her parents used to tell her she looked just like a fairy tale princess. Her dad actually called her Princess Kel Kel to make her giggle. She didn't feel much like a naïve little princess these days and wondered briefly what he'd think of her multiple ear piercings, blood red lips, black nail polish and a tattoo of an Egyptian Ankh above her left ankle. She was pretty sure he wouldn't have liked any of it.

She paid for her latte and couldn't help smirking at the shy counter clerk who could barely look her in the eye. Oh, how she loved playing with him. She leaned towards him, her jacket opening and her cleavage peeking from her V-neck T-shirt. "Hey, Jessie, you're looking super cute today. Is that some new flair on your hat?" The guy turned tomato red and mumbled something unintelligible. *Oh, why do I love torturing this guy so much?*

She considered pushing him further, but decided to give him a break. "See you tomorrow, Beautiful." She dropped a dollar into his tip jar as payment for her obnoxious flirting. As she made her way out of the shop, she turned back and took a mental note of the layout.

It was a game she played each morning. She'd select a location and then later, during breaks between classes, she'd recreate the scene on paper. It was her own mental exercise to keep her mind sharp.

That afternoon, between Arson Investigations and Human Behavior, both courses needed for her Master's degree in Forensics, she recreated the store on her sketch pad. She envisioned the serving bar, the three baristas, the two cashiers. In went the tables, six small round ones, customers on the two chairs at each one. The two green velour couches, filled with lounging guests reading newspapers and chatting. Brunettes with long hair tied back in ponytail holders and clips, blonds, a redhead with purple streaks, a really loud guy with a Mohawk and multiple piercings, a cute businessman immersed in his computer, Asians, African-Americans--in went everyone with all their idiosyncrasies. She was a talented artist with an exceptional eye and attention to detail. It was one of the reasons she was studying forensics. She had a burning need to solve things.

That evening as she strolled home to her apartment in Chelsea, she passed a man on a bench reading a newspaper. She tried not to pay him too much mind, and casually walked by him, humming a tune from her iPod.

She recognized him as one of the patrons from Starbucks that morning. He'd been engrossed in his computer, but she remembered his mop of thick and unruly brown hair and his handsome, wide-set features. She recalled the scene and was

14

certain it was the same businessman on the computer. Coincidence? She didn't think so.

She didn't believe in them. Not even a little.

Later that evening, she left her building through a basement side door which led to an alley on the next block. She circled back to her residence. The man was there, huddled in the doorway of a neighboring basement apartment, his gaze transfixed on her apartment window. She wasn't scared, like you'd expect a young girl to be when a stranger was stalking her. Instead, she was curious, wondering who he was and why he was following her. A quiver of excitement ran up her spine.

She decided to keep to her routine the next day. Starbucks, class, the gym, and then back home. While the stalker kept his distance, she noticed him two more times. He tried to blend into the crowd, but with that mop of hair she could pick him out easily. She had to remember both times not to stare too long at him and give herself away. But she could see him staring at her.

That night, sitting on the floor of her apartment on an orange plush pillow, she gazed at the small golden statue of the Buddha which sat on the coffee table in front of her. Fingering the smooth jade and opal beads on the bracelet on her wrist and twisting the silver rings on her fingers, she closed her eyes and took a few moments to reflect on her next moves. She opened them, at peace and content with her decision. It would set them both on even ground and she could find out what he wanted.

And how much he knew.

* * * * *

12 years earlier:

Location: TAR People's Hospital, Lingkhor Bei Lu northeast of Potala, Tibet

"*Mr. & Mrs. Goldman, I'm Dr. Shamar Chen. I'm sorry, but there's nothing more we can do for her. When you return to The States, I'm afraid she'll need to be institutionalized. It's the only humane thing to be done.*"

Mrs. Goldman sobbed quietly into a tissue. Wiping her eyes, she shook her head and held her husband's hand. "No, I can't do that to her. She'll come live with us. I'm qualified to take care of her."

The doctor shook his head. "She's been brutally traumatized and has been completely unresponsive for nearly two weeks. I'm not sure she will ever recover. She'll require extensive care."

Mr. Goldman spoke up, his voice soft. "Ever? No, we're her Godparents and her parents..." He couldn't finish and leaned over, placing his face in his hands. His wife squeezed his shoulders, giving him strength. Mr. Goldman sighed heavily and looked back at the doctor. "Even if she doesn't recover, we'll be there for her. It's what her mother and father would have wanted. Please have her released to our care."

"*As you wish. I'll sign the papers and you'll be free to take her home within the hour," he said. He stood up and left the room.*

The Goldmans turned to look upon the young child lying in the bed. The bright eyed, precocious little girl they'd known since infancy was now a former shadow of herself--so small, so pale, and so very still. Her big blue eyes stared unblinking at the ceiling from below a dressing wrapped around her forehead. With both her arms and one of her legs broken, she was a mass of bandages and casts. The only things that

16

moved were her fingers, up and down, up and down, making a continuous wave with the digits, fluttering over and over.

"What is she doing, Claire?"

"I don't know, Martin. I just don't know." They watched the child and her ceaseless movements, wondering how they were ever going to bring her back to reality, to heal from the horror she had experienced. How they were ever going to make her well.

Martin leaned over and placed his hands over the girl's fingers and they stilled. "Come back to us, angel." He released her hands, but within seconds, the dance continued.

It didn't stop.

Chapter 3

THE ENCOUNTER

The noise in the museum that evening was tumultuous, like a thousand voices caught in a maelstrom. Laughter and dialogue competed with each other as their echoes bounced through the corridors emanating within the cavernous space. The museum lights cast an exotic glow, making it both eerie and exceptional and throwing mammoth, distorted shadows along the pink marble floors and walkways. An impressive amount of illuminated treasures lined the walls.

Several exhibits were installed, markers discretely posted on free standing displays at the front of each corridor, but Kelsey had eyes for one thing only. She made her way through various galleries until she stood within the Tibetan exhibit. The room itself had been transformed. Decorated with hanging cloths and colorful silk sheets, it gave the room the appearance of the ancient gher tents Buddhist monks used for their traveling temples. Delicate Thangka scrolls adorned the walls along with numerous presentation posts. Some of the picture panels were embroidered and covered with silk, while others were ornately painted. All the scrolls had images of the Buddha, bodhisattvas or other deities on them. Kelsey stared around the room, recognizing the overwhelming theme of "The Wheel of Life," which was the Buddha's teachings of enlightenment. It was something near and dear to her heart and she felt comforted by simply standing in the room.

Her gaze strayed to the far wall where a ten foot copper statue of the Buddha, borrowed from a monastery in Mongolia, had been placed. Kelsey closed her eyes and took a moment to collect her thoughts. She breathed deeply and smiled.

Opening her eyes, she moved past the guards, the heels of her black boots clacking loudly on the marble floor. Many of the guards turned to her and she noted there were definitely more in attendance than normal, but you couldn't blame the museum for being overly cautious. Everything had to go perfectly for tomorrow's event.

She strolled towards the middle of the room where a set of monks worked on a five foot diameter sand mandala of incomparable beauty and complexity.

Two weeks earlier the museum began this exhibit, inviting Tibetan monks from the Wat Jokhang-Ling Monastery in the Catskills to work on this multifaceted masterpiece. They painstakingly laid millions of grains of colored sand, shaping them into hundreds of deities and a vision of the Buddha; a healing mandala to help the masses of people suffering in the world at this time. They were expecting to complete it by the next day and there would be a ceremony given by the Dalai Lama himself, who was traveling from India to New York City to lead a series of seminars on "The Art of Happiness." He'd be the one conducting the destruction of the mandala at the end of the ceremony.

Kelsey stood before the monks, their facial masks locked in place so a wayward breath wouldn't disrupt their creation. She was fascinated as she watched them use small tubes, funnels and scrapers to create their masterpiece. Their patience to the craft stunned her. Patience was not one of her strongest virtues. She couldn't imagine dropping grains of colored sand one granule at a time for hours and hours upon end. Only during meditation could she let herself relax completely and even then she couldn't do it for too long before her mind started its incessant whirl of crazy thoughts.

Visitors milled all around her, sometimes turning to stare in her direction and not at the display. She ignored them. People always stared at her and she was used to it. She twirled her dark brown braid in her fingers, turning her head this way and that, as if she were deep in thought, but she was really waiting for the stranger who had been stalking her the past two days.

A figure soon appeared at her side. *Ah, there you are. About time.* She felt his presence in a way that told her this wasn't just a random encounter.

"Did you know," the man began casually, "these monks had to undergo five years of training before they were even allowed to become sand mandala artists? Not to mention they had to learn all the rituals and all the oral texts. It's considered quite an honor to be chosen to create a mandala of this complexity."

Kelsey glanced over her shoulder at the man, craning her neck upwards to see his face. Yes, it was him, though he was taller than she'd originally thought, pegging him to be about six feet two. He was also significantly broader and more handsome, too, with what looked like a three-day growth of beard creating a dark shadow on his jaw. His full lips were posed in a quirky smile making him appear youthful. She couldn't fixate on his age, but she estimated him to be in his early thirties. She glanced at his unruly mop of brown hair, but it was his remarkable eyes that drew her in. They were a blue-green, with flecks of yellow dotting through them, making them appear to shine and sparkle.

With an effort, she pulled her gaze away and back to the artists.

Her stalker spoke again. "They say mandalas contain instructions by the Buddha himself for attaining enlightenment. That his very essence is in each painting and it's why dismantling it requires such a detailed ceremony. The media coverage is going to be relentless tomorrow for the procession to the East River where they'll scatter the sand into the water, releasing the mandala's healing powers back to nature."

Is he trying to impress me? Sure, of course he is. She couldn't stifle an amused grin and buoyed, he continued. "You know, each color and symbol has a deep meaning. See the blue thunderbolt?" He pointed, leaning towards her.

She caught a whiff of his cologne. It was an intoxicating, woodsy scent with exotic hints of patchouli and sandalwood. She'd never smelled anything like it before. *Man, that's nice, too. This is weird.*

He continued. "That represents compassion. The peaches on the upper corner symbolize taste and the band of lotus flowers signify purity." He glanced at a curtained section of the room where a guard checked the I.D. of visitors, confirming they were above eighteen years of age. "I'm surprised they convinced the museum board to add a display on tantric art for this exhibit. It's amazing how lenient the benefactors of the MET have become, isn't it?" He smiled and Kelsey remarked on how the right side tilted up more than the other, creating a dimple on his cheek.

"Up the attendance, and the exhibit is considered a success," Kelsey said. "Money's a good motivation for many things." She wondered when he was going to get to the point. She was sure he hadn't been following her just to discuss Tibetan Art Symbolism. *Time to make something happen.* "Thanks for the art history lesson. If you'll excuse me." She moved off to the right side of the exhibit and skipped behind a partition, wondering if he would follow. A display table was laid out on the other side with appetizers. She picked up a small moma, a Tibetan dumpling, and popped it in her mouth, savoring the taste. She moved along the table and took a sample of some warm buttered tea. *They got the food right. This is authentic.* As she sipped, she closed her eyes and could almost imagine she was a little girl, back in the gardens of Tibet. She could hear the tinkling of the monks' porcelain teacups and the yips of the spaniels as they raced throughout the monastery. Oh, how she had loved it there.

A gentle hand touched her shoulder and she sighed inwardly. So much for reminiscing. She turned to her stalker. "Yes?" she asked, innocently.

"I'm sorry, I should have introduced myself sooner. My name is Desmond Gisborne and I'm a New York City Police Detective." He reached into his suit pocket and flashed his badge.

She feigned surprise and took a hesitant step back. "Is there a problem?"

Desmond shook his head. "No, it's just I was hoping you could clear something up for me. You see, I'm working on a case and I think you might be able to help me."

Kelsey raised her eyebrows. "Well, sure, I guess. What can I do for you?"

The cop stared around at the crowd of people. "How about we find somewhere not so busy?"

Kelsey shrugged, threw her paper cup into the trash receptacle, and walked with him through the exhibit. He led her towards the tantric art presentation. That was fine with her.

They moved inside.

* * * * *

The little girl sat on the bed, her legs stretched out before her, her navy blue eyes wide open and staring into nothingness. A thin stream of drool suspended from her mouth and Claire Goldman gently wiped it away with a tissue. Only the child's fingers moved, fluttering in their ceaseless dance, the beaded jade and opal bracelet her father had given her tied securely with red string on her wrist. It had been a gift meant to bring the child good luck and good health and Kelsey had been wearing it when they found her. Claire cringed at the irony.

They had tended to her for over a month and they couldn't break her catatonia. Only at night did things change. In the wee hours of the morning, the screaming would begin. Nightmare induced shrieks so hideous the entire house shook from their torment. You could hear the absolute misery in her cries, feel the very torture she must have endured, but no matter what they tried to do, they could never get through to her or wake her up. She would scream and sob for hours, shouting out gibberish words, unintelligible to anyone but her, yet packed with such raw emotion and wretched misery, Claire would just sit outside her room and cry from the sheer heartbreak of listening to it.

It was like nothing she'd ever experienced in her twenty-two years as a child psychologist. She'd never encountered a situation this severe and she was determined to help this little girl. They met with doctor after doctor for consultations over the past few weeks, but not one had a clue as to what to do. "Institutionalization" floated in the air, words like "electric shock therapy" and "vagus nerve stimulation," but one look from Claire and those lines of thought were quickly abandoned. The only healing she'd been able to accomplish was getting the little girl's arm and leg casts off. At least her bones had healed well, and she was thankful for that. But how to help the ten year old heal after witnessing the murder of her parents and then being attacked by five men? She didn't know.

It was late, nearly eleven o'clock and Claire readied to put the little girl down for the evening. She had never met a child who slept so little. The bed creaked as her twelve year old son,

Ari, came in and sat down next to her. Claire turned to face him and gave him a tired smile as she wiped a stray strand of hair from his forehead. He was getting so big.

"You should be in bed by now, young man."

He bit his lip. "Mom, I want to try something. Do you mind?"

Claire peered at him questioningly, but nodded. "Sure, honey." She didn't hold out much hope as she slid off the bed.

Ari inched closer to the little girl until their faces were only inches apart. And then he spoke.

"Tedanalee."

Kelsey sucked in her breath and froze. Her fingers ceased moving.

Shocked, Claire raced to her side, placing her hand on her shoulder. "Kelsey, are you ok? Can you hear us?"

When Kelsey didn't react to her, Claire turned to her son. "What did you just say to her?"

Ignoring his mother, Ari turned back to Kelsey, staring into her unblinking eyes and spoke slowly, enunciating the words. "Tam ne tli Tedanalee."

Kelsey's eyes widened and she started shaking. Suddenly she turned her gaze to Ari, focusing so strongly on him that the intensity and lucidity in her expression took Claire aback. "Li, ti tli Tedanalee!" She started screaming, her fingers bunching into fists.

Ari shook his head sadly. "Ne, ne," he said softly.

Kelsey threw herself forward and violently pushed Ari backwards, throwing him off the bed. "Kalam nenot!" she shrieked. Then she sat back, rocking back and forth so forcibly the bedframe made a loud thump as it rammed against the wall. Her fingers began to move again ceaselessly. Within seconds she calmed, again the same mute child she had been only moments before, the intense clarity in her eyes replaced by the vapid stare they'd come to expect.

24

Martin Goldman stood in the doorway, where he'd been watching the exchange in shocked silence. He leaned down and helped his son off the floor. "What just happened?"

Ari stood up, took a piece of paper out of his pocket and unfolded it. "When Kelsey first came here and started screaming at night, I didn't notice anything, except how awful it was. Like someone was torturing her, but it was all senseless, nonsense words. After a few weeks of listening to them over and over, some words started to sound familiar to me, so I started writing them down. I mean, it's not like you can sleep once she starts." He showed the paper to his parents. "It's just like when I was learning Spanish and Hebrew. After a while, the words don't sound like gibberish all bunched together. Suddenly, you can start separating the words from one another. I started thinking maybe what she was yelling was really another language, but it's not one I've ever heard before. I even googled the words and checked out all these linguistic sites. None of them are popping ;up."

Martin scanned the sheet. Over twenty distinct words, with possible meanings, were written there in his son's perfect script. "Tedanalee means 'the place', tli means 'in',"" Martin read. "You know what this list implies if you're right, Ari?"

"Yeah, it means Kelsey's been speaking in a new language from a land called Tedanalee. And look here." He took another piece of paper from his pocket and unfolded it. It was a drawing of a butterfly, alien and colorful, but with wings curved in a strange, swirly fashion, as if it had come from another world. "When you were bringing over her things last week, I started looking through all the drawings she'd made in Tibet. I mean, she's like this amazing artist and I thought maybe there would be something in there which could help us. She's drawn all these crazy animals and plants and there are pictures of places that are definitely not a part of our world. It's like a fantasy reality."

Claire sucked in her breath. "Yes! That's it! She's escaped to an imaginary internal world. How could I not have seen this? Ari, you're absolutely brilliant."

Claire stared at Kelsey with renewed eyes, bright with excitement. "I think I finally have a plan to bring her back."

Chapter 4

SECRETS

They showed their ID and stepped past the guard and into the exhibit. The artwork was set up on a long, meandering path, to give one the impression you were strolling through a country garden. Sculptures of deities, statues of the Buddha, and large potted flowers dotted the colorful tiled walkway.

On display was an exquisite selection, ranging from Batik paintings on cotton fabric and watercolors on paper, to Thangka paintings. A multitude of sculpted brass displays were prominently displayed between the other artwork.

They moved along the pathway slowly, taking in the breathtaking images. Kelsey smiled in enjoyment as they passed the displays. She had always had an affinity for tantric art. There was something about it that spoke to her deep in her being. Everyone thought it had to only do with sex, but she knew tantric paintings were a celebration of one's inner soul and energy. They represented the body's window to the world, allowing the soul to flow anyplace it needed to get nourishment. If it had to do with sex for some, so be it. To Kelsey it was about a person's emotional response to things and an ability to recognize how one felt and what one needed, spiritually or physically, at any given time.

Desmond stood in front of an Indian Kama Sutra painting. It depicted a loving couple in the act of copulating.

Kelsey shook her head at their complicated position. *That's impossible. People just can't bend that way. Wait a second, could they?* A vaguely familiar thought flicked in the back of her mind and she tried to catch it, but it disappeared. She shook her head. *Stop it. Not now.* Things like this happened all the time to her. Her mind always raced with crazy ideas and thoughts that seemed to spur out of nowhere. At times she'd become so occupied with them she vaguely wondered if she were the most creative person on the planet or simply borderline schizophrenic.

Desmond stared at it silently for a few more seconds and then turned to her, his eyes shining brightly.

"You like tantric art?" Kelsey asked, skeptically.

"What's not to like?" He stared at her as if he were trying to figure something out about her, or make her say something. She didn't take the bait and waited him out, noticing how calm he appeared. Here he'd been stalking her for two days, finally had her alone, and he didn't seem nervous or unsure of himself in the least. In fact, his demeanor was the very opposite. He was relaxed and composed, and it intrigued her. Everything about him radiated confidence and power. She didn't encounter many people with that kind of aura about them.

She moved to a bench and he sat down next to her. She planned on starting a conversation about the philosophy of tantric art when Desmond pulled aside his jacket, took out a sheaf of photos, and laid them in her lap.

Remaining outwardly cool, Kelsey glanced at the photos curiously. She then looked up at Desmond innocently. "Yes?"

He smiled, and she remarked again on how quirky it was. *Why do I keep checking out his smile? Especially right now? Focus, Kelsey!*

She turned her head back as he pointed to the photo on the top, his voice now at odds with the amusement on his face. "The woman in this photograph is responsible for a murder in

Florida that happened three days ago. And, I believe this woman is you."

Kelsey hoped her expression was incredulous. "Me? What makes you think this is me?" She picked up the photo, which was a snapshot of a girl on an airport security line at Miami International Airport. She wore a baseball cap covering long blond hair.

Kelsey handed him back the snapshot and all the photos disappeared back in his jacket. "Are you serious?"

Desmond nodded. "Deadly serious."

Kelsey shook her head. "That girl doesn't look anything like me and I haven't been to Florida since I was seven years old when my folks took me to Disney World. Sorry, but you have the wrong person."

Desmond said nothing and just continued his intense stare. Finally, he spoke. "Do you want to know what this woman did?"

She crossed her arms. "No, not really."

There was a brief silence between them as some museum visitors strolled by, giggling into their hands and pointing at the artwork. Once they passed, Desmond turned to Kelsey again. "Well, I think you should." He took another photo out of his jacket and showed it to her, revealing the same woman on an airport security line in JFK. "Three days ago this woman traveled from JFK airport in New York, flew to Miami and then went to the home of Ricardo Perez, second-in-command to Raul Salazar, leader of the Colombian drug operation in the United States. She disabled the camera security system, broke through the barbed wire, and disposed of four guard dogs. Then she broke into the house, subdued and tied up one of Ricardo's guards, shot and beat the other so badly he is now in critical condition in ICU at Miami hospital. Then, she tortured and killed Ricardo before she ransacked the home. We believe she stole a computer disc that contained the translation of an ancient Buddhist text. After that, she flew home."

He sat back, a satisfied look on his face.

Kelsey stood up, her voice rising angrily. "Do I even look like I could do something like that?"

Ignoring the questioning stares of the other museum visitors, she took off her jacket and threw it on the floor, showing off her size four figure. *Enjoy, Detective Desmond.* To her surprise, he didn't stare at her D-cups, the way most men did, and kept his eyes trained on her face. *Gee, look at you. Congratulations, you've got some control.*

"Seriously, do I seem like I'm capable of beating up three men? I'm 5' 6" and 120 pounds soaking wet. The most exercise I do is jog in Central Park and three days ago I was at NYU taking a Forensics Statistics midterm exam, or didn't you check up on that? Oh, and I was also at a midterm party that night at *Impressions*. How in the hell do you think I could possibly have done all you're accusing me of? What, I've got this alter ego and I'm a superstar spy agent or something?"

Desmond glanced at one of the museum's security guards who now stared in their direction. "I suggest you lower your voice. Will you please sit down?"

Kelsey settled back onto the bench, huffing.

Desmond considered her for a minute and then leaned in, his voice a whisper. "And regardless of your elaborate acting skills, I think you did do it, and here's how. You took your exam and you completed it early. I did check and you got an "A" by the way. Then you put a blond wig over that braided black mane of yours, got rid of all the makeup and the black nail polish, changed your clothes and then shot over to JFK where you took the 11:15 a.m. Delta flight to Miami, landing at 2:17 p.m.. You went straight to Ricardo's address, disabled his security system and poisoned the dogs, but not before you were seen on one of the outside monitors from the street and taped. You subdued Ricardo and his men, beat them senseless, took what you needed and then made the 4:45 flight back to JFK, where you landed at 7:02, came home, changed and made it to *Impressions* by at least 8:35 pm, regardless of your name not being on either plane's manifest." He pulled out another photo and placed it on the bench. It was a shot of Kelsey at *Impressions* with her best friend, Julia, both of them mugging for the camera at the bar. A digital clock behind them glowed 8:35 in red neon.

Kelsey was stunned, but hid it. *How the hell did he get that photo? Damn, Julia must have tagged her on Facebook.* "You're absolutely crazy, you know that?"

Desmond was silent, but suddenly the mood in the room changed and Kelsey went on alert, her survival instincts kicked into high gear. Twelve years of intense martial arts training taught her hyperawareness and she knew deep in her core something was going to happen. The very air seemed charged. Suddenly, everything moved in slow motion. She could see Desmond's arm muscles tensing, the slight arch in his eyebrows, the subtle shift of his hips as they were about to lift from the bench.

I can't believe he's going to do this, right here in the middle of all these people. Doing her best not to react, she froze, watching Desmond jump off of the seat, lightning fast, and land an open handed smack to her face.

She could have blocked him. It would have been so easy to, but she knew it would be the worst thing she could do. *The sheer audacity of this guy!* She took the hit, letting the force of it cause her to fall backward off the bench and onto the marble floor where it connected with the back of her skull. *Okay, that hurt.*

As she lay there, playing stunned, she noticed many things. Visitors screaming, others with their hands covering their mouths in shock. Desmond stood stock still, his own

31

hand still raised, his face a mask of utter confusion and incredulity. A guard ran towards her.

The sounds of her fake sobs filled the gallery. The guard tried to help Kelsey to a sitting position and she held onto him protectively as she stood up. "Get this guy away from me. He's a crazy pervert!"

The guard stared at Desmond, gripping his walkie-talkie.

Desmond finally moved, whipping out his badge. "I'm a police officer. I was just questioning her." He took a hesitant step forward.

Kelsey flinched fearfully and jumped behind the guard so he was between her and Desmond.

The guard glanced at Kelsey, his gaze suddenly suspicious, but he still moved his arms around her shoulders protectively. "Is she under arrest? Did she do something?"

Desmond shook his head. "No, she's not. She didn't do anything. "

"Then why'd you hit her?"

"It was an... accident," Desmond said.

Kelsey wrapped her arm around the guard's waist. She leaned in, whispering in his ear. "He's been following me all around the museum. He tried to touch me and when I wouldn't let him, he hit me. Please don't leave me alone with him." Her cheek felt swollen from where Desmond had slapped her.

The officer glared at Desmond. "If you don't need her, then I think you should leave the museum. I'll see her out myself... *Detective.*"

Desmond nodded, never taking his eyes off Kelsey. Indecision flooded his features as he turned and quickly moved out of the gallery. Once he was gone, Kelsey thanked the guard profusely, put on her coat and asked the guard to accompany her until she found a cab.

As she got into the taxi, she waited until they were moving downtown before taking out her cell phone and dialing Julia. Her friend picked up on the first ring.

"So?"

"Jules, you're not going to believe this. He pinned me." Her heart beat hard against her chest.

Julia sucked in her breath. "Who? The guy following you? He knows it was you in Miami? How and who is he?"

"He's a cop and we missed a camera. Looks like he had a sting going on with Ricardo and it's how he pegged me. Talk about bad timing. The guy tracked me all the way back to New York and followed me to the MET exhibit tonight, thinking he knew everything, but now he's not so sure."

"Why? What did you do?"

Kelsey huffed and twirled the ring on her finger. "What I always do. I pretended. But this one's smart, Jules. Really intriguing and confident."

There was silence on the other end. Finally Julia spoke. "Oh, my God. Don't tell me you like him."

"What are you talking about?" Kelsey said.

Julia groaned. "There's something in your voice. Listen, don't go falling for this guy just because he figured out something you thought you'd kept hidden. As you know, you're not the only genius in this world. This man's been tracking you for days and trying to pin a murder on you. He's dangerous, a cop no less, and could screw things up for us."

Kelsey snorted. "Please, the guy's cute, but he's an ass. He's over-confident and thinks he's god's gift to detective work. You know what he did to try to pin me to the job? He hit me, Jules, thinking I would stop him. Right in the middle of the Tantric exhibit at the MET. He knocked me right off a bench and onto the marble floor!"

"Are you crazy? You let this man touch you?"

"Damned right I did. It screwed up his well-laid little scenario and now he has no idea about anything. Ari's plan was perfect. Or, nearly perfect." Kelsey bit her lip, thinking. *Something isn't right.* "What I want to know is why this cop was so interested in Ricardo in the first place? I mean, why would a New York City Police Detective be tracking a drug dealer, with my disc, in Miami? Unless he was after the same thing, but I don't see how that's possible. Who else even knows about this disc except us and the monks in Tibet?"

"I didn't think anyone else knew," Julia said. "But, at least that bastard, Ricardo, is dead. Fourth one down, Kelsey. It's just Raul left and you've already got one of the discs. You're almost there."

"It's not finished until I get rid of Raul and find Xanadu, Jules. That's all that matters."

"Patience. You can't kill him yet. We still need things from him."

"I know. But once I get my hands on all of it, it's open season on him."

"Hey," Julia said, brightening up and changing the topic. "You're coming to Bazaar's on Tuesday, right?"

"Of course. It's my turn to bring the food."

"Thank God. If I had one more salted duck egg from Seung I was going to throw up. I don't care if it's a delicacy. The stuff is disgusting."

"Well, that's balut for you. Nothing like a fertilized boiled duck egg as a snack. Ok, talk to you later. I've got to go find out more about this guy."

"Kelsey, don't get too caught up in this jerk. You've got way too much going on and I feel like this man could be trouble."

Kelsey snorted. "How much trouble could I possibly get into? And don't worry. I said he was intriguing, not that I wanted to go to bed with him." *Though I do wonder what it would be like to kiss him.*

"That wasn't what I was worried about. Okay, see you Tuesday."

Kelsey hung up the phone, her mind whirling. The taxi had just pulled up to her apartment. She paid the cab driver and walked into her building. She smiled at Viktor, the doorman, and then ran up the three flights of steps to her apartment.

Opening the door, she hung her jacket on the wooden coat tree and thought about Ricardo Perez. He was one of the men who had been in Tibet with Raul when he killed her parents. Was one of the men who had…" She shook her head, trying not to think about it, but she couldn't help it. Even after all this time, it was still so fresh in her mind. Rather than fight it, she closed her eyes and leaned her head against the wall, letting the painful images come, like waves in her mind, crashing down and spreading across the sands of her memory until she was right there lapping in the surf with them.

There had been five of them. Five men who had ambushed them in their camp in the mountains of Tibet.

She closed her eyes, remembering…

* * * * *

The setting sun streaked through the Tibetan mountains like a dusky rainbow. Mountain Abora rose in the distance, its glacier-capped peaks shining like a beacon.

A multi-roomed hut stood at the center of a cleared field in the forest, surrounded by groves of swaying bamboo trees. It was comprised of four rooms, three covered and one, the largest room, open to the sky. It was in this space that dinner was being cooked. The oily scent of yak meat permeated the air as a thin thread of smoke drifted up from a shallow pit.

35

The sound of laughter filled out the scene. It was a happy sound.

Standing in the center of the hut was a man, clutching a prized possession. He grinned at his wife, the poster sized, rolled scroll in his hand shaking from his excitement. He was dressed in non-descript long beige pants and a black sweatshirt to ward off the sudden chill of the evening air. His wife stood next to him, her hands on his face, leaning forward to plant a kiss on his lips.

In the shade of the bamboo trees, four men hid. They had been watching them for weeks, tracking their movements and waiting for them to discover this very scroll. It was a map to Xanadu, the mystical place supposedly in the heart of the Mongolian Empire. Not the fictional locale Samuel Taylor Coleridge wrote in the 19th century opium fantasy "Kubla Khan," but the real one. The one that supposedly housed treasures beyond imagination.

The couple was Margaret and Benjamin Porter. They'd been searching for this map ever since they'd met in college and had fallen in love with the fantastical idea of it all. They spent much of their early marriage learning and studying Tibetan culture. After the death of their toddler son to leukemia, they'd taken their daughter and moved to Tibet, spending the last two years there working on their quest to find Xanadu.

They'd befriended monks from the Bodhidharma Monastery and had finally found the missing link they'd been searching for. The lost scrolls of an ancient land, hidden for centuries deep in the catacombs of the monastery.

When Benjamin had first seen the scrolls in the hands of one of the senior monks, he knew it was only a matter of time before their contents would be lost to history. The ink was faded and paper rotted. The monks knew it wouldn't be long, too. More importantly, they were scared. Dangerous men searched for these scrolls and had threatened them for their secrets. They had feigned ignorance and the men had left, but the monks knew they needed to trust in someone outside the monastery to protect their secrets. They beseeched Benjamin for his aide, for they trusted him, knowing his goal was not to find Xanadu for profit or glory. The Porter's simply wanted the knowledge of its existence and only desired to protect its secrets.

Benjamin spent a year inscribing the words in the scrolls to computer discs. These words which were an ancient dialect and possibly the first true language of Tibet. He gave the discs to the monks and in turn, they handed over to him the very map he searched for. Armed with the translations of the ancient language, Benjamin could now decipher the map and finally start looking for the guiding force which had been his quest for his entire adult life. The family decided to remain in Tibet for a few more years, enough time to complete the translations and search for the land. They'd never been more excited in their lives.

The four men made their move and stormed into the hut. With their guns drawn, they surrounded the surprised couple.

"Give me the map," the leader demanded. He was Latin, dark, with a normal build, but something about him seemed to make the very air stale with his presence. He greedily eyed the rolled parchment in Benjamin's hand.

That man was Raul Salazar, the leader of the largest drug cartel in all of North and South America and one of the most powerful and evil men in the world.

Benjamin glanced at his wife and shook his head as she nervously peered behind the men.

"Of course, take it. We don't want any trouble. Just please don't hurt my family." He handed the prize over to the leader as if it were nothing more than a cheap trinket.

Once in his hands, Raul made to leave, turned, and then laughed, his gold tooth glinting in the light of the cooking fire. The sound was pure malevolence. He brandished a knife and plunged it into Benjamin Porter as his wife screamed in horror.

"You know too much." He turned his attention to Margaret.

She peered over Raul's shoulder, her eyes masks of terror. "Kelsey, run!" she shrieked. But before she could say anything further a fifth man loped into the clearing, dragging a fighting ten-year old with him by her hair.

"Ah, you found the imp, Ramone," Raul said, leering at the child. "Good job."

"Mommy?" the little girl cried. She turned and saw her father lying on the ground, his blood pooling in the dirt floor. She started wailing.

"Please, leave her alone," the mother begged. "She's just a baby. She knows nothing."

"No witnesses." Raul Salazar grabbed at Margaret. With a guttural cry, she reached out and ripped her nails down both his cheeks, his blood spurting from his eyes to his mouth in long, vicious streaks. They would scar him for the rest of his life.

Raul hit Margaret in the face and sliced her across her abdomen, eviscerating her. She fell to the ground, but she didn't die quickly. She lay there, unable to stop the horror which was to come.

She could do nothing as the men attacked her daughter. When they finished, they laughed at the scene they'd created, took the map and left, leaving the barely conscious child lying on the ground. Raul turned back to them just once before the forest overtook him. "No witnesses."

Two days later the little girl was found, catatonic in her dead mother's arms.

But alive.

* * * * *

Kelsey blinked back tears and moved through her apartment, past the living room and towards the den to her computer. Sniffling, she pulled up the various search engines and started googling one Desmond Gisborne.

Hours later she found what she was looking for.

Chapter 5

THE CONNECTION

It was late when Kelsey pulled back from the screen.

Googling Desmond proved to provide the basic fundamentals. He was thirty-four, born on July 19th. She had read through his dossier, finding out he had majored in Forensic Biology and minored in Asian Studies while at The University of Pennsylvania. He had stayed on to get his Masters in Criminal Justice from the same school. He was smart and educated, but instead he had chosen to become a cop? Why?

His parents were both scholars. His father had been a professor of mathematics, until he succumbed to prostate cancer the age of 62. His mother was still alive and was a professor of literature at Boston College.

Desmond had grown up in the prestigious Weston Hill neighborhood and attended a private school in northern Massachusetts. There were the usual awards of scholarship merit, a varsity letter in track, articles he published in trade journals while working on his thesis, but when she read further, something caught her eye and made her stomach jump.

A wedding announcement? She clicked the link.

Fourteen years ago, Desmond had married Charlotte Turlane.

Kelsey sat back, startled, and surprised at her reaction. *Why was she even remotely affected by this news? So, she hadn't realized he was married. What was the big deal about that?*

She moved her scrutiny to files from the NYPD police department, which she easily hacked into using codes Ari had provided just for occasions like this. What she didn't find on Google, she found here, but it only confused her more. The guy was a conundrum. He'd been awarded a lot of commendations, but after all this time, he should have moved up the ranks quicker. He'd only made Detective this year. It seemed he specialized in cold murder cases, finding missing children, and taking down drug dealers. He was solely responsible for finding the three kids last year who were kidnapped for a child prostitution ring, taking down the entire operation himself. She didn't remember hearing anything about his involvement in the media. Apparently, this guy wasn't in it for the personal glory. She felt a begrudging respect for him.

She searched a bit more for current assignments and there it was. She squinted in confusion. *How was this even possible?* Desmond was trying to solve a string of cold case murders of Tibetan Monks stemming from killings occurring twelve years ago at the Wat Jokhang-Ling Monastery, a Buddhist temple in upstate, New York. He had spent years trying to find the culprits and had finally pinned it to one Ricardo Perez and Raul Salazar.

Kelsey sucked in her breath, stunned. Both of them working on finding Raul and Ricardo? Murders that occurred the same year her own parents were killed. The Buddhist monastery link. Just the fact that the sand mandala artists at the MET that evening were from the same monastery startled her.

Breathing fast, she read further about the killings. The monks had been traveling to the monastery for a seminar and had been ambushed while they slept.

41

Kelsey sat back, shocked. Desmond searched for Ricardo and Raul and found her, instead. She had known for years Ricardo and Raul had carried out the murders at the monastery and knew Ricardo had taken a disc from one of the Monks. She also knew he had hidden it in his home in Miami.

She had just been waiting for the right time to strike. She had the disc, which was in Ari's office, and Seung was now decrypting and translating. The same disc her father had translated for the monks at the Bodhidharma monastery. This same disc, that for some reason, had been brought to the United States where Raul had found and confiscated it. But still, where was the connection to Desmond? Why was he interested in this specifically?

Her fingers flew back to the computer, pulling up the incident and rifled through old articles. Names and faces from the monastery massacre raced across the screen--the victims, Chen Doma, Dawa Li, Dolma Ju, Zhu Ki, Connor Gisborne...

She nearly tipped over in her chair. Connor Gisborne? She quickly focused on him. More articles appeared on the monitor. With a deep breath, she pulled up the first one.

A young American law student on pilgrimage in Tibet returned to the United States with a group of monks from the Bodhidharma Monastery in his company. Staying at a sister temple, the Wat Jokhang-Ling Monastery in the Catskills, he and other members of the cloister were attacked and brutally killed by multiple unknown assailants. Mr. Gisborne was found dead in his bed with multiple gunshot wounds to his body. His sparse room and belongings had been ransacked.

He is survived by his older brother, Desmond, and his parents, Charles and Collette Gisborne and grandparents...

She shook her head. It all clicked together now. Connor was Desmond's brother and now he was avenging his sibling's death. Connor and Tibet. The parallels between Desmond and her were staggering and here he was trying to pin a murder on her, when they probably should have been working together. Still, he didn't know the link and she was not about to tell him

None of it mattered. She had already taken care of Ricardo. Did Desmond really care about bringing justice to a horror of a man who had murdered his own brother? There had to be more. He had to have known something also about the disc. Had to be searching for it.

Well, he couldn't have it.

Kelsey pulled up some images of his family and a wedding photo that had run in the society pages surfaced. He looked nothing like his parents and brother. They were olive skinned, with dark hair and eyes. Desmond was like a beacon of light with his pale skin and blue-green eyes and towered over his parents. She vaguely wondered if he were adopted.

Kelsey pulled up Desmond's home address. 101 W 70th Street. The upper west side of Manhattan. She pictured the street in her mind. Tidy chocolate-colored brownstones lined the tree-rimmed block, his a full home, not one of those that were sectioned off into two hundred and fifty square foot studios for two thousand a month.

So he had money. Sure as hell wasn't his. Not with teachers as parents and his salary on the NYPD. It had to be his wife's money. She searched for Charlotte Turlane-Gisborne, and when the first article's title came up, she swallowed hard.

It was her obituary, dated four years after Charlotte and Desmond had gotten married.

Taking another deep breath, she pulled it up.

On November 11th, during a freak ice storm that blanketed the eastern seaboard, Charlotte Turlane-Gisborne and her six month old son, Tyler, were struck by a man in a silver colored

SUV on I-95 while returning from a trip to visit her parents. Her Lexus was shoved into the medium and then spun out of control, plummeting off the road and into a copse of trees where it crashed, bursting into flames. Witnesses say the speeding SUV careened wildly, but others claimed it looked like it tried to ram Charlotte's car from behind. When her vehicle crashed, the driver of the SUV ran over to it, appeared to speak to her, and then fled. She and her child did not survive the accident, despite every measure taken by the EMT's on scene. Charlotte was able to speak one word before she expired due to massive internal hemorrhaging and burns to nearly 60 percent of her body. She uttered the mysterious word, "Xanadu."

She is survived by her husband, Desmond Gisborne, a twin brother, two sisters and her parents, Roger Turlane and Suzanne Bowery Turlane. Burial services will be held..."

Kelsey stopped reading. Suzanne Bowery Turlane. Yes, of the Bowery's that owned the majority of the specialized organic grocery store chains in the continental United States.

Her hands started to shake. Charlotte had uttered the word Xanadu before she died. She knew. Desmond knew. This was more than just wanting her disc. He was trying to find Xanadu as well, and now he knew the only way to get there was to go after her.

Well, let him come. She could handle him.

Chapter 6

BACK TO REALITY

Desmond sulked across Central Park and tried to let the cold night air clear his head. *What had he been thinking?* He had been so sure Kelsey was the girl from Miami.

Her image filled in his mind. When she had taken off her jacket, revealing her incredible, well-proportioned physique, it was all he could do not to stare. He'd been appreciating her from afar, but when he was up close to her, her beauty startled him. Those eyes, so sharp and intelligent, bore into him. And that attitude. He didn't think she took crap from anyone. Her confidence and acting skills were impressive. But, man, that body. Something about her pulled at his very being and it had taken all his will to stay on point.

He shook his head. Dammit! What was wrong with him? This girl was lethal, his main suspect, and here he was thinking about her body.

He inhaled deeply, his breath smoking in the air and managed to regain his control. Regardless of what had happened in the museum, he felt Kelsey had been capable of the attack and murder, and if so, she was one of the most calculating individuals he'd ever encountered. That made her supremely dangerous. He had taken down many a felon who thought they were too smart for him. But he was smarter.

Well, most of the time he was.

He thought about his job and how much he'd sacrificed to stay on the force on cold cases, just so he could keep the one with his brother and wife alive in the background. Two murder cases he'd never been able to close, but he was sure they were intrinsically linked to one another.

He'd finally made detective and that's when he had a break in his case and found Ricardo hiding in Miami. He was too close to solving this to let anyone else screw it up and so instead of bringing in the Florida police and dealing with the mountain of paperwork that would be required, he decided to do it himself. The rest was easy. He put in for three weeks vacation, staked out Ricardo's location, planted his own camera right alongside the other surveillance cameras and waited. He was about to make his move when this spit of a girl showed herself on his own surveillance camera. Shocked was not the word.

He followed her back to NYC, lost her in the airport until he finally located the cabbie who'd taken her to her apartment.

He followed her for a few days, still not sure if it was the same woman, but after researching her background thoroughly, he knew she was capable of doing this crime. Yet for the life of him, he couldn't figure out her connection or reasoning. What was she, a hired gun or something? A regular student by day and sexy lethal assassin by night? He groaned. It sounded too much like a bad "B" movie.

A homeless man shuffled past him and Desmond gave him a wide berth. He wondered suddenly if he was too close to the case. Perhaps he was blinded, trying so hard to avenge Connor's death and pin it on someone that he'd latched onto Kelsey too hard. For god's sake, she was barely twenty-two years old, but his research showed she was one of the most accomplished individuals he'd ever come across. He found a copy of her Stanford-Benet Test and was stunned to see she scored the high figure of 178. Wasn't Einstein 189 or something close to that? She had been schooled at the elite Woolard Academy where she received straight As. She graduated at the age of seventeen with perfect SAT and ACT scores, a year's worth of AP credits, and multi-level and upper level graduate school lab work. After that it was a bachelor's degree at Columbia within two years and now going for either her Master's or a Ph.D at NYU.

Not to mention this beautiful young woman was also a multi Dan black belt in Tae Kwon Do, ranked #1 in the ITF league in sparring throughout her teenage years.

Still, when he hit her she fell to the floor like a wilted flower. He squinted in sheer frustration. He'd never intended to strike her, but he was maddened when she seemed to be playing him. He wanted her to show herself. What he needed was proof she was the girl from Miami, not what she was capable of, yet he had struck her anyway, trying to provoke her.

Desmond suddenly stopped in mid-stride, his breath catching and his stomach turning over as realization hit him. Oh, my God. She had let him hit her. In fact, she probably saw it coming and purposely didn't stop him. If that was the case, it meant she knew who he was and may even have known he was following her the past few days.

Groaning, he ran his hands through his hair and started walking furiously, angry at himself. Because if Kelsey knew he'd been following her, she purposely set him up to meet her at the MET. Set him up to find out what he knew! He'd fallen right into her trap.

What if he was wrong? So she took Tae Kwon Do. Lots of teenagers took martial arts to keep in shape and get some discipline. That was a huge jump to Miami and Ricardo Perez, six years later, no less. He could just imagine dragging her into the station and getting his ass laughed off the force when they got a good look at her. It was one of the main reasons he hadn't hauled her down to the precinct in the first place. He was so damned frustrated with the lack of cooperation he'd been getting on this case that he was determined to do it himself. If he were on vacation, well then, he could do things his way, not the department's, and they'd have no say about it if he didn't have to check in.

He came out of the park by 72nd Street and walked south the two blocks to his residence. With each step he became more and more certain Kelsey was the woman in Miami. He was determined to spend the next two weeks finding out why she did it, why she took that disc and what it had to do with the theft at the monastery all those years ago.

He thought about his brother and sighed. Connor had been such a gentle soul. Naïve in so many ways. What happened to him was a travesty that Desmond still couldn't make right. Connor had just graduated from Harvard and had wanted to take some time off. He'd always been interested in Buddhism and had decided to study with the monks in Tibet before beginning law school and before another set of foreign visitor restrictions came down from the Chinese government. How excited he'd been on that last phone call.

"Desmond," Connor had said. "I met an American couple who are working on something unbelievable. It's spiritual and it has to do with the mystical land of Xanadu. They gave me something on a disc that I'm bringing back to the States to show you. It will change everything."

He never got a chance to see it. Connor returned to the States and mere hours before he was to meet him, he was murdered.

Desmond climbed the steps and unlocked the door to his brownstone. Stepping inside, he shut the door and leaned against the wooden frame. Poor Connor. He never had a chance.

He didn't turn on the lights as he moved down the hall, his footsteps echoing hollowly on the bare wooden floor. Once in the kitchen, he opened the refrigerator, its light seeping into the room and reflecting off the mica chips in the black granite countertop. Desmond grabbed a carton of milk, one of the only things in the fridge. Forgoing a glass, he chugged down a quarter of the carton before putting it back and wiping his mouth on the back of his sleeve.

He thought about the last connection he had. The one that kept the link between Kelsey and him alive. Kelsey's parents were killed in Tibet the same year as the murder of his brother. That had been easy enough to find out once he had started digging up her background. Now he believed they were the same couple Connor had spoken about, and if that was the case, then Kelsey might have also known Connor. Of course, she was still alive, so it made sense she was not there during the attack and could have been staying somewhere else at the time of her parents' murder. It didn't seem plausible Raul would ever leave anyone alive to ID him.

He moved back down the hallway, kicked off his shoes and threw his jacket on the banister before walking upstairs. Without even taking off his clothes, he fell onto his bed, exhausted. He stretched and picked up a photo of a smiling blond infant sitting in a frame on his nightstand. Staring at it in the moonlight seeping through the windows, he breathed a deep sigh and placed it back on the stand. He turned his attention toward the ceiling, his thoughts drifting back to Kelsey Porter.

What if she was avenging the deaths of her parents and that's why she killed Ricardo and took the disc? If so, then she might even know what was on the disc and might even know what it had to do with Xanadu.

Closing his eyes, he tried not to think of her, but it was so hard. Those brilliant blue eyes kept staring at him and he fell asleep thinking about them peering into his very soul.

* * * * *

One week after Ari's discovery, they brought the little girl to the back of the house. The scent of fresh plaster and paint permeated the air.

Both nervous and excited, Claire stood in front of a plain wooden door and unlocked it. Then, with a deep breath, she turned to Kelsey, bending to her eye level. Though the child didn't respond, or even acknowledge her, Claire spoke to her as if she could hear and understand everything.

"Honey, we know you've gone through one of the worst things imaginable, but we're all here to help you. I know you've been hiding away in a land called Tedanalee. It sounds like a beautiful and wonderful place to help you cope with the pain of this world. But honey, Tedanalee isn't real and I think deep inside you know that. You can't stay hidden away there forever. We want you to come back to us."

She opened the door and guided Kelsey inside. It was a 12 x 12 foot room with white bleached hardwood floors and walls painted a stark white. In the center of the room were buckets of paint in a multitude of colors, along with numerous tubes of oil paints, brushes in varying sizes, water soluble pencils and crayons as well.

Claire faced the child, again bending down so their eyes were only inches apart. "Kelsey, this is your room to do with as you will. You can do whatever you want in here, whatever you feel like. You can paint the entire room black, or yellow or green. You can dump all the paint on the floor, write curse words or hateful things, anything you want. You can even put holes in the walls and break the door. I promise you that you

50

won't get into trouble. Never, ever. This room is your Tedanalee in this world, your safe haven, a bridge to help you back to this reality. Please honey, come back to us."

Claire stood up. "I'm going to leave now. Do whatever you wish in here."

She left the room and closed the door. Martin stood outside it, hesitant. "Do you think she'll actually do anything?"

Claire put her ear to the door and shrugged. "I don't know. Let's give her some time."

They sat down on the floor in the hallway to wait. For a full ten minutes there was nothing but silence and they were about to give up hope, when they heard light footsteps on the wooden floor coming from inside the room. Claire peeked under the doorframe and saw Kelsey bend down to pick up a paintbrush. She held it in front of her face, staring at it, her expression unreadable.

Claire turned back to her husband, triumph in her eyes. "Let's let her be." They got up and moved into the family room.

Nearly three hours later Kelsey stood in the doorway to the family room, covered from head to toe in black and red paint. Claire had been reading a psychology journal on the couch, Martin and Ari played chess, and seven-year old Patricia was reading a book.

Claire stared at the child, noting the differences. Her blue eyes were now clear and focused, but desolate. Her lips quivered when she spoke.

"I'm done," Kelsey said. Her voice was so soft Claire had to strain to hear her.

Claire slowly rose and inched over to the child, bending down gradually so as not to startle her. "I'm so glad, honey." She stared at Kelsey, who was stiff, her hands rigid at her sides and her fists clenched so tightly her knuckles were white.

51

Suddenly, the child rushed forward into Claire's arms and sobbed uncontrollably. Claire hugged her fiercely, ignoring the paint sticking to her clothing and her hair, holding her for hours until the child cried herself out.

After they cleaned her up and put her to bed that night they went into the back room to see what Kelsey had created. Claire couldn't process what she saw and didn't understand the drawings Kelsey had made of at least twenty dead little girls, each and every one being tortured in the most horrific of ways.

Claire had nightmares for weeks after that.

The child was damaged and distressed, but at least she was back.

Chapter 7

BAZAAR'S

Bazaar was a private club located on a quiet tree-lined street in the middle of a residential block in Chelsea. You could faintly hear the deep beating bass from the gay bar on the corner where gorgeous muscled men in tight designer jeans and expensive shirts moved in pairs down the street. The entrance to Bazaar's, via a basement doorway of an elegant brownstone, led one into a world time seemed to have forgotten. Privy only to those allowed entrance by Reginald Shevchek, the present owner and great grandson of the first proprietor, Baron Maxim Shevchek.

Maxim had been a former concert violinist in the USSR. He had also been a spy for the United States. When his comrades finally came looking for him, he quickly defected, whisked himself to the US, and created a place of refuge for those who "knew more than they should." It was a safe haven for those both in and outside the government who worked "around the law," though their efforts were always at the agenda of helping the United States.

Ari Goldman, Kelsey's brother, had been contacted by Reginald a few years back to reclaim a set of letters that had once belonged to his great grandfather. One of Ari's former clients, an ex-agent from the CIA, knew of his uncanny abilities in surveillance and ops, and even at his young age, he recommended him to Reginald for the job.

The letters had been intended for a Senator on the actions the KGB was committing. A museum in Prague had refused to part with the set and Ari had assisted Shevchek in "acquiring it." Reginald's family was an intensely private one and it mortified him that the letters were displayed in the public domain for all to see.

It had been child's play. Kelsey and Josh had been on scene. They disabled the cameras with some fun new lasers Ari had gotten from the Middle East, and broke into the museum. The letters were now in the hands of Shevchek and he was forever in Ari's debt. Now Ari, and those who had helped acquire those letters, were honorary members of the club.

* * * * *

Kelsey turned back to Bazaar and balancing a tray on her left leg and a large shoulder bag filled with drinks, she grasped the bronze knocker, striking it three times.

Reginald himself opened the massive, mahogany door with a warm, wrinkled smile and his perfectly appointed Italian tuxedo and tails.

"Miss Porter, always a pleasure. They're already waiting for you in the back room. May I assist you?" His handlebar mustache twitched when he spoke.

Together they made their way through the luxuriously decorated space. Sumptuous runners covered the sparkling hardwood floors and dark cherry wood adorned every archway and staircase banister. Original oil paintings from the early Renaissance era hung in ornate gold and silver frames in the richly wallpapered rooms. It had the distinctive feel of a men's club. Thick, deep plush arm chairs, leather couches and the smell of expensive cigars and cognac wafted through the rooms.

Pushing aside a set of red velvet curtains, Kelsey moved into the private back room. Five smiling faces greeted her warmly from around a massive cherry wood table.

"It's about time you got here," Julia said, clapping her hands. "We're starving! So, what did you bring us?"

"For someone so small, you'd never guess you eat like a cow," Kelsey said.

"Oh, yeah, like you don't," Julia said, but she blushed profusely.

Kelsey glanced to the food. It was her turn for the embellishments this evening and the group traditionally settled on a specific theme each time. Based on the success of the recent mission, Tibet was definitely the order of the night.

These Tuesday night get-togethers started right after the Shevchek job four years prior and every fourth Tuesday whoever could make it would come.

Reginald stepped from behind Kelsey and placed the large round serving tray on the table. Meanwhile Kelsey started pulling dishes out from her bag.

As the wrappings came off, her friends leaned in expectantly and her heart nearly burst with joy. She loved each and every one of them fiercely. Here she could be exactly who she was. No one judged her, no one expected her to dumb herself down. They were her lifeline, her family and her own Knights Templar. There were too many people in the world she simply had to put up with on a daily basis, but these people weren't them.

"So, based on recent events," Kelsey began. "I thought it only fitting we honor the Buddhists the proper way." She pointed out the delicacies. "This is a sampling of Tsampa with yak butter, over here is a course of dried mutton, and in this dish is a heaping bowl of Momo, which I got for you, Dennis." She glanced kindly at a slip of a man who grinned back at her. His mop of dark curls bobbed around his face as he leaned in to peer at the dishes. Dennis's glasses slid down his nose and he pushed them up as he grabbed a dumpling and popped it into his mouth.

He nodded and chewed enthusiastically.

Knew you'd like them. Dennis was one of Kelsey's best friends since the sixth grade. Not to mention he was also their group's resident computer programmer and one of the best hackers in the country.

She continued, pointing. "I also brought an order of Thenthuk, which are Tibetan noodles."

Julia squinted and picked at the dishes with chopsticks. "I never had the yak tongue before. Just tell me it's not like balut." She turned her glare to Seung, who just laughed at her.

Kelsey waved her off. "Don't worry, it's nothing like balut. First of all, it's yak, not duck and I tasted it at the restaurant. It's as good as if you'd eaten it right off the grasslands."

Kelsey glanced at her brother Ari, a mix of emotions running through her. Ever since she had joined their family, their relationship had been complicated. She loved him dearly, but he was so damned obnoxious and condescending. On the flip side, he was also ridiculously protective of her and their fights about it had been vicious over the years.

"So, did you at least remember to bring the wine?" he asked, sarcastically.

You, obnoxious little nit. "Like I would forget your precious drinks? Yeah, I've got them. It wouldn't be Tibet if we didn't have salted butter tea, barley beer and Baijiu. That's a barley wine the Tibetans call white spirit, if you didn't know, smartass." She handed to the bottle to a waiter, who poured the wine for Ari to taste.

He swirled the liquid in his glass and sniffed. He took a sip and let it settle on his tongue, and nodded at the waiter. "It's actually excellent. Hey, Porter, you going to try some, this time?" he teased, arching his eyebrows.

Kelsey wrinkled her nose. "I'll pass. I'll just stick with the tea."

He smirked. Okay, he had one thing on her. She had no palate for alcohol. So kill her.

The other guests were comprised of individuals who had entered Ari and Kelsey's lives during their academy years. Kelsey couldn't help laughing at Julia, who was presently unceremoniously shoving her beautiful face into a heaping mound of noodles, her hand holding a section of her long, flaming red hair so it wouldn't fall into the bowl. That girl was as lithe as a dancer, but had the table manners of a teenage boy.

Seung called out to her. "Hey, Kelsey, you're not holding out on me, are you? I know you've got something else hidden in that bag you're carrying."

Oh, I certainly do, my friend. Kelsey pulled out a final plastic container, pushing it towards him. She was looking forward to making him squirm. "You think I'd forget about getting you one of the most disgusting ethnic delicacies I could find?" Seung was always looking to try new things. Nothing seemed to phase him. Well, if duck with caterpillar fungus didn't do the trick this time, nothing would.

His excitement made his dark brown eyes shine and he leaned over to take a peek at the dish. Kelsey loved watching him. He was so enthusiastic and singular in his appearance with his exotic Asian good looks and his straight, glossy black hair that cascaded down his back and reached the waistband of his tight black jeans.

"You know, when you move, you think you sound tough, but you really sound like a chorus of jingle bells with all those belt chains rattling around you," Julia said, between chews. "Like a little Christmas Elf, or something."

Seung grabbed his chopsticks and dug into the bowl. "And a ho, ho, ho to you, too. It's so you'll know when I'm sneaking up behind you, Jules." He took a bite and nodded. "Not bad, Kelsey. Tender, kind of sweet, even with the ginger and onions, but then again, I've had this before." His eyes twinkled behind the black eyeliner.

"You have?" *I can't surprise this guy!*

He nodded. "Caterpillar fungus, or cordyceps of you want to be more specific, is supposed to be an aphrodisiac. Melie thought we should give it a try one evening, though I can assure you I didn't need it."

Joshua shook his head. "Kelsey, you can't put one over on him."

"No, I apparently can't." She watched Joshua dig into the yak tongue. He was a one man colossal of muscle, bravado, and sheer passion and was Ari's best friend from the moment they had met at the academy. Kelsey knew if there was ever anyone who would survive Armageddon, it would be Joshua. Working with him on assignments was such a rush because he could keep up with her, both physically and mentally. Not a lot of guys could do that. Unfortunately, he was also a pain in the ass the way he hit on her whenever he had the chance. Not that she didn't wonder why she didn't take him up on it. It wasn't like she wasn't attracted to him, too. He was cute, and sexy, and perfect for her, but something always stopped her from taking that next step.

There's something so very wrong with me. On the outside she appeared to be a sexual dynamo, but for some reason, every time she had the opportunity to be with a guy for more than just the casual kissing or foreplay, something deep within her pulled her back. She didn't understand it at all, unless it was because of her attack when she was ten. *Yes, that has to be it.* So, at twenty-two, she was still technically a virgin, something Ari thankfully didn't tease her about. He seemed to be pretty pleased about it, actually.

She turned to her brother, who was staring at her over his wineglass. He was tall and dark, with handsome Sephardic good looks, and he really did know her better than anyone else on the planet. A computer and business genius, at the tender age of nineteen the guy had quit Harvard and took over a fledgling revenue and profit sharing company. Within five years, he had turned it into a multi-million dollar enterprise, working with the top Fortune 500 companies across the globe. That was just one of his jobs and just a cover. The real thrill was in the freelance assignments, like what he had done for Shevchek and of course, what he was doing for her now.

After her attack, Kelsey had moved in with Ari's family. It had taken her brilliant brother awhile to comprehend and accept that the little spit of a girl who came to live with him might just be as smart as he was. Or smarter. She remembered the first time he realized it.

* * * * *

"Dad, this thing's not working!" Frustrated, twelve-year old Ari threw the manual on the couch in disgust, where it bounced and fell to the floor.

Martin glanced up from the circuit board. "Having a tantrum isn't going to fix the problem. Now, go pick it up."

They had built an incredible structure, four feet across and three feet high. A complex system of electrical networks, when assembled together properly, would make a train move up a slope and give it enough juice to circle around the architecture. There were hundreds of different circuits and breakers and battery-operated fuse boxes, and it had taken them the good part of two days putting the unit together. But, the train wouldn't run and for the past hour they couldn't figure out where they'd gone wrong. Whenever they flicked the switch, the train would just sit there.

Kelsey had been with them for a little over two months by this time and watched them from the doorway. "Can I help?" she asked.

Eyebrows raised in contempt, Ari snorted. "I don't think so."

"Ari, hold your tongue." Martin turned to Kelsey, nodding towards the couch. "Sure, Kelsey. The manual's over there if you want to give it a try."

Kelsey moved over to the thick instruction guide, limping slightly, and began reading, to much chortling by Ari.

When she was finished ten minutes later, she moved slowly over to the structure and stared at it intently for a few minutes. Martin and Ari watched her cock her head this way and that for quite some time, considering, before she swiftly moved her hand deep inside, switched a set of breakers and then hit the switch.

Martin and Ari sat dumbstruck as the train started to slowly chug up the slope.

Kelsey turned to Ari. "Next time, I won't help you if you're going to be mean to me, you big stupid know-it-all." With that, she turned in a huff and limped from the room.

A week later the Goldmans started testing her and shortly after that, Martin and Claire contacted the academy.

* * * * *

Julia finally spoke up. "So, Kelsey. Tell us about Desmond."

She felt their gazes upon her. She took another sip of tea and stared at Ari over the rim of the cup. He watched her intently, his brows furrowed. "As you know, we missed a camera."

60

She enjoyed watching Ari click his tongue in disgust. "That wasn't my fault. It was a camera this rogue cop added. How could we possibly have known he had his own sting going on?" She could tell he was mad and embarrassed. He hated when things went wrong when he was responsible. Not that it humbled him much.

Kelsey shrugged. "The problem is, he knows I took the disc and even though he's not a hundred percent certain any longer that I'm the girl in Miami, I don't think he's going to go away so easily."

"Well, we have the disc, so I wouldn't worry about him getting it," Ari said.

Julia reached over to grab the wine bottle and poured herself a glass. "Say what you will, Ari, but the guy seems pretty persistent. He could make things really difficult for her. He could decide to charge her for the crime, bring her into the spotlight, or even try to threaten her to give him what he needs. You know, he hit her. Smacked her right in the face in the middle of the museum."

Ari whipped his head around and stared at Kelsey. His face was beet red with anger. "What do you mean, he hit you? Why the hell didn't you tell me this?" He pounded his hands on the table, rattling the dishes.

"Ari, will you just calm down?" Kelsey said, the others around the table echoing her. "I didn't tell you because I knew you'd get crazy and freak out over it." She turned her glare onto Julia. "Sometimes you just vomit from the mouth, you know that? You like instigating things, don't you?"

Julia grinned behind her glass of wine while Ari continued yelling at Kelsey.

"You have to tell me these things. You can't leave me in the dark with information like this. I have to profile him, find out what he's doing, what he's thinking and I need to know everything that happens. Otherwise the entire run is for naught."

Kelsey rolled her eyes. "I don't need a personality run to know what he was doing. He was testing me. He knew I took down Ricardo and his guards, so Desmond probably figured if he tried to physically hit me, I'd stop him. To prove a point that I was capable of committing the crime. I don't need a profiler for that."

"Yeah, but you didn't stop him. Did you even put up a fight at all?" He searched her face. "Where'd he hit you? Did he hurt you? I'll friggin' kill him if he did."

Joshua spoke up. "Ari, come on, like anyone is going to be able to actually hurt this girl. So, she's got a bruise on her cheek she's hiding with make-up. Big deal. She just took down Ricardo. I think she can handle a smack to the face. I've given her much worse myself," he said jokingly.

Ari crossed his arms. "Yes, but we all know she has a tendency to take things too far. One day your luck just might run out, Kelsey."

Kelsey huffed and shook her head, but the truth was, she was a little scared Ari might be right.

Chapter 8

ARI

They sat, side by side under the big oak tree on the main lawn of the academy. He, with his ever-present laptop and she with a collection of poems by Kipling. One would think they were studying, or talking to each other about their schoolwork, but if you moved closer, you'd realize they taught each other something entirely different.

"Thank you, in the familiar form, is "tedalink." Love is "Titidalaah." Kelsey pronounced the words as Ari typed them into the computer.

"I thought love was "Limili?" Ari asked.

Kelsey shook her head. "That's "like." And don't forget, you have to say it fast. It should have the effect of the wind whistling through the trees. Also, don't forget to click those consonants with the back of your tongue and blow air out of the back of your throat when you say the last letter for most of the words, almost like you're trying to fog up your sunglasses."

Ari nodded. "That's the hard part, like I'm talking with my epiglottis and blowing through it all the time without sounding like I'm coughing up phlegm. How you came up with this entire language with this complex syntax and diction, while catatonic, continues to blow my mind. And you remember all of it and keep adding to it every time you have a freaking nightmare." He scanned the database. "Kelsey, there's over eight thousand words in here right now. I can't believe we're just getting to other uses for the words love and like."

She shrugged. "Well, these are used specifically when referring to animals, not people. There's a lot more, too. I just wish you were smarter so you could catch on faster." He gave her a face and she playfully punched him in the arm. "I'm just glad you want to learn it. It's nice to be able to tell it to someone and not keep it a secret."

For the past three years, she'd been teaching Ari the complicated language of Tedanalee. He was a linguistics genius and was fascinated by the different enunciations and complexly structured context Kelsey had created. He could already speak what he'd learned fairly well, but she added words as fast as he could memorize them. It drove their parents crazy when they would converse to each other in their secret language.

"Ok, enough for now," Ari begged. "I've actually got to study for both a Latin and Mandarin test for this afternoon. I keep doing this and I'll start throwing in Tedanalee words and my professors will think I've lost my mind."

Kelsey smiled. "Ah, crazy... that's "Kitataza," by the way."

He exhaled loudly, plugged in the adjective and then shut the laptop.

"Tamas samala poplola dinkilola, Kelsey. (We shall rule the world, Kelsey.)"

She smiled. "Li, fi dididi lkinkilia. (Yes, if the gods allow.)

* * * * *

The midtown office building was a construction marvel. Covered in dark beveled glass and sixty-five stories high, it was built to withstand everything from an 8.9 earthquake to an airplane attack.

Ari's offices took up the entire fifty-second and fifty-third floor's and were designed with the intent of being retro-hip. The floors were gray cement and the ceiling had been removed to expose the internal copper piping. The inside walls were bright white and bare except for an occasional modern art painting. Wide floor to ceiling windows offered a breathtaking 360 degree view of New York City. Lines of computer banks and cubicles stretched across both floors and the place was filled with the hum of over a hundred people bustling by, typing code and researching. Open and airy, you could see almost the entire operation at once. A multi-colored glass staircase in the center of the office separated the two levels. The southwest corner of the lower floor was a communal center complete with both a pool and foosball table, multiple sets of couches and lounge chairs. There was even a kitchen area housing a top-notch coffee bar and manned with its own barista. The office buzzed with caffeine-fueled activity as the workers got their free afternoon fixes.

Within conference room B, one of only three rooms on the upper floor with actual solid walls and a door, a group was crowded around the large conference room table. Refilled mugs of coffee, half eaten muffins and empty yogurt parfait cups covered the table. Computer screens were embedded in the table itself and the people stared into their own monitors.

"So everyone understand the plan?" Ari said. "It's a quick in and out job. Get the second disc locked in Raul's office and hit the road. Got that?"

Everyone nodded.

"Good. We've been monitoring his activity for days now. The perps have seen Kelsey for two nights in a row and they're sure to make a play for her tonight. Raul is leaving to visit his mother in Brooklyn and shouldn't return until the morning, as he does each time he visits her. Only his security crew will be in the vicinity."

Ari turned to Kelsey. "I'm having someone come work with you on this assignment."

Is he serious? "It's an easy recovery job. I don't need anyone to help me."

He picked up some documents and scanned them as he spoke. "You will tonight. The entrance to Raul's office building is personally coded. When you disable the men, you'll need to place one of their handprints on the keypad to gain access. You won't be able to pick them up yourself. One of the guys is pushing two-fifty."

"I expected to just get the little one."

He shook his head, looking at her. "He's still heavier than you. Easier if you had another pair of hands when it goes down."

"So who's coming with me? Joshua?"

"He can't. He just left for a job in California and won't be back until next week. I've already got someone else lined up for you."

"Who is it?"

"I'd rather not say."

You and your damned secrets. Kelsey blew out a sharp breath. "Ari, come on. Stop with the games already. You know how much I hate surprises."

He shook her off. "I don't have him fully briefed yet, but don't worry. He'll be qualified and it will go smoothly." He called across the room. "Seung, how you doing?"

Seung lifted his head briefly, his eyes never leaving the screen. "Fine, but I'm not ready yet. You can't rush these things, man. The disc was encrypted with a virus and I've got to decrypt each and every word if you want to read it."

"Fine, just let us know as soon as you're done."

Dennis called out to them and they turned to their table screens. Kelsey's eyes drew to deep slits as she watched Raul come out the front door and climb into the black Towncar waiting for him.

Ari squeezed her shoulder. "Kelsey, we're getting close. You keep your cool until this is over and then you can destroy the bastard. But not until we have the map and are one hundred percent sure there's nothing else that animal has that we need."

Kelsey turned to stare at her brother. *Keep my cool. How about you practicing what you preach, bro?* Still, only he knew how much she could take and how far she would go to get what she wanted.

* * * * *

"Enough! Both of you!" Claire yelled. She threw the hand towel to the ground in frustration and stormed over to Kelsey, grasped her chin in her hands and turned her face left and right. Her daughter's cheeks were bruised, her top lip was swollen and her right eye was literally blackening right in front of her.

She glared at Ari, his face a mass of contusions. "Why you both persist in doing this to each other is absolutely beyond me. Fine, you want to beat each other up, go to it, but I won't be privy to it any longer, helping you both pick up the pieces." She stormed out of the kitchen, but not before turning back to level a threatening gaze at both of them. "And you can both make yourselves your own dinner tonight and tomorrow night because there's no way in hell I'm going to sit here and look at either of you for the next few days!"

As their mother stomped away, Ari turned to Kelsey and grinned. "You lotht." He lisped, dabbing his bloody lip on a napkin.

Kelsey squinted at him and placed an icepack on her cheek. "Don't worry. I won't renege on the bet."

67

A year into Kelsey's martial arts training, Ari had decided to join up as well. Damned if he was going to let Kelsey be better at anything than him if he could help it. Their father even constructed a dojo in their basement and the two of them sparred constantly. Although he was older and bigger, Kelsey was quicker and sharper, which evened things out beautifully for them.

To keep things exciting, they made little bets with each other on who would win. Household chores and homework assignments were usually the prizes over the years, but their fights had started to escalate and become more vicious and so the stakes had increased as well.

Kelsey wanted to spar every free chance she had. She didn't know why, but she had this burning need to fight. It gave her a thrill to hit something. It seemed to release energy pent up in her body. Her mother told her once she figured it had to do with her attack and it was Kelsey's need to feel in control, but Kelsey didn't think that was it entirely. It actually excited her, deep in her gut. Touching someone and hurting them, even it was Ari. That was something she didn't feel the need to tell her mom.

So this past evening she pushed Ari to spar with her and he didn't want to. They had a big argument about it and finally he made a bet with her that if he won, she had to do something for him very different than the other bets. Something much more dangerous.

Kelsey thought about it for mere seconds and then agreed. It had been a heated battle, and they had gone after each other much longer than the three minute match limit. Neither of them would back down as they were both committed to winning. And, since neither of them was scared of being hit, or of being hurt, it made things even more dangerous.

But today, Kelsey lost her focus for just a moment. It was enough for Ari to get inside. He punched her in the face, kicked her legs out from under her, threw her to the ground and won the match.

Now she had to pay up.

✦ ✦ ✹ ✹ ✹

It was one a.m. and Kelsey stood outside the administration office at Woolard Academy, hidden under the branches of a weeping willow tree. This particular building was one of the most beautiful on campus with its red brick façade and Tudor design, but she wasn't admiring its beauty at this time. She was excited, waiting for one of the two security guards who drove around campus on their golf-carts, to pass by. The school didn't have cameras within the buildings, so all she had to do was avoid the ones outside, which had been easy to do.

She waited until one of them finally circled by her on his never ending loop and then left the safety of the tree, climbed up the fire escape, and jimmied the old window of President Hamilton's office. She glanced around one more time to see if she'd been seen and when she didn't notice anyone, she slipped inside.

She put on her penlight and made her way to the secretary's office. The top desk drawer was ajar. She reached inside and rummaged in the back, easily finding the key the secretary used to lock the files each day. She discovered this just yesterday while creating a fake medical reason for the woman to locate one of her own school files for the nurse. With her split lip and bruised cheek, the backstory about a fall down her house stairs wasn't too complicated. Her boyfriend of the moment wasn't as easily fooled, though. He knew she had sparred with Ari and didn't appreciate him beating up his girlfriend and messing with her face. Her brother was going to *have to watch his back around the guy for a while. That made her smile.*

Kelsey had pretended to be immersed in a book while the woman tried to be discreet about where she hid the key, but Kelsey saw everything.

Headlights swung into the room and she ducked under the desk, waiting for the security guard to continue his loop again. Seconds later she heard his golf cart chug past and continue to another part of the school.

She moved to the metal filing cabinet behind the desks and unlocked them. After rifling quickly through the student personnel and staff files, she found the list of codes to the school databases that Ari specifically said he wanted. She made copies of an extensive set of financial documents and put the file away. She was about to replace the key in the drawer and leave when she changed her mind. She slinked into President Hamilton's office and inserted the key in the filing cabinet she knew he hid in a closet in his office.

She marveled at their ineptness when the same key worked. The cabinet was filled with additional personnel records. Kelsey scanned through the folders and found hers. It was very thick and included a complete psychological profile. Her eyes widened as she rifled through the documents and she read quickly. She'd had no idea how much testing the Goldmans had done to get her well. Not to mention the underlying belief many of the institutions had about her own personal well-being. She glanced back in the cabinet folder and saw an additional extensive collection of the medical work-ups that had been done on her. Anomalies popped up throughout it.

My stomachaches? Apparently as a young child she suffered bouts of unexplained illness. The doctors attributed all of it to the stress of losing her brother and then her parents at such a young age. Of course that didn't explain the three other hospitalizations at the age of two, three and six. Again, no conclusive evidence was discovered for her symptoms and they seemed to disappear on their own.

She turned to another series of files and her stomach clenched. Oh, no. Report after report discussed her nightmares and the strange language she'd speak at night. A language no one understood or could figure out. There was talk she might have a split personality or schizophrenia and she'd need to be watched. Kelsey was taken aback. No one had discussed this with her, ever. It was one thing for her to think she was a little crazy herself, but to have the authorities think so as well? And the principal and teachers at school? It was a bitter pill to swallow. She realized she'd have to hide the stomachaches and queasiness that still occasionally popped up. She'd also have to hide the fear of her nightmares and keep them stored deep inside. There was no way anyone was going to "put her away" or incur intense psycho-therapy as some doctors in the file had suggested.

Swallowing hard, Kelsey returned the documents, locked the cabinet and returned the key to the secretary's desk.

Then she grabbed Ari's papers and left the way she'd come in, skirting around the cameras and catching up with Ari who waited for her in their parent's car behind the gym. Neither of them paid much mind to the fact that Ari wasn't of age to drive at night, nor did their parents even know they had taken the car. Their mother was barely talking to them anyway. She was still mad at them, so it made it that much easier.

She jumped into the car and tossed the papers in his lap.

"You took longer than you should have." He shot her an accusing look. He put the papers in a manila folder and placed them in the backseat. "I thought I was going to have to go in after you."

71

"I got distracted. There were a lot of things to read in there."

He raised his eyebrows. "Care to share?"

"Are you going to share with me why you needed the financials of all these people?" she shot back.

The stared each other down.

"No."

She clucked her tongue. "Then I have nothing to tell you, either."

"I'm sure I can find out."

She eyeballed him. "You scare me sometimes, you know that?"

He turned onto the highway, his jaw set. "Good. Then the feelings mutual."

Chapter 9

THE MEET UP

New York City at night is like no other place on Earth. With six million people living in just a few square miles, it's never entirely silent. Yellow cabs flew by on streets so congested during the day, you could spend twenty minutes just trying to travel four avenue blocks across town.

It was ten o'clock at night and the city was just waking up. Couples were leaving to go to the clubs and the restaurants were packed with late night diners. The homeless, who you didn't notice as much during the daytime since the mayor came down on them, were in force once the sun set. They slept on the various church steps around the city or shuffled through town with their ever present shopping carts filled with whatever bric-a-brac their antipsychotic medication made them collect. Police cars cruised the streets, their red flashing lights on but sirens off, and in the relative din you could hear the sounds of the subway trains clearly as they rumbled below, whisking passengers from one end of the borough to the other.

The diner on 70th and Broadway was quiet this evening. It was only ten o'clock and its business usually picked up after one in the morning. A lone waitress, an actress wanabee with blond hair and pink streaks, her septum piercing making her resemble a young bull, read a script as she sat on a bar stool. A couple of college-aged kids made out in a booth by the back wall, their omelets cold in front of them. An elderly man sat at the bar drinking a cup of coffee and reading the day's newspaper.

The door opened and the bell tinkled. Ari strolled in, letting in a cool stream of air that rustled the remaining newspapers across the pink Formica countertop. He was formidable in his long black leather coat and boots. He nodded at the waitress who cocked her chin towards the lone gentleman sitting in a booth against the window. Ari sauntered over and sat opposite him, laying his leather briefcase on the seat.

"Hello, Desmond." He eyed the cop, the man who'd had the audacity to hit his sister. He wanted to reach over and beat the shit out of him, but he didn't. This man wasn't an idiot. He was smart and had figured too much out all on his own.

They would use him.

"I'd say hello back, but I don't know who you are, how you found me or why you even called this meeting. If you hadn't mentioned Kelsey Porter, there's a good chance I wouldn't have come."

The chimes above the door tinkled again and two teenagers dressed in Goth sulked in. They took a table by the counter, their belt chains jangling as they sat down. The waitress put down her script, grabbed her pad and pen and ambled over to them.

"Then it's a good thing I mentioned her, isn't it?" Ari said. He stared at Desmond. Pretty obvious to see why Kelsey liked him. He was her type to a "T". Smart, calculating and muscular. She had a thing for guys who were strong and could take care of themselves. Not to mention good looking and an agenda that was too good to be true. He was perfect for what was coming. Ari leaned forwards. "I want to make a deal with you."

Desmond raised his eyebrows. "A deal about what?"

Ari took a picture from his briefcase and laid it on the table in front of Desmond, who started slightly.

It was a picture of Connor Gisborne with his arms around Benjamin Porter's shoulders. The Bodhidharma Monastery was behind them in the background.

Desmond greedily reached for the photo, his eyes drinking it in. "Where'd you get this?"

Ari took the photo from him and put it back in his briefcase. "It was found in the personal effects of Kelsey Porter's parents. You know, the girl you've been following for the past few days? The one you decided to smack in the face in the middle of the art museum?" He leaned towards him, squinting. "You're lucky she didn't take you out right in the middle of the tantric exhibit, because she could have easily. While you were trying to test her, she was actually testing you."

Desmond leaned back, exhaling loudly. "So it was her all along. I knew it."

Ari clicked his fingers at the waitress, who nodded and quickly brought him over a cup of coffee. Ari grabbed a sweetener and stirred the contents into his cup. Taking a sip, he considered Desmond and made a decision. "I say we make a deal. One that will make you forget my sister had anything to do with that job in Miami."

"Your sister?" Desmond said, staring at him. "Ok, tell me, why would I ever let a known murderer walk scot-free?"

"Because I don't think you had any intention of arresting her in the first place and because we're going to help you avenge your brother's death."

Desmond's eyes widened and Ari waved his hands indifferently. "Yes, we know the entire connection between your brother and the Porter's. We know about the murder at the monastery, the slaughter at the hands of Raul Salazar and Ricardo Perez. And Xanadu." Ari took another sip and leaned back, considering. "You need us, Desmond. We know things you don't and with your background in Asian Studies, your experience as a cop, and your own personal involvement in this case, we can make quite a formidable team. Together we're going to get you the answers you need as to what Connor and the Porter's were working on in Tibet and why they were all killed for it."

Desmond gripped his hands on the table's edge. "You know what it was he was working on? You know what was on the disc they took from him?"

Ari smiled. "Yes, we know what he was working on. As to the contents of the disc? We're close to finding out. There are just a few things which need to be done first and we could use your help. Starting tonight."

Desmond sat back, considering.

Finally, he nodded. "Fine, I'm in. Go on."

Chapter 10

THE SECOND DISC

The office of Raul Salazar was in a building located on a narrow street in the South Bronx. Gutted cars cluttered the pot-holed filled road, with prostitutes and homeless drug addicts shuffling by looking for tricks or their next fix.

It was two a.m. and Kelsey was in an abandoned lot across the street from the office, crouching behind a dumpster the sanitation department had long since forgotten. Used condoms and needles littered the ground and the smell of urine permeated the air, but she ignored all of it. She was focused on the two guards who stood outside the front door of Raul's building. They patrolled the perimeter, their handguns drawn as if they were expecting trouble. She saw their breath smoke in the cold night air.

She had pretended to be a prostitute and worked the block the previous two nights, strolling by the building and the guard's post, so they were well aware this street was her territory. She'd eye them in a way that told them it was more than just a friendly hello, but a strategically placed yell from her "pimp" caused her to scurry away in apparent fear. She would disappear into a stark white Cadillac with tinted windows and gold tire rims, Ari disguised behind the wheel.

Well, tonight she had no intention of running anywhere.

She glanced around the corner, waiting for her team member to arrive. She'd worked with contracted men before on other assignments when their particular expertise was needed. As long as they didn't screw things up and get in her way, she was fine with it.

There was movement to her left and she turned, shocked to see Desmond strolling towards her in civilian clothing.

What the hell? "What are you doing here?" she asked, incredulous.

"Your brother thought you could use my help," Desmond said.

I'm going to kill you, Ari. Kelsey pulled out her cell phone and punched the speed dial button savagely. "Is this your idea of a joke? Why the hell did you bring the cops into this? You know who this man is?"

She listened for a few angry moments, then huffing, shut her phone.

"Fine, you can stay, but don't fuck anything up."

"I'll try not to," Desmond said sarcastically, pulling out a Ruger P95. Certainly not the standard issue the New York City cops used. "But you should know I have as much invested in getting this last disc as you do."

Kelsey raised her eyebrows. "Oh, really? And then what are you going to do? Arrest me for getting rid of that rotten piece of shit in Miami? Or maybe you'll hit me again?" She tilted her head mockingly. "That went down well for you at the MET, didn't it, genius?"

They stared at each other in stony silence. Finally Desmond spoke. "The plan, please?"

Kelsey took off her winter coat and placed it on the ground. "The plan," Kelsey said, as she kicked off her sneakers and then brazenly pulled off her T-shirt and blue jeans to Desmond's shocked surprise, "is for you to not get in my way." She stood there clad only in a lacy red bra and black thong. Goosebumps popped up on her arms from the cold. She pulled out a sheer black camisole from her bag and slipped it on, the bra now peeking out sexily from underneath.

78

Reaching into her bag again, she pulled out a tight red leather mini-skirt and eyeballed Desmond as she shimmied it on over her hips. Desmond just stood there in silent amazement.

Yeah, now you're looking. Like what you see, buddy?

"I'm going to go over there with those two thugs. Don't be a hero and try to save me. I'll be just fine. Trust me when I say they aren't going to want to see you." Grabbing a pair of scuffed, gold high-heeled sandals, she slipped them on and then spritzed some cheap perfume down her cleavage.

"After I disable them, then and only then, do you come over. I'll need a second pair of hands to lift up one of the guys."

Desmond nodded in understanding. "The handprint sensor."

She huffed. *Thank God he knows something.* She expertly applied cheap pink lipstick without a mirror. "Are you planning on coming inside with me?"

"Yes."

She raised her eyebrows questioningly. "You bring a car?"

He tossed his head. "Two blocks back, parked in the alley by Raul's office window."

Good, good. She pulled a few strands of hair out from her ponytail, where they fell messily around her face, then leaned into her bag and removed a spiky metal roller. It was the kind holistic chiropractors used for topical acupuncture treatments. Squaring her shoulders and squinting, she started at her wrists and then rolled it hard up her arm. Tiny red pinpricks of blood sprang up.

"What the hell are you doing?" Desmond asked aghast, reaching out to stop her.

She smacked his hand away. "Making needle tracks." She quickly ripped a second track on her other arm.

"You're unbelievable," he breathed, stepping back.

79

You haven't seen anything yet, cop. Kelsey then took out a small vial and squeezed out two drops of liquid in each eye, flinching from the burn. Seconds later she looked up, her eyes beet red, her nose runny, and her costume complete.

A beautiful, used-up young hooker now stood before Desmond. Staring at her, you knew she would have been pretty if she hadn't succumbed to drugs and the street. Now she just looked worn and tired. Kelsey knew Desmond had seen enough of them back at the precinct to know she could have fit right in with the best of them.

Kelsey placed everything back in her pack and adjusted her bra, hoisting up her breasts so her cleavage was even more revealing. From Desmond's expression, she knew they looked fine. *As good as having a mirror.* "Seriously, don't come over until I disable both of them. Come too soon and it's my ass on the line. I won't have my gun with me. Just remember to bring my bag. Got it?"

With that she turned away from Desmond's stunned expression and sauntered down the street, her high heels clicking languidly on the concrete sidewalk.

Kelsey closed in on the two guards, smiling as she strolled towards them. She marveled that she wasn't even nervous, just excited at the prospect of trying to seduce them. *God, she was one of the weirdest chicks she knew. There really was something seriously wrong with her.*

"Hey, boys. Looking for a good time tonight?" She slid into a strong New York accent ;and slurred her words just slightly as if she were drunk.

One of the guards called out to her. "We're always looking for a good time, beautiful. Seen you around here a few times. Been waiting for you to come on over and say hello."

"Is that so?" She moved over to the speaker, a massive specimen pushing two hundred and fifty pounds of pure muscle. With his ugly, cragged face and bald dome, he exuded the kind of power only gotten with steroids. The pimples on his collarbone peeking out from his unzipped leather jacket confirmed it.

Kelsey placed her hand on his chest and then traced her fingers up and down his muscled arm. His friend giggled. He was a small guy with jet black greasy hair, a weasel-like face and jumpy eyes.

"Hey, Gino, I think she likes you," he chirped, his voice high and pitchy.

"Course she likes me, asshole. You got enough money, she'll like a donkey." He peered down at her, and then over her shoulder. "Where's your pimp tonight?"

Kelsey pouted. "Don't worry about him. He won't be bothering me. He's working a new girl on 161st Street."

Gino stared at her breasts and she breathed in deeply, pushing them up for his benefit. It was cold and her nipples were hard as rocks. Gino grinned lasciviously. "Is that so? Hey Chaz, she says no one's going to bother us tonight."

Chaz giggled excitedly, practically jumping up and down in anticipation. His gun bobbed in his hands. She could already see he was getting sexually excited.

Guys are so friggin' easy to manipulate.

Kelsey moved closer to Gino, her breasts rubbing against his chest. "I can be very good to you."

Gino cupped her breast and then grabbed her ass. "Chaz, hold my gun while I take care of some business," he said, tossing Chaz his Browning. He leaned down and kissed her neck, roughly grabbing her hair with his other hand.

Kelsey spoke up, a petulant whine now in her voice now. "Baby, not out here. My pimp will go crazy if he comes back and sees us. He's scared of Raul and doesn't want me to bother his men. Says he'll beat the shit out of me if he catches me. Let's go inside where it's warm. I'll make it worth it, I promise."

81

She ran her chipped nails down his arm and gently cupped his crotch.

Gino grasped her shoulder, a little too hard. "Fine, inside, but you gotta do both of us."

She melted into him, kissing his neck. "That definitely won't be a problem."

Squealing with excitement, Chaz scurried to the door and punched in a twelve digit code. Kelsey waited until she heard the click as it unlocked and then landed a sharp upwards elbow jab right under Gino's chin, shoving his head backwards so hard it rocked his brain. At the same time, she grabbed his belt with her free hand and pulled his body forward, nearly fracturing his neck. He fell to the floor, momentarily stunned. She turned to Chaz, who fumbled with his gun. Kelsey smacked it out of his hand and landed a ridge hand strike to his temple. He flew backwards into the brick building. His head hit the wall with a sickening sound and he fell to the ground, unconscious.

Seconds later Desmond appeared at her side. Gino tried to get up and Desmond punched him in his face twice. He collapsed back to the ground.

Desmond threw Kelsey her backpack. She reached inside, pushed aside her jacket, and pulled out her gun.

"Get the little one," she ordered, but Desmond had already lifted Chaz up and was pushing him forward. A moment later she heard the second door unlock.

She grabbed Gino's legs and started dragging him behind a dumpster. *God, he's freaking heavy.* Desmond came out and together they hid him, running back to the door to get Chaz. Once they disposed of him, Kelsey put on her backpack and followed Desmond into the building.

It was only a step up from the decay of the outside. Bare industrial floors and dirty, yellowed walls, filthy with hundreds of greasy handprints. It was apparent an enormous amount of traffic had frequented these hallways. Cigarette butts collected in the corners and a lone metal folding chair sat just inside the hallway. The smell of marijuana, tobacco and a hint of disinfectant hung in the air. It was also very warm. Old radiators clanked, banged and hissed as water moved through them. ;

"Raul's office is at the end of the hall, and up a flight of steps," she whispered, catching her breath.

He nodded, breathing hard, his own gun at the ready. They moved stealthily down the deserted corridor. They ducked their heads into the various apartments, each filled with ratty couches, tables holding scales and various sorts of drug paraphernalia.

"How long have you known about Raul's whereabouts?" Desmond asked.

Kelsey glanced at him. "About three years. Why?"

"You should have reported it to the police."

"Yeah, right. I report it to the police, he flies or lands in jail and I can't get to him, his discs or the map. As soon as I'm done with Raul, you can have him, but not a moment before."

They moved cautiously down the hallway.

"I don't understand," Desmond whispered. "You and your brother aren't cops. For Christ's sake, you're barely legal. How the hell do you get all your information and how do you know how to do any of this? And that gun? What is that, a Korth Semi Auto? That pistol is worth over four thousand dollars."

More than that. "I'll bet you just hate not knowing something, don't you?" She glanced at his face and threw him a bone. "We get our information from a Mexican girl who cleans up for Raul every week. By helping her with her family's immigration status, she's willing to give us what we need."

They moved further down the hall and ducked into another apartment, broken out into very small rooms, each with a single bed. Old condoms, filled ashtrays and drug paraphernalia littered the tables and floor. They moved back out to the hallway.

He whispered to her again. "And what about your gun?"

God, he was so damn nosey. "What's the matter? Are you jealous, thinking your Wilson might not be longer than mine? Didn't know you were so self-conscious that way, Detective."

When Desmond only stared at her, she huffed. "The gun is mine and registered. Feel free to check when we're done here. Now will you shut up about it, already?"

Footsteps clicking on the staircase sounded and they froze.

With a swiftness which threw her off guard, Desmond grabbed her around the waist and thrust her into a hall closet. She dropped her backpack to the floor and Desmond pulled her close, quietly shutting the door behind her.

As she stood there, chest-to-chest with Desmond, she noticed many things. The way the closet door pressed tightly against her backside, the way Desmond's hands held her at her waist, his gun still in his hand, and how hard and surprisingly muscular his chest was. She leaned in closer and sniffed. *He smells amazing again, too.* Her stomach jumped. Footsteps sounded outside the door.

She held her breath as a male Latino voice spoke into a walkie-talkie. "Chaz, Gino, come in. Where the hell are you guys?"

When there was only a static reply, the man cursed and they heard him stomping down the hall to find his guards. They heard the first click of the inner door and then it slamming shut.

Desmond released Kelsey and opened the door. "After you."

Did he look amused? Smart ass. She pursed her lips and put on her backpack. With a huff she moved back down the hallway, quickly up the stairs and down to the last door on the left.

Putting her ear to the door, she heard nothing, and opened it, gun drawn. No one was there, but the scene startled her. *Whoa.* Given the evident sparseness and state of disrepair of the outer offices, she was expecting more of the same, but it wasn't. A collection of treasures from ancient lands adorned the room. Baubles and trinkets shone brightly on ornate tables and filled lighted, glass display cabinets. Persian rugs hung on the walls and covered the floor. Every corner of the room held Ming Dynasty vases in various sizes. Antique maps competed for space on the wall with what looked like original masterpiece paintings. The man was a treasure hunter. A collector. A drug lord.

A murderer.

"The safe is behind that painting." Kelsey stepped up to the work of art. She was about to remove it, but paused for a moment, studying it. *This isn't possible. Could it be?* It was a stunning, gloomy painting with a depiction of a homeless man begging on a Parisian street.

Desmond whistled. "I think this is an original Picasso. Look at the signature. *Pablo Ruiz y Picasso.* It must have been one of his early works."

Kelsey nodded. "I think it is, too. This is probably one of the paintings he made when he first went to live in Paris. It's probably worth millions." She picked it off the wall and gently laid it on the desk. Behind it was a basic wall safe. Kelsey snorted. "You'd think he'd splurge on a decent safe."

Desmond moved back over to the office door and peered out. The other guard hadn't returned. "All clear."

She nodded, placed her backpack on the floor and took out a small drill and hammer. Leaning over to the locking bars on

85

the safe, she punched a small hole in the side of them. She struck the locking bar with the hammer and less than sixty seconds later, the safe popped open.

Desmond came over, clicking his tongue. "Impressive and quick. Where the hell did you learn to do all this?"

"*Law & Order.*" She reached inside, ignoring the wad of hundred dollar bills, the three bricks of cocaine, a multi-carat diamond necklace, and sighed in relief when she saw the disc holder. She removed her booted laptop from her backpack, opened the disc holder and shoved the disc into the drive. Seconds later ancient text in code popped up and flashed across her screen.

"Why don't we just take the disc and get out of here?" Desmond asked.

She shook her head. "I don't want him to know we have it. He already knows someone took Ricardo's disc. Let him think this was a regular robbery and we have no idea what the real prize in the safe is. We're buying us time."

She dialed her cell phone. "This it, Seung?" she asked, noticing Desmond's questioning glance. At the same time, the cursor jumped across the screen as Seung took control of the computer.

She listened intently, before nodding. "Give me control back." She downloaded the information to her laptop and then sent it back to Seung. Seconds later she got a confirmation it had been received and shut the phone.

Quickly and efficiently, Kelsey uploaded a virus onto the disc, corrupted the document and then placed it back in the holder and into the safe. Once Raul removed the painting, he would know it had been compromised. She took out the cash, the coke and the necklace and placed them in her knapsack. Then she quickly replaced the priceless painting, opened his closets and placed various tracking devices in the soles of his extra pairs of shoes and jackets stored there. As they turned to the window to leave, Kelsey noticed a jewelry box on the table and opened it. Inside housed a collection of charm trinkets. She pushed them around with her fingers and then snatched up a small golden elephant charm and pocketed it, "For good luck."

Then they quickly made their way down the fire escape to the unmarked sedan below.

Now it was time to get the key.

Chapter 11

TEDANALEE

It was three a.m. and Kelsey had been asleep for nearly three hours when the dream came. It was quiet outside her apartment with just the traffic from the city streets humming from fifteen floors below.

Her bedroom was dark, save for the blinking green fire alarm light in the corner of her room.

Nights when she dreamed of Tedanalee were fitful. The Goldmans always knew when she was deep in her imaginary land because they would hear her cries and the strange language she would speak.

She lay on her back with her eyes closed and her hands on top of the soft covers. Her fingers moved ceaselessly in their repetitive motions, picking up one finger, then the other, repeating with the rest, up and down, up and down like a wave as she went deeper and deeper into her dream. She started talking rapidly, kicking her feet. At times she even opened her eyes, though they stared vapidly into nothingness. Only her fingers never ceased their strange dance…

* * * * *

The bright yellow sun streaked across the sky, cutting through the Aurora Borealis, which were constant dancing ribbons of color that never completely left the sky. They reminded her of Chinese Dragon kites and streamers the way they weaved and flowed into each other. During the daytime, they were streaks of pinks and yellows and greens, while at night, the colors deepened to oranges, blues, purples and deep reds. In the distance, the peaks of the Himalayas loomed, surrounding the valley and hiding it from view behind the sheer cliff walls which protected it.

Kelsey moved through the tall grass, soft tufts of greenery enveloping her feet. Nearby her a small stream rippled over moss covered rocks. Clusters of fish, flat versions of miniature flounder collected in the deeper pools, then righted themselves and propelled their lithe bodies along with the current down the stream's path.

A tickle at her ankle made her glance down. A creature sniffed her foot, making little wet chortling noises. Its ferret-like body spun around in its excitement, as it wound its way up her leg and then suddenly, whipped itself away to scuttle into the trees on its eight little legs.

Kelsey glanced up as the call of a dungchen, a Tibetan long horn, sounded in the distance. The sentry from the castle was announcing a meeting of arms. The instrument was otherworldly and haunting, creating a long, deep wail that always gave her goose bumps.

A soft fluttering brushed her cheek and caused her to turn. She smiled brightly. The butterflies were back, but they were unlike any others of their kind that roamed the Earth. They were much bigger, more beautiful, intricate, and tame. She held out her hand and the creature floated down to her open palm. It was six inches high, with purple and black patterns adorning wings that curled at the ends with spiral threads. Even the antennae ended in a helix of feathery wisps. It gently opened and closed its wings and then softly lifted off, flying towards a group of the tiniest pink and white flowers of such devastating beauty it brought tears to her eyes.

She loved this place she had created and visited it often in her dreams. It made her feel safe and whole, like no one could ever hurt her there.

The long horn sounded again and she rose. A darkness filled the sky as an animal of immense size flew down towards her, but she wasn't afraid. She glanced up in exhilaration, her arms open wide.

It was her Fedelia. The massive creature alighted next to her and bent low, allowing her to climb onto its creamy white back, a streak the color of buttercream running from its mane straight down to its long, bushy tail.

A cross between a horse and a winged dragon, it was a creature of myth--loyal and fierce, intelligent and beautiful. Kelsey leaned forward and kissed her side. "Klikila Ishu." (Hello, my Caring Friend)

Ishu whinnied and turned her enormous snout to gently nuzzle Kelsey's face. With practiced ease, Kelsey gripped the sides of its back with her knees, grabbed the thick mane and they took off, soaring through the sky towards the golden city of Tedanalee where she would find the Emperor and Empress waiting for her.

As they soared, the long horn sounded again, but this time another joined in, the pair's call filled with urgency. The bass whirring of the instruments echoed across the land. Black bands bled through the ribbons of color streaking across the sky, cutting and spreading, like ink falling onto a master's painting and smearing the beauty that was underneath.

The Fedelia whinnied in fear.

"Ne fledili, tamas fishala," (Don't worry, we will be safe) she said, though a familiar sharp pain began in her chest.

They soared faster, desperately trying to beat the impending blackness. They were joined by other fedelia riders as they too raced past the streaks towards the city.

Suddenly, there was a terrific tearing sound, as if the very fabric of the universe had ruptured and the sky was being ripped apart. The air shook with fury, throwing Kelsey and her steed off course, but the fedelia pushed through the torrent. The air in front of them split and opened to reveal a nothingness so great that Kelsey's soul froze. It pulled at her, beckoned to her as if it were searching to destroy her very essence.

The fedelia reared back, trying to avoid it, but it was like a vacuum and began pulling her in, faster and faster. Riders fell off their mares, flying through the air and were sucked into the black void. Just before Kelsey was to be eternally lost, her mare tried one last time to free herself, but they plummeted into the abyss.

The nightmare changed, switching immediately to the never-ending horror that greeted her each time. A young girl's scream ripped the night... the scene appeared and Kelsey watched from afar, as this time, a young Mayan girl in a white ceremonial robe was dragged to the edge of a cenote, a limestone sinkhole filled with water. The teenager struggled desperately to be free of her captors, but they held onto her tight, gripping her shoulders and pulling her by her long hair.

The girl begged and pleaded, but her cries fell on deaf ears. Kelsey realized she knew this girl. How she knew her, she didn't know, but her name was Itzel.

Kelsey could do nothing except watch in horror as the girl was thrown over the edge, her nightmarish screams filling the darkness until Kelsey couldn't handle the pain of it anymore.

* * * * *

Kelsey awoke with a start, her own scream stuck in her throat. She clutched her chest as the cramp gripping her slowly subsided. Leaning over, she grabbed her cell phone on the night table and dialed Ari.

He picked up by the second ring. "You have a bad dream again?"

"Yes," she said, trying to catch her breath. She told him about it. "What does it mean, Ari? And don't give me psychobabble, I can't bear it tonight."

She heard him sigh. "Kelsey, it means what it means. Maybe internally you feel like you're coming full circle with Raul and it's all finally coming to an end. Maybe the blackness is him and you're trying to rationalize your fears in fighting him."

"And the girl?"

"Who was it this time?"

"Her name was Itzel. She was a young Mayan sacrifice. And like the others I've dreamed about, she seemed so familiar to me. And her pain. It felt real to me, too."

"The pain is as real as you believe it is, Kelsey. No more than that."

He's mocking me? Anger lathered her words. "I know what a dream is, Ari. I know the creatures in my dream of Tedanalee aren't part of this reality. But every time I have this delusional fantasy, it's like I'm back in that land just as I was when our parents brought me home. Real dreams are disjointed. They change and they have a different feel than in real life. In this place, I can smell the flowers, I can feel the cool water of the stream and it makes my hands wet. The grass on my bare feet is soft. I hear music and can see things in the distance like cities, temples and mountains. And the colors of the sky are constantly changing. The entire experience is linear and doesn't move around or fluctuate in a disjointed fashion like real dreams do. People don't just suddenly disappear or turn into animals. Nothing shifts or changes and I'm familiar with everything there. I know the rules, what's around the corner, what's in the glen and down in the valleys. I know every part of the city from the basement keeps, to the storage sheds in back of the huts, to the inner rooms of the sanctuary. It's like I'm *from* there, Ari. Even that horrible blackness has a familiarity to it.

"And, then at the end, when the dream shifts and brings me the vision of another dead girl? I somehow know these girls and feel each of their deaths personally. Each time when they die, it's like a lance to my heart."

Ari was quiet. "I don't know what to tell you. You want me to say the fantasy place is real? I've seen your drawings. Flowers no one has ever seen before. Fish that swim sideways. Cities of gold. What about the flying animals? Or the language only you seem to know and no one else on the planet, save what you've taught me? You want me tell you it's all real and this place truly exists? You're brilliant, Kelsey. Who's to say there's any limit to your imagination?"

"And the girls? What about them?"

He was silent for a moment. "You really want to know what I think?"

No, I really don't. "Of course, I do."

"I think each time you dream about one of them you're reliving your attack from when you were ten and projecting it onto a random victim so that you can cope. They're symbols of you, which is why they feel so familiar."

"So I'm conjuring them to help me cope?"

"Yes, that's what I think. What else could it be, Kelsey?"

It could be that I'm damaged. That thought hurt to think about, but it plagued her. "Maybe I'm sick. Or mentally ill, because sometimes I feel like I might be."

"I don't think that's it. In fact, you're the least crazy person I know, and that's not something I say easily, Sis."

You do have a soft side to you, Brother. "Ok, I won't get too used to it. I'm sorry I woke you."

"Want me to come over?"

"No, I'm okay. I'll talk to you tomorrow." She was about to hang up when she remembered something. "Oh, new word. Plummet is 'flitaladat.' Don't forget to say it fast and make it sound like raindrops plinking on water."

He chuckled. "Flitaladat. Ok, I'll input it in the morning. Get some sleep." She heard him hang up and then closed her eyes. She thought about how Ishu's mane felt in her hands and how earthy she smelled. Her thoughts turned to the doomed girl. It was the way all her dreams ended. With the death of one girl after another, each death more horrifying than the last and she was helpless to stop any of them.

Kelsey closed her eyes and tried to sleep, but it didn't come easily.

Chapter 12

DECODED

Ari's offices were literally humming. With projects ranging from profit and loss reports for foreign companies to developing code for websites, the constant tap of computer keys sounded like a thousand monkeys tap dancing on parquet floors.

There were other operations being run behind the scenes, operations surrounding assignments for "special projects" he and his team took on occasionally. The biggest one active right now was for the hunt for Xanadu.

The group was assembled in the conference room, waiting for Seung to give the word. He sat hunched over his computer screen, his straight black hair tied in a ponytail that stretched down his back and brushed his waist. A flaming red phoenix tattoo could be seen on his right arm, peeking out from under the rolled up sleeve of his rock t-shirt.

Ari dribbled a basketball on the concrete floor, the sound sharp and loud, echoing hollowly against the walls. He moved to the front of the massive space, took aim and tossed the ball against the hoop on the door frame. "Nothing but net," he said proudly, as he continued shooting.

Julia sat at her own computer with Dennis, watching various computer screens and cameras presently tracking Raul Salazar. He was currently in his office in the South Bronx, but he'd be on the move soon. He was like clockwork, predictable.

They still monitored him though, waiting for their next move in the game -- this one would be the hardest so far.

Kelsey leaned back on a chair, staring at the ceiling in deep thought. The mission two nights before had gone perfectly and she had Desmond to thank for that. They worked together seamlessly and he was capable and dependable. After Ari briefed her today, she realized he was right to have chosen him. Desmond's agenda was so similar to her own it was mind-boggling, but he didn't know everything and she had no intention of letting him in on all her secrets.

Still, he had come through. Now they had the contents of the second coded disc and Seung used the information from the first disc to translate the decoding syntax to the second one. He had been working all night and the table was a mess with his empty coffee cups and chocolate candy wrappers.

Kelsey closed her eyes, thinking of Desmond. More specifically, to the moment she had been shoved up against him in the closet. It should have been terrifying, the knowledge they could have been caught, but instead, she had been excited and stimulated. She remembered her surprise when her face pressed against his chest. It was strong and muscular and he smelled great, as if he bathed in some exotic scent. She vaguely wondered how he felt about her.

Frustrated, she opened her eyes. It didn't matter. She couldn't lose control like this, especially if she was going to have to continue to work with him, now that Joshua was on assignment. Josh was one of her very best friends and they had a flirty relationship. Still, they both knew where they stood with each other and she knew how far she could push him. She remembered a scene only a few years before…

* * * * *

The apartment was finally quiet. For the past ten hours Kelsey, Ari, Julia, Dennis, Seung and Joshua had been playing a marathon game of Dungeons and Dragons. Ari was a genius Dragon Master and they had traversed so far tonight no one wanted it to end. It was now three a.m. and everyone had passed out in various bedrooms, on the couches, wherever there was space.

Kelsey and Joshua were still awake, talking quietly on the balcony. It was a warm night, the stars visible and shining brightly in New York City, which was unusual because of all the air pollution. It was a beautiful evening, the lights from all the buildings blinking brilliantly and the hum of the city just a soft purr in the background.

Joshua sat next to Kelsey on the outdoor sofa, her head resting on his shoulder. She adored this man. At nineteen-years old, and he at twenty-one, they would have made an exquisite couple, so strong, so beautiful and brilliant, but Kelsey simply didn't feel that way about him. At least not usually.

Joshua stroked Kelsey's hand and played with her fingers. At one point he turned to her, took her chin in his hand and brazenly kissed her, and she let him. It was late and she was so tired, but more than that, it felt just nice to have someone to hold and touch.

"Kelsey, my little elf," Joshua whispered, grasping her chin gently.

Little elf. He was obviously referring to her Dungeons & Dragons character, but conveniently forgot she was a super powerful four hundred year old being with amazing fighting techniques and an ability to lull her victims with her voice-- thank you very much. Kelsey instinctually moved closer to him, and as he leaned back on the loveseat, in a fluid motion, she moved on top of him and he wrapped his arms around her. Her long hair fell around his face and she pressed her lips to his. He kissed her back, strongly and without a thought, while she straddled him, pushing her body against his. Everything felt so perfect. She heard his breathing quicken. She didn't want the moment to end when suddenly a wave of icy cold water was thrown on her from behind and she jumped up, shocked.

Ari, dressed only in a pair of boxer shorts stood in the balcony doorway, an empty ice bucket in his hands. "Thought you both might need that." He said it teasingly, but the look he gave Joshua lying stunned on the lounge was anything but friendly.

Kelsey stood there, glaring at her brother, water dripping off of her and onto the floor, speechless. He was so damned over-protective. She couldn't even find the words to yell at him.

"That's better." He turned and stepped back into the apartment.

Kelsey glanced at Joshua and he shrugged. "It was probably for the best. Last thing I need is to get Ari all pissed off at me. Felt like I was kissing my sister anyway."

Kelsey moved back over to the sofa, leaned over Joshua, water droplets falling onto his chest, and gave him one last lingering kiss, her tongue teasing his mouth. "Really, this is just like kissing your sister?"

He nodded, swallowing hard. "Yeah, I felt nothing. Absolutely nothing."

With that Kelsey smirked and slinked back into the apartment, leaving Joshua alone to regain his composure.

* * * * *

Still, she knew with Joshua there'd be no lasting repercussions. He'd never do anything to betray his trust with Ari, so she knew he would only take it so far. Not like it would be with Desmond. Ari wouldn't be there with a cold glass of water to stop her if things got out of control. *Why would they get out of control? What in the heck was wrong with her suddenly?*

"It's time," Seung announced, waking her from her reveries. They all crowded around him.

Seung glanced over his shoulder at Kelsey. "Your father was brilliant. When he turned these discs over to the monks, he must have known to encrypt them so no one would be able to easily translate the information. I can tell Raul and his men have tried to decode it. There are different language decryption programs I can see that have been applied, but none of them have worked so far. We're lucky they weren't destroyed in the process.

"It took me awhile to figure out what your father had actually done, but here it is. There are no symbols for a standard alphabet, so no way to get any language algorithms going. What it looks like is that your dad translated everything phonetically. Don't ask me to tell you what language this is or what any of the words mean though, because I've never heard of it before. The world structure appears to be similar to many of the Eastern and Central Asian languages, so I've tried to find obscure or abandoned dialects for Tibetan, Chinese and even Burmese, but none fit. Maybe even Hindi or Thai, but it's not any of them either. Ari, you're the linguistics genius, maybe you can figure it out."

He sat back while they all leaned in. One look and Kelsey sucked in her breath and nearly fell backwards. Ari caught her and they both stared at each other in abject shock.

"What? What?" Julia, Seung and Dennis all said together.

No, this isn't possible. Kelsey shook, her fingers moving repetitively in the age old motion. Ari grabbed her hands, stilling them and she stared at him, wide-eyed and frightful.

"What does this mean? How can this be?" She started to hyperventilate.

He shook his head, for once, completely and utterly speechless.

Julia spoke up. "If one of you doesn't explain what the hell is going on, I'm going to scream."

Ari stared at the screen, and then back at Julia. "That language... it's... the language of Tedanalee," he stammered.

Seung raised his eyebrows. "Kelsey's made-up language? The one she dreams about? That's impossible."

I thought so, too. Kelsey gently removed her hands from Ari's, took a deep, disjointed breath and slowly returned her gaze to the screen. She leaned in, saying the words silently, her lips moving. She glanced at her friends. "I understand everything on this screen. I can translate all of it. It's a Tibetan Buddhist Prayer. *'May I become at all times, both now and forever a protector for those without protection, a guide for those who have lost their way, a ship for those with oceans to cross, a bridge for those with rivers to cross, a sanctuary for those in danger, a lamp for those without light, a place of refuge for those who lack shelter and a servant to all in need.'"*

Seung shook his head. "Your Dad transcribed the words from old scrolls he got from the monks directly to this disc, right?"

Kelsey nodded.

"Did your parents ever speak this language to you?"

Speak Tedanaleese? Of course not, it's not even a real language. Kelsey shook her head. "And I never saw it written either, so I'd have no idea how to read it if it weren't written out phonetically on paper. That's how I've been teaching it to Ari."

"How many languages did your dad know?" Seung asked.

THE HUNT FOR XANADU

Kelsey pursed her lips. "Four. English, Tibetan, Mandarin and French. And a little bit of Egyptian, too."

Ari ran his hands through his hair. "Then how in the hell is the language of Tedanalee on this disc, Kelsey?"

I don't know, I don't know! She swallowed hard, staring wordlessly at the sentences as they flashed on the screen, clicking page after page.

Seung sat back, crossing his arms. "So you're telling us you are fluent in a language that, apparently, the monks have been keeping secret for thousands of years?"

She stared at all of them silently and then nodded. "I guess I do."

There was nothing else to say.

* * * * *

They were in Desmond's townhouse in a comfortably-appointed family room decorated to resemble a country ski lodge. Rustic furniture and heavy oak coffee tables were placed strategically around the room, giving it the illusion of great space. A bookshelf filled with biographies of musicians and poets and family photographs lined the back wall. A large flat screen TV hung over the fireplace. The fireplace itself was a real one, not like the fake ones many apartments in New York City boasted. This one was presently burning with two *Duraflame* logs, their colors dancing upwards through the draft, like colorful ribbons of light.

Kelsey tore her eyes from it. They reminded her too much of the sky in Tedanalee and she simply couldn't think about it after the revelation she somehow knew a secret language the monks had kept hidden. A language she was never taught. She and Ari had sat up for hours discussing how and why and they still had no answers. Instead, they decided to move on to the last part of the plan. The last, most dangerous part and one which would test her beyond anything she had experienced so far.

"So, what's the next step?" Desmond asked, sitting on one of the sumptuous leather couches. He was finishing up a grilled chicken sandwich.

Kelsey paced the room, having already shoved down a tuna sub, barely even tasting it. She ran her fingers along the fireplace mantle and stared thoughtfully at the framed photograph showing a much younger version of Desmond playfully holding a blond infant in his arms. He seemed so happy. She turned back to the burning log. "*Hritili ooch tlashaphah* (ribbons of light)," she whispered as she fixated on the colors streaking upwards. She turned back to Desmond, a little unsure of how to begin. She hardly knew this man. How she wished Joshua could do this assignment with her. At least she knew where he stood. He'd relish the job and then tease her about it mercilessly for years on end.

On second thought, maybe that wasn't such a good idea.

"Look, I know you just made detective and found Ricardo, but there's nothing in the logs anywhere that the Miami trip was sanctioned by the department."

"How do you know this?" Desmond frowned.

"We checked up on you."

Desmond stared at her for a full minute and then sighed. "No, the trip wasn't sanctioned by the department. Let's just say my cold cases haven't been getting the highest priority and I decided to see what I could do myself."

Kelsey nodded. *So he could play outside the rules. Maybe he could do this after all.* "Raul keeps the map he stole from my father locked in a wooden box. The key to this box is kept on a chain he wears around his neck and he never takes it off. The concern is with me stealing the disc from Ricardo, he may do something rash. It's time for me to take the map before something happens to it."

Desmond took a swig from his water bottle. "So you want to steal the box to get to the map?"

"We'll steal it eventually, but not yet. First, we need the key to open it. Supposedly, if you open the box without the key, it'll destroy the object inside. Some sort of trigger, a liquid or something inside it. I don't know how much of it I believe. It's a little too *Da Vinci Code* for my taste, but I'm not prepared to take the risk after all these years."

Desmond wiped his hands on his napkin. "So, how do you expect to get your hands on this key if he keeps it around his neck all the time?"

"I'll just have to get close to him."

Desmond raised his eyebrows. "And how do you expect to do that?"

Ok, here we go. "The last Thursday of every month, Raul travels to South Beach where he frequents a high-end swingers club called "Garters." Raul isn't into swinging himself, but likes to have sex with women who are with their own devoted men and who like to watch their partners with other people." She let that sink in.

Desmond lean back and exhaled with a blasting breath. "Let me get this straight. You intend to have sex with Raul to get this key?"

Kelsey rolled her eyes disgustedly. "Are you out of your mind? Have sex voluntarily with the man who killed my parents?" *That was the least of her reasons.* She shook her head, pacing. "Raul likes younger girls and always chooses the same type. They've got long dark hair, blue eyes, fair skin, about five-six, five-seven, big chests. That remind you of anyone in this room?"

Desmond sighed.

She smirked. "Good, so we have an understanding. I could do this myself, could possibly get him to choose me, where I would hope to get him into one of the private rooms, do the job and then get out, all on my own. But, it would be much easier, and according to Ari, a much greater chance of success, if I could play the part the way it goes down each and every time. I'd rather not blow the one opportunity he gets to have a good look at me without a disguise on and then not get selected. So, if I had a partner, the entire operation will go more smoothly. Just know if you intend to help me, you'll have to play the part of my husband. This isn't going to be a Sunday School lecture or a square dance. It's a sex club."

"Why me? Why not have Ari help you?" Desmond asked.

"You want me to do this with my own brother? No, thanks. Besides the obvious, he's too much of a live wire, has anger issues and while he is brilliant in support, planning and maneuvers, on-point, he'd have a problem controlling himself. The first time Raul touches me Ari would probably hit him. I need someone with more of a level head who can control himself. Don't take this the wrong way Desmond, but I had someone else in mind for this assignment. Unfortunately, he's presently unavailable and I can't afford to wait for him to get back in town. I have to move now and with your connections to the case, we thought you would be a good fit."

Desmond considered this. "Just how much of a part am I playing?"

Exactly how much would you like to play, Desmond? "I'm not intending to sleep with you either."

He reddened. "Um, I wasn't expecting you to." He drummed his knees with his fingers. "Ok, I'll do it. Just tell me what I'd have to do."

She eyed his rumpled blue jeans and polo shirt. "Well, first of all, you need to get some club clothes, something black, tight and designer. Then we have to get a flight to Miami by tomorrow night." She paused, staring at him. "Listen, I don't know you that well. In fact, except for what I've read online and the amount of time we spent on the last job, I don't know you at all. I can fake this with the best of them. You saw me with Gino and Chaz, so you know I can handle this, but I need to make sure you won't freak out on me or get all weird when we're in there. You'll have to play your part well if we want Raul to be convinced of the ruse and be interested enough in us to take us to one of the back rooms. Are you going to be able to do this? Tell me now so if I have to, I can come up with an alternate plan."

Desmond stared at her coolly. "I think I can handle this, Kelsey. I may hate this man with everything in my being, but I won't freak out seeing him. And for another matter, you won't be the first woman I've ever been close with. I was married before and for the record, I can improvise with the best of them."

Oh really? We'll see about that. Without warning, she hopped over to Desmond, straddled his lap, took his startled face in both her hands and kissed him, passionately and deeply. For a brief, tense moment, he didn't move, but then he relaxed, moved his hands to her waist and started kissing her back. She felt him draw her close to him, his tongue enter her mouth. Her stomach fluttered and after a few more tantalizing seconds she pulled back, staring headily into his eyes.

That had been... incredible.

"Yeah, you'll do just fine," she said quickly, jumping off of him and moving to the couch on the far side of the room.

Desmond sat there, staring at the ceiling and trying to get his breath back.

* * * * *

The fire was dying down in the bedroom fireplace, the colored embers drawing into small tufts of orange and yellow light, one by one fading to ash. Desmond sat on the floor in front of the hearth on the area rug, thinking.

So many people he loved had died at the hands of Raul Salazar and Ricardo Perez. Innocents caught up in something which had nothing to even do with them. He thought about his baby boy. He had barely gotten the chance to know him. And Charlotte. So sweet and humble and unaffected by the amount of money she had. Even this brownstone he was living in now. It had been a wedding gift from her parents. They'd been content living in Desmond's West Side Village studio.

Desmond held a photograph of his family, staring at Tyler as Charlotte held him in her lap, both of them smiling at him behind the camera. Charlotte's round Irish face was beaming, her light blue eyes happy as she held her baby, her strawberry blond curls bouncing gently on Tyler's shoulders. Tyler laughed, his new baby teeth peeking through his smile.

Ten years since they'd been murdered. He was sure it hadn't been a simple hit and run. Perhaps their murderers had found out he tried to avenge his brother's death and punished him. Perhaps they had thought he was in the car with them.

None of it mattered. They were dead and gone and now he was avenging all of them. He had given up opportunities to advance his career, wanting only to be on the street and to be assigned to cold cases where he could solve crimes--and to always have this case active in the background.

He'd had his share of partners over the years. Men and women who were loyal, good cops, but they never lasted long. They simply didn't fit into his world and they slowly took other assignments. There were a few casual girlfriends over the years, but they never lasted long either. He kept mostly to himself, both on and off the force.

Then he finally got a break in the case.

A few weeks ago, right at the time he got his promotion to detective, he had busted a young drug dealer who knew Ricardo. He spilled his guts to Desmond to get a lighter sentence. The fact that Ricardo was in Miami drastically complicated things. The paperwork alone to coordinate between state departments would take days, maybe weeks, and he just couldn't afford to waste any more time. So, he decided to do it on his own.

He closed his eyes and his mind drifted to Kelsey Porter.

Her face came unbidden to him. Those big, succulent lips, those eyes, the way she'd kissed him. It was so brazen and cocky. She was like no other woman he'd ever met before and while he had been with his share, Kelsey seemed different than all of them. Something about her appealed to his very being, as if she had been physically made for him. He remembered being thrust up against her in Raul's office closet. It felt so good holding her and he was disappointed when it ended. He thought she might have felt the same by the way her heart had started racing. He could literally feel it pounding through her shirt when her breasts were pressed against him.

What was he thinking? That was probably all adrenaline because they were inches away from getting caught. The girl was a professional, for god's sake.

The question begged, was he going to be able to get through the next assignment with the evident desire he felt for her? There was no doubt in his mind she'd be able to play her part well. Just the way she'd handled Gino and Chaz told him she was experienced. Normally it would have disturbed him, but for some reason he didn't care. It was her past and none of his business. What he did care about was that she was also brilliant and fearless and those things fueled his desire for her, making him question his own resolve. And her hair smelled good, too, dammit.

So much he still didn't know. He thought about Ari, knowing there was no way they were blood relations with his dark Sephardic looks and her lily white complexion. More so than not, she had gone to live with him and his family after the deaths of her parents. Between that time and this, she'd become a powerhouse, and apparently, her brother as well. There was just too much to think about.

He concentrated on his own brother and his son, imprinting those faces in his mind so if he started to get swayed while on assignment with Kelsey, he'd think of them. Maybe he could think of baseball.

He just hoped all of it would be enough.

Chapter 13

SMOKE AND MIRRORS

They checked into their rooms at a hotel in South Beach, Miami. It was a modest space for a suite--two bedrooms with queen-sized beds, a small living room, dining table and open kitchen.

It was now ten o'clock in the evening and Desmond stood by his bathroom mirror, trying to tame his mane with hair gel. Freshly shaven and wearing expensive designer black slacks, a button down shirt and new black shoes, he could have passed for any of the fashionable men roaming the streets of Miami.

He stared at his reflection and suddenly wondered what on God's earth he was doing here? How in the hell was he going to pull this off? He realized he'd agreed to this assignment without fully thinking it through and now he was nervous as hell. To actually stand next to Raul Salazar, the man responsible for his family's death, and not do anything about it? Turning, he moved into the adjoining room just as the other bedroom door opened. He froze, mid-step.

Kelsey breezed into the living room and it was as if the very air had been electrified. She was breathtaking. Her hair, which she always seemed to keep tied back, was now down, cascading in deep, thick waves swaying to the middle of her back. She wore a sexy, glittering silver sequined mini-dress with a deep v-neck and mile high stiletto heels. Her face is what shook Desmond to his core. Expertly applied make-up made her navy blue eyes alluringly sexy. Her lips were wet and glossy and her porcelain skin was flawless. Exotic earrings sparkled from her ears and an intricate cuff bracelet graced her arm. She looked like a model or a movie star and he was stunned to silence.

She paused at his expression and then rolled her eyes. "Easy, Desmond. It's all just smoke and mirrors. A little pancake and nothing else."

Desmond found his breath. "No offense, but I'm not exactly sure what mirror you're looking into." He spread his hands wide and turned in a circle, a little embarrassed. "Um, is this okay?"

She stared at him appreciatively, a light blush coming to her cheeks. "Yeah, you look great. I like what you did with your hair." She leaned towards him and sniffed. "And you smell nice again, too. You put that on for me?"

He grinned, both embarrassed and relieved. "Maybe a little. I guess we both clean up well. Just for the record, no matter what happens tonight, know I'll only be thinking of your mind."

That made her laugh. It was so genuine, it released any tension in the room, the awkwardness for the moment disappearing.

Chapter 14

GARTERS

It was eleven o'clock in the evening and it was hot and muggy on the strip. A sleek black limousine slowly pulled up to the entrance of the social club. A long line extended from the front of the building and around the block, packed tight with beautiful young things in slinky, glittery clothing. There was a mix of different types of couples ranging from older men with young women, to middle-aged couples looking for a good time. Two enormous bouncers stood at the head of the line, a velvet rope separating them from the crowd, slowly letting in those who fit the profile of the clientele they wished to entertain that evening.

A hired driver climbed out of the car, resplendent in his chauffer's uniform, and opened the door for his passengers. Desmond rolled out first. The bouncer glanced his way, but what he waited for was his guest. Desmond held out his hand and helped Kelsey out of the vehicle. One look exchanged between the two bouncers and the velvet line parted. Desmond and Kelsey breezed inside to the complaints of those still waiting on line.

The club was mystical and intoxicating. Rose-colored filters played with the light and essential oils permeated the air. Deep, sexy music streamed through speakers hidden in the walls. They came first to the entrance lobby where they were served a glass of high quality champagne. Then they passed through a security check and turned over any cellphones and

111

cameras. Once cleared, they were ushered through the thick tapestried curtain and into the vast open space which reminded one of an airline hanger. Throughout the club were multiple dance floors, high stage platforms for pole dancers to move provocatively for their partners, as well as multi-level seating areas, flush with couches, chairs and even communal king-sized beds. To the back of the building was a flight of steps which led up to a long hallway to the private rooms, for those guests who wanted to take their desires to the next level.

Kelsey held Desmond's hand as she negotiated him further into the club, past sumptuous booths occupied with people drinking and cavorting, now and again clicking the lamplights in front of them to indicate their needs and desires.

He whispered in her ear. "What do all the different light colors mean?"

She stopped walking and leaned her back against him, holding his arms about her waist. *This feels nice.* "They're a guide to let others know what you're seeking. There are three types of lights. Yellow if you're looking for a man, red for a female, and green if you're looking for a couple. You flick your light to show your desire and then interested parties will come over to you. If you like one of them, you hit a second light of the same color, but only if you see someone you would consider going into one of those back rooms with. At that point, they decide if they're going to take you up on your offer and they'll either come over or buy you a drink and you take it from there."

"Been here before?" he asked, sarcastically.

She eyed him. "No, but Ari staked it out for me last month, thank you very much. Apparently, he had a very nice time."

She started walking again, aiming towards an open booth in the middle of the room. It had a clear view of the entrance to the club and they could observe anyone entering or leaving.

A narrow, low table sat in front of an oversized couch, an unlit lamp resting on top of it.

She moved in and Desmond joined her. A waitress appeared immediately. "May I get you something to drink?"

Kelsey slid over to Desmond and wrapped her arms around his neck. "I'll have an appletini, please. And you, my love?" She turned and tilted her head so she could nuzzle his earlobe.

"I'll have a gin and tonic, thanks."

She could tell she was tickling him by the way he squirmed.

The waitress sauntered away and Kelsey leaned back, watching her go.

"How long before Raul shows up?" Desmond asked.

Hopefully, soon. While teasing you is fun, seeing Raul and not killing him is the last thing I want to do. She cocked her head. "Could be an hour, maybe two."

The waitress was quick, their drinks placed on the low table. Desmond slipped her two twenties and she was gone. He took a sip of his drink, but Kelsey didn't move towards hers. "You're not drinking?"

She shook her head. "I hate the stuff. Just ordered it for show."

They made small talk as they casually watched the decadent displays going on around them. To their right, an attractive middle-aged woman in a skin tight gold lame dress had jumped up on one of the platforms and gyrated for her husband and another couple- to great applause. On their other side, a lesbian couple kissed each other passionately. It was interesting to note the light in front of them was yellow. Waiting for a man.

The other booths quickly filled with customers in various stages of undress or flirtations. Kelsey leaned over and flicked the yellow switch on their lamp, then turned back to Desmond and straddled his lap. *Showtime. Let's see if you can handle me.* She leaned towards him and started nuzzling his neck.

He exhaled, his hands resting gently on her waist. "Kelsey, is this really necessary?"

She ran her lips and the tip of her nose up and down his throat. "Well, unless we want to look like complete voyeurs we could just sit back and talk, but that's like going to a nude beach and never removing your towel. Look around, Desmond. We have to play the game or we'll stand out. Don't worry, I promise I won't hurt you." She teased, nibbling on his ear.

An Asian man in his fifties strolled over to them and grinned. He wore a diamond ring bigger than the cherry in Kelsey's drink. Kelsey glanced at him and then turned back to Desmond, ignoring the man completely.

The guy took the hint and moved away.

Desmond grabbed her wrist and held it up. "Nice bracelet."

"It's a Kundalini cuff bracelet. Do you really like it or are you just trying to get me to stop messing with you?"

Desmond swallowed hard. The image on the silver bracelet was of a serpant coiled three and a half times around a smokey grey lingam.

"Maybe a little of both, though I can't believe you're wearing a bracelet with a phallus on it."

What a prude. "I thought it would be appropriate. We are in a sex club, Desmond. Actually, this is a charm bracelet which will supposedly give me the power of pure desire." She leaned in and continued to nuzzle his neck, feeling Desmond's pulse racing.

"Just tell me what it is you like about places like this?"

Like? She didn't know if she liked them or not. Watching all the couples cavorting around her didn't seem to affect her at all, though it did have a slight familiarity to it. She wondered about that. She moved to his jawbone and ran her lips across it, kissing it lightly. *Man, he smelled good.* "I don't really care either way. People can do whatever they want, though personally, I see no reason to bring someone else into my relationships. I'd think one person who you care about would be enough to satisfy you, don't you?"

"Yeah, sure."

She tantalized him with her mouth, and she hadn't even done anything more than playfully toy with his neck and ears.

"So how would you like your first time with someone to be?" he said.

What did he just say? Does he know? Kelsey pulled back and peered into Desmond's eyes, searching. *No, he can't possibly know about my past.* She leaned forwards and continued playing with his neck. "I'd want it to be special, fairy tale stuff. Have a decadent dinner, walk hand in hand in a garden with flowers and violins, and end up in a sumptuous, luxurious hotel room entangled in each other's arms." She started kissing him under his chin, running her lips across his neck.

Desmond closed his eyes. "I didn't know you were such a romantic."

"There's a lot of things you don't know about me." Suddenly, she froze glancing towards the entranceway. Her blood felt like it had turned to ice. "He's here, Desmond. Make it good."

With that, she sat up on her knees, faced Desmond and brought her face to his, kissing him. He responded and she felt him wrap his arms around her and give in, content to let her lead.

Raul stepped into the room, moving slowly past the couples cavorting on the couches, searching for those couples seeking men only. He passed by Kelsey and Desmond and

115

Kelsey turned to face him smiling coyly. *Get a good look, you disgusting pile of scum, because I'm going to kill you one day.*

She eyed Raul and while she bit her bottom lip seductively, she didn't hit her light for him to come over. Instead, she shrugged her shoulders, turned back to Desmond and began kissing him again. Raul squinted his eyes and laughed loudly, his back gold tooth glinting in the light, and moved past them towards the bar.

When he was out of sight, Desmond pulled back. "Why did you do that?" he asked, slightly out of breath. "We had him."

"I'm toying with him. Trust me, he'll be back." With that, she planted her lips on him again before he could stop her and it was even more fiery than before.

* * * * *

Minutes later Raul sauntered back with a cognac in his hand and leaned against a column opposite Kelsey and Desmond. He watched them, appearing as if they had no desire for anyone else in the club but themselves.

"Desmond, grab my bottom," Kelsey breathed.

"What?" he asked, startled.

"Just grab my tush and don't freak out," she said, planting her mouth on him again and rising up on her knees slightly.

Desmond ran his hands under her dress and froze. She wasn't wearing any underwear.

"Stay cool. Raul loves this. Just sealing the deal."

He pulled her towards him, running his hands up dress, holding her waist and for another few tantalizing seconds they both seemed to forget where they were until Desmond tore himself away from her mouth. "Kelsey… Raul."

What just happened? Did I just lose control? Kelsey blinked a few times to clear her head. She turned towards

Raul, who now watched them from the opposite couch where he sipped his drink. He tipped his glass in her direction, his eyes flooded with lust. This time, without hesitation, she leaned over and flicked a second switch on her lamp.

Yellow.

Raul put down his drink and sauntered over to them. The scumbag was of medium height, dark complexioned and had a full head of slick, curly black hair. You could see the ends curling up on the nape of his neck, glistening from hair gel. When he smiled, his gold crown glinted amidst bleached white teeth. A two carat diamond earring pierced his left ear and a small gold hoop hung in the right ear. Two deep, jagged scars ran down both his pock-marked cheeks. *My mother gave you those, you bastard.*

Kelsey slowly slid off Desmond's lap and pulled down her dress. She grabbed Desmond's hand and led him over to Raul like a puppy. Ignoring Desmond, Raul leaned over and grabbed the back of Kelsey's head, bringing her forwards and kissing   her. She tasted the cognac on his lips. It was all she could do not to vomit. *Desmond, don't do anything, please. Play your part.*

"Yes, you'll do just fine," Raul said, pulling back. His voice was deep, guttural and made her skin crawl. Together the three of them sauntered towards the rooms in the back of the club. Desmond took Kelsey's hand as they moved through the cavernous space.

He leaned towards her. "Your fingers are ice cold."

She shushed him, squeezing his hand as they proceeded up the steps and down the hallway where they were given one of the special private VIP rooms.

Raul slid the door open and slipped inside the perfumed chamber, scented with musk and other essential oils. The space was the size of a small hotel room with a king-sized bed, a couch and sitting area. The walls were a dusky rose and the lights in the wall sconces exuded a soft yellow glow. There was approximately five feet of space before the bed, with a small upholstered armchair and petite side table flush against the wall.

"Have a seat, my love," Kelsey told Desmond, nodding towards the chair. Raul moved over to her and took her in his arms, grabbing her and rubbing her against him roughly. Kelsey casually reached her hands behind her back, pulled her dress off her left shoulder and as she kissed Raul, removed the syringe taped to her shoulder blade. She used her other hand to squeeze Raul's neck and inserted the needle. Before he even knew what happened, he collapsed.

Desmond grabbed him before he hit the ground and Kelsey shuddered, quickly moving away from Raul and up against the wall. Desmond laid him on the couch and turned to her. "You okay?"

I will be. She nodded. "Let's just get this over with."

Taking a deep breath, she moved over to Raul and took off his necklace. It was rawhide with the silver key attached to it. Desmond pulled up his own shirt and removed some modeling clay he had flattened and taped to his torso and began kneading it until it became pliable. Kelsey grabbed an ashtray and Desmond put the clay inside, using his fingers to work out any bubbles and making it as even as possible. Kelsey handed him the key. He pressed it into the clay with his thumbs to keep the pressure even before pulling it up. It was perfect. The clay now held an exact imprint of the key. He wrapped the top of the clay and ashtray with the tape and put it on the small table.

Suddenly the door opened and a waitress stuck her head in, asking for drink orders. Desmond grabbed Kelsey and threw her onto the bed. She knew immediately what he was doing. She wrapped her legs and arms around him and started kissing him.

The waitress nodded knowingly and closed the door, never noticing Raul on the couch on the opposite wall, hidden within the shadows of the room.

When the lock clicked shut, Desmond pulled back. *No, Desmond, don't stop kissing me.* Kelsey looked deeply into his beautiful eyes. They were misty with desire. She knew that look.

Between the deep bass music, the scents in the air and the way they touched each other, Kelsey was overwhelmed. Even with Raul unconscious on the couch across the room, part of her wanted Desmond badly and she could swear he felt the same. The question was, how far would she let it go?

Desmond bent forward and kissed her again. He caressed her face and ran his hands up and down her body, his mouth never leaving hers. There was a strange familiarity to it and desire and pure need flooded her being.

Reaching down, he pulled up her dress.

Wait, wait! I have to stop! Why did she have to stop? She didn't want to. Conflicting thoughts tore through her brain. *No, you have to. Get yourself under control, Kelsey. You must. This isn't the way it should be your first time.*

With effort, Kelsey pulled her lips away. "Desmond, please. I have to tell you something--before we do anything further."

"What?"

She saw his pants fall to the floor. He was definitely ready. *Oh my God. What am I doing?*

"I've – I've never done this before. Not really."

He laughed. "I know. This is the craziest thing I've ever done, too." He planted his lips on hers again.

She desperately needed to talk to him and simply explain herself, but she was having such a hard time. His smell and the way he touched her overwhelmed her. The way he felt as he pressed his body against hers was driving her wild. "No," she said finally, between kisses. "It's not… what I meant exactly. It's just," she paused, trying to speak.

He wasn't giving her a chance to answer. He ran his lips up her neck, right under her earlobe and she moaned softly. *I don't want this to ever, ever stop.* "Oh… just forget it."

Desmond moved on top of her and it happened so quickly she flinched in surprise and winced for a moment in pain. At that moment, Desmond froze, apparently suddenly and completely aware what she'd been trying to tell him.

"You mean you've never done *this* before? You're a virgin?"

Oh, the expression on his face! Kelsey shrugged helplessly. "Well… technically, I'm not. Raul and his men took care of that in Tibet."

Desmond immediately turned to roll off her, but she wrapped her legs around him. "No… don't, please."

He stared at her in disbelief. "What do you expect me to do?"

What did she expect him to do? "I don't know. It's … maybe you can show me… what the big deal is?" *Oh, my God, she was so pathetic. This wasn't how it was supposed to happen.*

He shook his head. "I don't know if I can do that."

Grimacing, Kelsey nodded and released her legs. She felt Desmond stall in sheer indecision. She was about to ask him to get off of her when he bent down to her and gently ran his fingers against her jaw, making her shiver. Leaning in slowly, he kissed her again, but this time it was so much gentler than before. He began to move slowly and she felt her body tingle everywhere.

It went on for excruciating, tantalizing minutes, and then Desmond upped his pace, watching her intently. Kelsey couldn't catch her breath. It was as if her entire body was on fire, when suddenly she gasped and her entire being shuddered.

She heard Desmond groan and felt him drop his head to her shoulders and press himself even closer to her.

As they lay there, her senses slowly returning, she was keenly aware that she had let a man she hardly knew take her "virginity," in a sex club, with Raul Salazar, her rapist and the murderer of her parents lying unconscious in the room with them.

And she had enjoyed it.

Disgusted wasn't even the word.

Chapter 15

REPERCUSSIONS

As gently as possible, Desmond rolled over and lay on his back atop the rumpled sheets next to Kelsey. Raul was still unconscious on the couch. Kelsey sat up and glanced at Desmond, staring at his nakedness. *What did I just do?* She wanted to talk to him and make sure things were okay, but when he didn't move or say anything after a full minute, she scooted off the bed. The sudden awkwardness was agonizing.

She quickly pulled down her dress, and grimacing, moved across the room to unzip Raul's pants, pulling them down a bit. Part of her wanted to kill him right then and there. It would have been so easy. She glanced at the bed pillow, imagining shoving it in his face until he suffocated.

Instead, she removed a micro-sized lipstick taped under her arm, quickly applied it and then leaned in and kissed Raul's collar cuff, her lip-prints smearing and staining it. While he wouldn't remember anything, he would have at least thought he had done something that night and wouldn't get suspicious. She didn't glance at Desmond, who still hadn't said a word to her. She untied Raul's shoes and then removed two micro tracking devices taped under her breasts and placed them under the soles. They were so small and flat, he would never even feel them. Lastly, she placed the key back around his neck.

"We should leave. He'll be coming around in a few minutes." She couldn't even look at Desmond, realizing she'd mistaken how he felt. He didn't like her or have any feelings for her. He had just gotten excited by what she had been doing to him, the job, having sex with her, and now he was uncomfortable at the ramifications. *Oh, she had made such a mistake. So stupid of her to let herself get out of control and finally let her feelings sway her.*

Desmond sat up and silently buckled his pants. Kelsey realized he was probably repulsed by her behavior. Could she blame him? How much class could she possibly have to allow this to happen? Letting men like Gino and Raul Salazar touch her, going out in public places without her underwear on. She'd acted like a promiscuous slut, so he'd treated her like one. What did she expect?

When he finished dressing he turned to her. "Kelsey, can we talk about this?" He picked up the ashtray and put it in his pocket.

She shook her head, embarrassed. All she wanted to do was get out of there and get as far away from Desmond as possible. "Not now, let's just leave." Without another word, she opened the door, planted a plastic smile on her face, grabbed his hand and they ambled slowly down the hallway, down the steps and across the club floor.

They retrieved their cellphones and wallets and left the club. Their driver waited for them outside in the limo.

He opened the back door and without a word Kelsey jumped in. Desmond moved inside and sat opposite her before the driver sped away. She laid her head on the backseat and closed her eyes so she didn't have to talk to him. Not that it mattered. He never uttered a single word the entire ride back.

Before they even came to a full stop in front of the hotel, Kelsey flew out of the car and raced up the front steps. Desmond shot out after her. "Kelsey, we need to talk about what happened."

No, we most certainly don't. She stopped and turned to him. "Please, it's okay. Don't worry about it. I'm fine."

His eyes pleaded with her. "I didn't understand what you meant. You should have told me."

She shook her head. "I tried to, but it doesn't matter. I could have stopped you. I just got carried away. Really, it's not that big a deal. We've got the key and that's all that matters, so let's just forget about this and move on." She held out her hand. "The cast, please?"

Desmond took the ashtray out of his pocket and handed it to her.

She turned and walked up the steps.

Desmond wouldn't let it go. "No, it is a big deal. Please, I'm so sorry, but I didn't know what to do. I just felt so bad, I didn't realize what was happening... and you looked so pitiful!"

Revulsion tore through her and her stomach clenched violently. She turned to him, her features contorting. "You pitied me? That's the reason you continued to have sex with me? Only because you felt bad for me?"

He raised his eyebrows. "No, that's not what I meant!"

Get away, get away, get away. Without a word, she turned, opened the door to the hotel and ran to her room.

* * * * *

As Desmond watched her retreating back, he kicked himself. How many times was he going to screw up with this girl? He had never forced himself on anyone in his entire life and while he knew what happened wasn't entirely his fault, it shook him to his very core. To be so torn between shock and incredulity, but at the same time so flooded with desire, was something he'd never experienced. He had started to have feelings for this girl, strong feelings he hadn't had since his wife had died, but he'd misjudged her. He would have bet everything he owned she was one of the most experienced young women he knew and then to find out it was all an act?

Then he screwed it up further by not being able to explain himself properly. She must be mortified by his behavior.

He rubbed his face with both his hands, and ran his fingers through his hair. *"I'm an idiot."* As he trudged up the hotel steps, he knew he had to explain himself. He went into their suite, but her bedroom door was shut and she was silent behind it. He decided not to make things worse and would talk to her in the morning.

That never happened. When Desmond knocked on Kelsey's door at ten o'clock to catch their flight home, he found she'd left hours before. She was probably already halfway home to New York by then.

Chapter 16

YOU DID WHAT?

The screaming could be heard throughout the entire floor.
"You slept with him?"

The very air in the room seemed to ripple in waves of contempt and frustration as Ari hovered over Kelsey at the conference table. He was livid, his face a beet red and his body language so threatening, Dennis, Seung and Julia sat dead silent on the other side of the table, grimacing. Ari's fists were clenched so tightly his knuckles were white and he slammed them hard on the tabletop on either side of Kelsey. She didn't move, remaining as rigid as a stone statue.

Ari hit the table again, toppling over the empty coffee mugs. The porcelain cups clattered on the glass top loudly. "That wasn't part of the plan, Kelsey! What the hell were you thinking?" Infuriated, he picked up a set of binders and threw them violently across the room. They slammed into the wall and they could hear the scared shrieks of the interns in the cubes on the other side of the partition.

Kelsey stared at him stonily. "You need to calm down. It's not a big deal."

His eyes bulged. "Not a big deal? Are you out of your goddamn mind? You waited twenty-two years to have sex with someone on your own volition and you finally decide to do it in the middle of a stinking sex club with a guy you hardly know? Not to mention that disgusting pile of filth who raped you and murdered your parents in the same room? What? You suddenly decide to go slumming and become a goddamn slut?"

Her eyes flashed. "It's none of your business. You're not my father."

He shoved a finger in her face and she smacked him aside. "Damned right I'm not your father. He would have kicked your ass and told you what an absolute and utter stupid fool you were. You acted like a stinking whore, Kelsey!"

She flew to her feet and pushed him back. "Shut up, Ari. You don't know how it was. I just got carried away. I liked this guy. And for god's sake, I'm twenty-two years old. None of it matters. We got the cast of the damned key, so just leave me alone, because it's over and it's not going to happen again."

"Damned right it's not, because I'm going to kill him before he ever gets within twenty feet of you again." Ari paced the room, grabbing the baseball bat he kept in the corner. He regularly swung the bat to release tension and now he swung it with such force that it made a whistling sound as it whipped through the air.

"Carried away," he mumbled, taking a viciously fast swing. "You should have known better. You should have been able to control yourself."

Julia spoke up. "Ari, give her a break."

He pointed the bat at Julia. "Stay out of this, Jules. You're the one who brought this up to me in the first place with your big mouth, and damned if I'm going to give her a break. She knows how guys act around her. Anyone in a ten foot radius of this chick wants to have sex with her and if she's gyrating all over them half-naked, you think any guy is going to contain himself if she gives him the get go? So, it gets hot and heavy and instead of using her head like she usually does, and was supposed to, she acts like a promiscuous little whore and eggs him on. Mark my words, I'm going to rip that guy apart. I brought him into this to help her, not to fuck her. That wasn't part of the plan!"

There was a knock at the door and Ari's secretary stuck her head into the room. She had obviously heard Ari screaming and was usually immune to his outbursts, but when he was like this she continued to watch for flying objects when she walked into a room. "Mr. Goldman, I'm very sorry to bother you, but you have a visitor. He said it was urgent."

"Clarice, tell him I'm busy."

"Yes, sir," she said, but Desmond breezed by her and into the conference room.

They all froze.

Fuming, Ari clenched the bat and flew across the room. "You're a dead man."

"Leave him alone!" Kelsey yelled.

Desmond deftly dove out of the way, lightning fast as the bat swung and hit empty air. Even Ari seemed surprised that he missed. He righted himself, reared up to swing again, but Kelsey had made it to Ari by that time and shoved him roughly aside, screaming into his face. "Stop it! This was my decision and no one else's and if I want to have sex with someone, I will, you hear me? It's none of your business what I do. I'm not a child!"

Ari and Kelsey stood there fuming at each other, each of them shaking violently. Kelsey finally turned to Desmond, her voice cold and clipped. "What do you want?"

He kept his eyes on Ari and his bat. "Raul is getting ready to leave somewhere. He has a wooden box with him."

The very air in the room dropped ten degrees. It was still for mere seconds, and then everyone was in motion. Ari flew to Dennis and they booted up the live web cam, Julia started scouring the internet for any flights or travel sites Raul was tapped into and Kelsey raced over to Seung where together they started locating all the GPS tracking devices placed on Raul's cars and clothing.

"There he is leaving his office, complete with luggage," Dennis said, as they all crowded around the screen. "He was supposed to leave next week for Colombia. Something's happened to spook him." He raised his eyebrows at Kelsey. "You sure he doesn't know anything about the other night?"

She shook her head. "No, he was unconscious the entire time we..." she paused and bit her lip.

Ari glared at her. "Yeah, you'd think he'd have woken up with the sex show going on next to him." He stared over Kelsey's head at Desmond, his disgust apparent. "Have a good time breaking her in, Desmond?"

Kelsey turned to Ari, her voice tight. "Shut. Up. Now. Raul has no idea we have the key. He's probably just feeling the pressure about what happened to Ricardo and then the robbery at his office. It's expected. It was your own damned psychological runs which declared it as one of the possible outcomes." She turned back to the webcams.

The GPS tracked him towards the Throgs Neck Bridge.

"Looks like he's going to the airport," Kelsey said, turning to Ari. "Or do we need an in-depth psychological profile for that, too?"

"That's confirmed, Kelsey," Julia said, ignoring the jabs flying back and forth. Travel logs filled her screen. "He's on his way to JFK. Changed his flights from next week to today and is now on the 11:00 Avianca flight to Medellin, Colombia, and then on a connecting flight to Bogota." Her fingers flew as she pulled up the reservation screen. She glanced at Kelsey. "Um, how many am I booking for?"

"One," Kelsey said.

"Two," Desmond said at the same time.

"You're not going anywhere with her," Ari spit out.

129

Desmond stared at both of them, his face a mask of conflicting emotions. "I'm going after him, whether you let me help or not. It would be better for all of us if we did this together. What happened at Garters was a mistake that should never have happened and it won't happen again."

Why don't I just slice open my chest and you can pour a bucket of salt on my heart, Desmond? Kelsey swallowed hard, her face reddening as he reminded her again of how much he regretted what had occurred. How much he'd pitied her.

He saw her reaction and tried to speak, but she put up her hand to stay him. "Just book two, Jules."

Ari grunted in frustration and tossed the bat wildly across the room where it crashed in the corner, overturned a garbage can and broke a clay planter.

"Done," Julia said. She turned to Kelsey. "Downstairs now. We've got twenty minutes to get you ready and then you're out of here." She eyed Desmond. "You, too. Raul's seen you and we can't risk him recognizing you on the plane. Seung, start getting the gear ready. Dennis, help him. Ari, if you can calm down, we could use your help as well." There was a flurry of activity and regardless of the scene which had just happened, they all moved together fluidly and efficiently.

Desmond braved speaking to Kelsey as they moved briskly across the floor. "These people all work here, just to help you get Raul? Ari's entire business is a cover for this?"

She passed her hand over her eyes. She didn't want to talk to him and couldn't face even looking at him. She was so ashamed and disgusted with herself.

Julia answered for her as they took the steps two at a time. "This is a legitimate, successful company, Desmond. Kelsey's agenda is a side job and yes, his business is a cover for it."

They moved into a group of rooms in the back of Ari's office--a top of the line design studio with mirrors, dressing tables, and clothing arranged by category on every available space. Against one wall were shelves filled with various weapons and cases of ammunition, military gear, tents, and any supplies needed for an advanced covert operation.

Desmond whistled softly. Most of the stuff in the room was classified, even illegal. There was a shelf of improvised explosive devices, nunchakus, fiber optic cables, scopes and silencers.

Ari walked in behind him, noticing his expression.

"You even think of reporting any of this and I'll have you taken out before you even get out of my building. You understand me, cop?"

Desmond turned to him, his voice hard. "I suggest you stop with the constant threats. They're meaningless to me. You obviously have something going on with your sister, so why don't you take it up with her?"

Ari squinted. "Don't be as ass. There's nothing going on with her. I just don't like guys who can't keep it in their pants when they're around her."

"Then maybe you should have done the job with her yourself and none of this would have happened," he murmured. "Or maybe you would have screwed it up even further, with her writhing on top of you without her underwear on? She does have a way of being very... persuasive."

Ari gripped his hands into fists and took a threatening step towards Desmond, but when Desmond didn't back down, he moved to the other side of the room, helping Seung pull out various boxes and gear.

Out of the corner of his eye, Desmond watched Kelsey remove a wig and hat from the closet--the same one he noticed she had worn for the Miami job. She placed it on her head, covering her braid, then rummaged inside another bin before turning to the mirror.

"Desmond, put these on," Julia said, kindly, handing him a tight, curly blond wig and a pair of wire-rimmed glasses.

Seung brought two carry-on bags over to a table against the far wall and they all crowded around.

He started organizing the equipment they would need for a very advanced undercover mission. Out came a GPS tracker, a pair of night-vision goggles, flashlights, transmitters and extra magazines for their guns.

Kelsey put on a lightweight blue blouse with multiple pockets and started storing some of the supplies in her shirt. She stored her unloaded gun, the goggles and a small laptop computer in her carry-on bag. They'd declare their guns to the TSA agents when they got to the airport.

They handed Desmond a shirt of his own, filling it with spare magazines, a small flashlight, and the Garmin GPS receiver. They stowed his bag with two of the smallest sleeping bags he had ever seen, each folded up to the size of his palm.

"Are we camping out?" he asked.

Dennis piped up, adding energy and protein bars to their supplies. "Most likely. Raul's drug operations are run in the middle of the forest and when he's there, it's usually for a week at a time. But, he's taken the map with him, so we believe he's more than likely going to be headed to the nearby Buddhist monastery. Remember, these sleeping bags are built for two and biodegradable. Use it once and then crumple it up and bury it. Eventually it'll just disappear."

"Did you say Buddhist monastery?" Desmond asked. "I didn't think there were any monasteries in South America other than the single one in Brazil."

Everyone stared at Kelsey, their resident Buddhist expert.

"They just opened this one a month ago," she said quietly, checking the inside of her bag. "It's the only other one in the country and they come from a sect in Tibet that worked directly with the members of the Bodhidharma Monastery, so we can be sure Raul is going to go there and try to get them to give him some answers."

Ari spoke up as he brought canteens over to them. He shoved Desmond aside. "Kelsey, there's a good chance you'll have to intervene, because if Raul doesn't get what he wants, he'll probably kill them. There's no way they'll be able to protect themselves."

Julia handed Kelsey her passport. Then they all glanced at Desmond questioningly. He put his hand in his pocket and held his up. "Once I saw Raul leave, I thought I might need it."

Chapter 17

RAUL

The first class cabin was richly appointed with video flat-screens, plush carpeting and wide cream-colored leather bucket seats that converted into beds. A sexy stewardess who could have posed for Playboy handed out beverages.

She offered him his cognac and scooted away. She had smiled pleasantly, but it was plastic and seemingly painted on her face. He knew she was terrified of him, as she should be. Everyone was scared of him, and that's how he liked it. He took this flight regularly and his reputation was well known. He didn't get to where he was by letting people walk all over him. Kill or be killed was his motto. No witnesses.

Raul Salazar held up the glass of Pierre Ferrand, admiring the tawny brown color. He twirled the liquid in the thick, tulip-shaped cup and sniffed it. The spicy aromas of licorice, ginger, caramel and vanilla permeated his senses. He took a sip and leaned back, thinking about the box in the overhead bin. The box that held the secrets to the land of Xanadu, a world of riches meant for him alone.

He remembered when he first learned about Xanadu and had realized the mystical land was actually real. At the age of twenty-five, he was working the streets and met a monk who had been kicked out of the order because of his addiction to crack cocaine. He would sell everything he ever owned for another score of the drug and Raul was only too willing to comply. Quickly moving up the chain of command as the

United States emissary to the Colombian drug trade, he was already building up a fierce reputation. No one went against him.

When the monk no longer had any money to pay for his fix, he made a desperate plea to Raul. He would tell him a secret of a place that held riches and powers beyond belief. Raul didn't believe him until the man started speaking. It was then Raul plied him with drugs to get him to tell him all he knew.

* * * * *

"Please, Señor," the young monk begged, scratching his skin. "I beg of you. If you give me some, I'll tell you a secret my order has been protecting for centuries. It's a powerful secret."

"A secret? What type of secret?" Raul was not normally a curious man, but powerful things always intrigued him.

"There's a land called Xanadu, a mystical land that the Buddhist Monks protect. They say an ancient secret order in Tibet holds scrolls and maps to this land. I can tell you more about them if you will simply provide me my fix."

Raul did. For the next few days, he provided the monk daily hits of cocaine, watched the high he achieved, listened as he told of a land beyond beauty, cities made of gold, fantastical animals and mythical creatures. A hidden world that held riches to claim for those who could simply find a way to get there. He listened until he had learned all the monk knew. Then, he watched him crash, relishing the way he begged for his fix.

Then he killed him.

The next week he was on a plane to Tibet and began his quest to find Xanadu. The monk had said there was a monastery at the base of Mount Abora and that in order to

135

travel through the land, he would have to bribe the Chinese officials to roam Tibet freely. That wasn't going to be a problem. Raul was comfortable in a world where anything could be had for the right amount of money, including access to places others normally couldn't go.

Raul traveled far and wide, visiting many monasteries, some closed, some secreted, threatening them all, but he didn't find what he sought. Then, at the Bodhidharma Monastery, he found a couple with a daughter, who were also searching for the land of Xanadu. They helped the monks and while he didn't know what their reward would be, he could wait them out, monitor them, and find out what they had discovered.

For a year, he did. He watched them surreptitiously, waited until they had transcribed some discs and were given a map. The Map! The one that would lead him to Xanadu.

It had been so easy. While based in New York, he had Sherpa's working for him, spying on the couple. As soon as it was known the map was found, he went straight to Tibet with his men. He attacked the monks and took their disc and then dealt with the stupid Americans. They held the map to a valuable land in their little hut in the woods with no security and no weapons. Apparently, even the Chinese military didn't know they were there. He smiled as he remembered murdering them both and defiling their daughter. He vaguely wondered if she had lived. Probably not, and he didn't care.

Right after that, he discovered the Porter's had given one of the discs to a visiting American who had brought it back to The United States with him. It was easy to locate him and dispose of those who knew too much. He took the disc, not caring at all that he killed innocent men. All he cared about was being the only one in the world who now had both the discs and the map. It was his lifelong quest to decode them and find Xanadu. Once he did, he would be powerful beyond belief. He didn't believe Coleridge's poem, Kubla Khan, was simply created from an opium-induced dream. Coleridge must have gotten the information from somewhere because if it were just a dream, why would the monks be hiding it? If you took the words in the poem literally, "a sacred river and powerful fountain," then it meant there were incredible riches to be had, possibly the true fountain of youth. When he finally found this land, he'd dominate it like he dominated everything else in his life and he'd truly become the most formidable man in the world. No one could ever touch him.

The problem was, how to get there? None of his people could decode anything on the discs yet. The American had encrypted them somehow. Only once had one of the analysts been able to even read a small decoded copy and the words were still unintelligible. Raul had been enraged when it happened and nearly shot the man, but the man had begged for mercy and gave him clues as to how to get the information he needed. Go to the other monasteries, question the other monks, see what secrets they might still be hiding.

First, he went back to the Bodhidharma monastery, but they told him nothing. They had now hired Shaolin Monks to protect them and after a week of attacks, they forced him out. Many of the monks from that particular monastery fled to other temples around the world. He tracked a small cloister to Africa, but they still kept their silence, so he murdered them. He attacked six more Buddhist temples around the world in twelve years, and it had yielded him nothing.

* * * * *

He took another sip of cognac, the taste suddenly bitter and put it down, rubbing his scarred cheeks with his hands. They itched when he was stressed or frustrated, and now he was both. Someone was out to take his prize. For years after he had first acquired the map, things were steadily being worked on, visiting monasteries, decoding the discs, decoding the map, creating the box to house it in. Then, four years ago the killings began. First his cousin, Ramone, had been murdered while on vacation in the Bahamas. He was found naked in his bed with a gunshot to his temple and burns riddling fifty percent of his body. The autopsy report showed the burns had been inflicted while he was still alive. A year later it was Chico, killed in his home in East Hampton and beaten so badly it took dental records to identify him. They say the attacker took a bat to his face and entire body. Every single bone had been broken. He'd been tied up when they found him. Again, the autopsy results indicated he'd been alive as the killer bludgeoned him to death, bit by torturous bit.

There were no witnesses for either murder, and no note, but Raul had a gut feeling their deaths were connected to him, to the map, and to the murders of the American couple and their child in Tibet. Both men had been with him at the time and were now dead. He had learned to trust his gut over the years and it had yet to steer him wrong. But who could have done it? There had been no witnesses.

It was then the rest of them went even further underground. Juan took his family to Mexico and hid away in a remote coastal town. Ricardo moved to Miami into a heavily guarded estate. Only Raul remained where he was. He wasn't afraid of anyone. Let them come.

Six months before Juan was found floating face down in his swimming pool, a nylon cord wrapped around his neck. His home had been robbed.

It was not long after that Ricardo had been killed. Raul felt his rage starting to build again. Like a white hot flame obscuring all rational thought, the rage had the all-consuming ability to overtake him. It made him want to kill, to destroy, to annihilate. Ricardo had been his right-hand man and best friend, but at least now they had a lead as to who had been doing this.

A stinking woman.

Ricardo and his two bodyguards were attacked by a young blond who had the audacity to confront and kill him in his own home and then take one of the discs. How the hell she even knew about them concerned him. If she knew about the discs and knew about the murders of the Americans abroad, then he had to assume she'd be coming after him next. Maybe she knew about the second disc, maybe she even knew about the map. How she knew was beyond him.

He wasn't worried about being attacked and killed, himself. He glanced around the first class cabin, three other seats taken by his bodyguards. Let the bitch come. He'd take her in every way imaginable, and then let his guards have their way, before he slit her throat.

He took another sip, trying to calm himself. All she had was a single disc and the real prize still sat above his head. The remaining disc was back in his safe. A safe which had been compromised by another young girl, a prostitute no less, who had assaulted his men only days before to get money for her own fix. Taking his necklace, the money and bars of coke, she had left the disc and his paperwork, never realizing the real prize she overlooked. Fine, let her have those other trinkets. Stupid bitch.

He closed his eyes, picturing the map in his mind. He had stared at it for years and every detail was etched in his brain. For the past decade, he'd tried to find anyone who could make heads or tails of it. All anyone could say was that it was a perfect replica of the landscape surrounding Mount Abora in relation to the Bodhidharma Monastery and the adjacent countryside. But that's where any knowledge ended. In every margin and written between the topography were words inscribed all over the map. Words that were unintelligible and unlike a language any linguist had ever heard of before.

So, now he was off to Colombia to confront a new set of monks at the recently erected Chi Wong Po Monastery which had opened just five miles from his base of operations. The proximity and obscurity of the location astounded him. Maybe his luck was turning. He'd demand they translate the map for him, and if they didn't, he'd kill them. He was done playing games.

He quieted his mind, breathing deeply, and absentmindedly toyed with the key that hung around his neck. He was trying to understand why things were getting so out of control.

He rubbed his face, feeling the scars that were a constant reminder of letting a woman once get the best of him. The anger grew again and he breathed deeply. He was just stressed with the death of Ricardo. He remembered Ricardo's call after Juan's death. He'd been so scared.

* * * * *

"Raul, someone is coming after us. Someone knows about what we did in Tibet."

"And what did we do in Tibet, Ricardo?" Raul said. "What did we do that was any different than what we do every day? Kill a bunch of stupid Americans? Big fucking deal. What, you think, their ghosts are after us?"

"No," Ricardo had said. "But someone is. Someone who might know about what we did to all those monks and that family, or someone who knows about the map."

"Don't you worry about the map. I've got it locked up tight, the only key kept around my neck. I've got one disc, you've got the other. You just remember the riches we'll get when we find that land. You hear me?"

"I hear you, Raul."

"Good, don't worry. There's no way anyone is going to be able to get to you."

* * * * *

Well, he would find the one responsible and destroy her. Then things would go back to normal. His mind turned to that recent night at Garters when he had blacked out. So unlike him to not remember anything that happened.

He did remember the hot young thing he had kissed. Those dark blue eyes and that amazing ass. Everything had been perfect, right down to her man watching--then nothing. He took another sip of his cognac, knocking back the contents and grimacing. He knew something had happened because he'd woken up undressed with her lipstick stains on his clothes and her perfume in his hair. Still, he would have liked to have remembered fucking her.

The stewardess returned, her plastic smile frozen on her face. "Another drink, Senor Salazar? Anything else I can get for you?"

"No, just get the hell out of here and leave me alone. I'll call you when I need you." She flinched, but obediently backed away without another word.

Let the bitch flinch. He'd bang her in the bathroom before the flight was over and shove a year's worth of salary in her underwear as thanks. More than enough money to silence her.

Chapter 18

DREAMS

Kelsey woke with a start, staring wide-eyed around her with her hands in mid-flutter in her lap. She sat in the aisle seat next to two elderly Spanish women who chatted and knit baby blankets. Pink and aqua-colored yarn spilled from their ample laps and onto the floor.

She glanced across the aisle. Desmond stared at her curiously through his wire rimmed glasses, his eyebrows raised questioningly.

She ignored him, laid her head back on her seat and closed her eyes, keeping her hands balled into tight fists. She didn't want him to know anything about this part of her life, but wasn't sure how long she was going to be able to hide it.

The dreams had been coming more frequently. Even in little catnaps, they made their appearance, as if her subconscious was trying to sabotage her.

This time, she flew through the air on Ishu, racing to the sanctuary to save the Emperor and Empress. The sky was filled with warriors like herself, whose only mission was to rid the world against the blackness streaking across the sky. Yet, in this dream, the blackness was closer, with the dark malignancy spreading out not just over Tedanalee, but across the entire land. Soon it would overtake the world and the beauty and secrecy of this land would no longer exist. The dream switched and she was again privy to another senseless murder. She watched three men storm the shack of a young family from a small town in Kenya. Watched helplessly as they ripped a two-year old girl from her screaming mother's arms. They brought the child out to the savanna and threw her into the middle of a den of wild dogs. In moments, the toddler had been torn to shreds. Her name had been... Halima. Yes, Halima.

It didn't take someone with a master's degree in psychology to know the source of the dream. The cause of this cancer sat in the first class cabin, fifteen rows ahead of her, while the source of an impending ulcer sat just three feet next to her.

Desmond. What the hell was she going to do about him?

Kelsey risked a glance in his direction, but he had turned back to his novel. Her heart skipped just looking at him. *Oh, why does he pull at me so strongly?* A terrible thought came to her. *Am I in love with him? Is this why he affects me so much?* How desperately she wished things were different. Her stomach tingled as she remembered how he had kissed her and how she felt in his arms when they had... *Just stop it!* She squeezed her eyes shut in frustration. She couldn't even bring herself to speak to him, and how she was going to be able to work together with this man was a mystery to her. She was still startled by how fast it had happened. One second she was in control, and the next, it was as if her mind and body had lives of their own and she had simply disappeared and become someone else. But it hadn't felt wrong at the time. It had felt like the most natural thing in the world.

Why now? Why, with him? This kind of thing had never happened to her before. She had dated other people before Desmond, but had never let herself get too worked up or do anything she would have regretted. She had thought she loved those boys, too. The thing was, she just didn't sleep around, period. Some people might have thought that was prudish, but it was far from that. It was all about control. After her attack, she wanted to have the final say over that part of her life and damned if she was going to let another man determine when she would give it up to him.

Desmond was like no one else she'd ever met before. He was strong and smart and capable. And so damned sensual. She peeked at him again. Even now in her own miserable disgust, he pulled at her and it mortified her. To think she had feelings for a man who didn't feel the same way and who actually pitied her? She remembered the expression on his face at the hotel when he made that comment. It was still a bitter pill to swallow. She realized he'd just felt badly he had taken her virginity and nothing more.

"Kelsey, can I please talk to you?"

She turned to him, to that smooth, sultry voice and that beautiful face and tried to keep her expression completely neutral.

He looked so earnest, those blue-green eyes usually sparkling, but now dark and frustrated. *I won't let you sway me.*

Desmond waited for her to respond, but when she didn't, he took a deep breath, exhaling loudly. "I want to talk about what I said at Ari's office. I never meant what had happened in Garters was a mistake. It was again a bad word choice. And I never pitied you. I just said you looked so pitiful. It was – I was just… so surprised… just shocked and confused. I was just trying to do the right thing."

Feel nothing. Be a blank slate, Kelsey. Get rid of your feelings and emotions. It will be so much easier. Stay in control.

"You're not going to say anything? You won't talk to me about this?"

She couldn't do it, no matter how hard she tried to not let this hurt her, she just couldn't, so she let the anger, frustration and shame come forward. It was so much easier to be angry than sad anyway. "You're wrong. The entire thing was a mistake, but it was my mistake, not yours. I never should have let Ari bring you into this, thinking nothing would happen. I should have held out for my first choice for this assignment. Things would have turned out much differently and you wouldn't feel such regret."

Desmond looked stunned. "Kelsey, that's not fair. You were right there with me. I didn't do this by myself. I could have sworn..." He didn't finish the thought.

The two elderly ladies next to Kelsey glanced up curiously, but Kelsey waved her hands at them indifferently. "No se preocupen." (*Don't worry yourselves.*) They went back to their blankets.

Frustrated, she turned away, shaking in embarrassment.

"Kelsey, I'd really like to talk to you about this. I'm really so sorry this happened."

Let's cut the crap already. I can't keep talking about this. She turned to him, her voice as cold as ice. "Do me a favor and don't make this anything more than what it was. You're the same as any other guy. You get a little action, do a little heavy petting and suddenly you get all excited and want to go to bed. I've seen it hundreds of times and all of the other times I've ignored it, but this time I wanted it too, okay? There you go. Blame released and put it all on me. I could have stopped you and I didn't. So it's done and over with and I don't need your regret or your pity. Trust me, it wasn't that big a deal, so drop it."

She couldn't believe she just said that. It had been a big deal, the biggest deal ever. She had wanted him to keep touching her so much that it had made her confused. *Ugh.* Better not to let him know how strongly she felt about him. It was behind her and she had no intention of sleeping with him again and complicating her life any further.

With that, she leaned back and refused to speak to him for the rest of the trip, drawing the hat low over her brow. God, how she hated not being in control and feeling so helpless.

Chapter 19

CUSTOMS

José María Córdova International Airport was the main airport serving Medellin, Colombia, and it bustled with activity. Its newly paved runway and modernisation systems made it attractive for the new airlines coming in, but nothing could erase the lingering thoughts of what four decades of conflict had done to the country. As one of the world's worst humanitarian locals, it was still a place where tourists could unfailingly be caught up in the internal war between cocaine drug smugglers, the leftist rebels, guerillas and paramilitary militias.

It was a place where Raul Salazar felt right at home.

Kelsey waited for all the passengers to disembark and then she and Desmond grabbed their bags from the overhead and moved through customs, keeping a steady pace behind Raul and his men. To match their passport photos, they threw their wigs and glasses into a trash bin inside the main building.

They watched as Raul breezed through security by an official with an overzealous demeanor, shaking his hand enthusiastically and moving him to a special line. A quick exchange of cash greased between palms, and Raul was through.

They'd catch up with him later.

"Senorita, necesito examinar sus maletas," the security guard said.

Kelsey handed him her passport and documentation and was pulled aside to have her bag checked.

A short, stocky man with a thick mustache went through her things, finding the goggles and laptop and looked at her questioningly. "¿Para que necesita estos?"

She turned to a female customs agent, who translated. While Kelsey could speak fluent Spanish, she didn't want it to appear she could. "I'm an ornithologist, working on a study at Harvard investigating the sleeping habits of the Red Tailed Hawks in northern South America versus their habits in North America. It's a striking brown and white bird with a brilliant red tail. As a nocturnal animal, my night goggles will help me to see them in the open country when they're feeding."

He held up her gun.

She handed him her paperwork. "For protection in the jungle, of course. It's registered, as is my traveling companion's. You'll see both guns are unloaded and extra casings are in my luggage."

The guard stared at her for some time and kept rechecking her identification. Then he nodded to Desmond and checked his bag. Afer a few more cursory nods, he released them.

They moved through the airport to their connecting flight. Kelsey stopped to tie her hair into a bun and put on sunglasses. They were the last to board the puddle jumper to El Dorado Airport in Bogata. Kelsey breezed by Raul, who sat in front reading the day's edition of the El Colombiano and moved to the back of the plane. Desmond followed her and squeezed into the last seat next to her. They sat so close, their shoulders and hips touched. Desmond had to keep his legs crossed and his hands on his lap or he would have fallen into Kelsey.

This is just great. Now I have to touch you the entire time, too. She glanced at him exasperated, crossed her own legs to give him more room and then stared out the window for the rest of the flight, trying to ignore him.

148

She thought about the mission and her heart raced. She was getting close. She'd dreamed for so long of the moment she would avenge her parents and kill every last person involved in their deaths. Then, she would get the chance to begin the same quest her parents had started so long ago.

It had taken time and it had taken patience to get to this point in her life, but she was ready.

Chapter 20

TRACKING

The midday sun blazed down through the tops of the hardwood evergreens sitting at the upper quadrant of the forest, their tips reaching nearly one hundred and eighty feet in height. The sunlight barely penetrated the deeper layers of the rainforest, which were stopped by the thick vines and branches of the tree's canopy.

It was dim on the forest floor. The ground was soft and pliant under their feet, rife with rotting fruit, decomposing animals and old fallen leaves. As they moved through the mystical jungle, over fallen tree trunks and decaying branches covered with moss and ferns, Kelsey and Desmond continuously checked their GPS tracking devices and compasses so they wouldn't get lost.

A rustling made them glance up, but it was just a disturbance by some unseen creature in the canopy leaves. Filled with howler monkeys, tropical birds, and a multitude of other creatures, the forest was alive above them.

They stopped for a moment to take a drink from their canteens and eat energy bars. Their gazes stretched up to the understory blocking the sky. The canopy was even further up, hidden by the mass of solar collecting dark green leaves that were so large they could hide an army of small animals.

This part of the jungle, a hundred miles south of Bogota, was close to Raul's base camp. Kelsey glanced at her tracking device and slit her eyes. Raul was up ahead, no more than two miles away. As Desmond had moved past Raul on the plane, he'd rested his hand on Raul's chair seat, catching the back of his shirt. A quick "lo siento" and he'd moved on, Raul never realizing Desmond had attached a final tracking device to the inside of his shirt collar. Another one was in his right shoe, placed there by Kelsey during the Garter's mission. Others were placed in various jackets, suits and wallets by them and the cleaning woman at his office.

They jumped over a mass of downed trees and fell right into a pile of insects. Beetles and spiders scattered under their feet and Desmond jumped back with a squeal. A tarantula scuttled by quickly.

He glanced up sheepishly, his face reddening. "I don't like spiders."

Kelsey stifled a smirk and moved on. *Big baby.* She had been aloof with him since landing at the airport, but watching how Desmond conducted himself on this assignment, her respect for him grew. He really was the perfect partner - adept, capable and thoughtful. If they weren't on a mission and they weren't having these personal issues, she would have enjoyed her time with him immensely. The thought of exploring this exotic and mysterious world with an interesting person who could keep up with her both physically and mentally? Not a lot of people could do that. She stared above her again and thought about the way the canopy stretched out and hid the world. Kind of like how she hid within herself. The irony wasn't lost on her.

She turned back to the forest floor, noticing chowchillas and fernwrens pecking at the ground and into rotting logs, searching for grubs and other small insects. She picked her foot up as another tarantula skittered across her path. The forest was an intoxicating and dangerous place and she could understand how people could succumb to its perils.

151

Something's wrong. She stopped walking and held her hand up. Without question, Desmond froze next to her. The howler monkeys had ceased their shrieking and the chirping birds had disappeared. Even the insects had silenced their incessant droning. Everything had become strangely quiet.

And then it wasn't.

"Run!" she yelled.

Gunfire erupted just inches above their heads. They pushed through the forest as fast as they could, deep into the brush, with unseen assailants chasing them. They splashed through a small stream bed, wading to their knees and came out on the other side, forcing themselves to move faster through the harsh, dense jungle. Harsh shouts followed and pursued them.

They pummeled through the bush and up a small hill, over a series of rock outcroppings and fell behind the trunk of a Kapok tree. Kelsey pinned herself against it and Desmond pushed himself against her side. Her backpack was shoved uncomfortably against her hip.

Kelsey peered around the trunk. "FARC-EPs?" she whispered.

Desmond drew his gun, nodding. "Looks that way. They control about thirty percent of the jungle territory. Always a risk running into them. They'll be looking for hostages." He put his finger to his lips.

The guerillas came into view, their rifles at the ready, spreading out and searching.

As Kelsey drew her gun, she felt Desmond's breath come faster against her neck. He apparently saw the amount of men they were up against.

Gunshots sounded, and Kelsey flinched. A flurry of activity sounded above them as the revolutionaries tried to scare them out of hiding. Dead birds and leaves rained down upon them, but Kelsey and Desmond didn't move or make a sound.

The rebels worked in closer until they were only yards away. Kelsey peeked around the tree using the foliage as camouflage. They were a team of six of the nastiest men Kelsey had seen in a long while. Stealthily, they moved through the forest floor, searching. Close enough for her to smell their unwashed bodies. Ropes and handcuffs attached to chains on their belts jingled as they tracked them.

"¿A dónde fueron ?" *(Where did they go?)*

Another man moved to the front of the group and bent down to the dirt. Their tracker. He glanced ahead. "They came this way." He peered around, his eyes meeting a mass of dead animals and dung mounds littering the ground. "They're not far, but we scared them. There's a good chance they're going to try to hide in the drug lab up ahead. I'll bet that's where they're headed. With only two of them, they can't get far. Probably journalists. We can use them." The men moved a few feet further away.

Desmond leaned down and picked up a rock at his feet. With a great effort, he heaved it across the clearing where it landed ahead of their location, nearly fifty feet away.

With a flurry of excited shouts and curses, the militants took off. "They're up ahead, go… go… go!"

Good thinking, Desmond. Kelsey turned to him, inches from his face, and he was staring at her with a strange expression.

He pulled his gaze away and glanced around the tree. "Come on, we saved a few minutes. Let's not waste it and put some distance between them and us."

With that they moved quickly through the jungle, still needing to cover another two miles before dark.

Chapter 21

I WAS DREAMING!

Raul's largest drug facility was housed deep in the Amazon jungle. The complex was hidden from the air by the massive forest canopy. Entering the compound through a guarded gate, you passed multiple storage buildings and loading garages. The activity was endless as workers hauled cocaine, marijuana and illegal contraband to and from these warehouses and into waiting vehicles. Guards with rifles and a set of Dobermans milled throughout the brightly-lit complex, their watchful eyes on alert for anything out of the ordinary. Secreted beyond these buildings was the drug lab. Past that, at the very back of the compound, stood a low, rambling hacienda, flush against the jungle. It resembled an island escape with its pink stucco walls, colorful archways and wide open bay windows positioned throughout the home to give it the illusion of space. Trees and indoor gardens could be seen through the windows along with statues, sculptures and a multitude of artwork Raul had collected over the years. In the front of the house, across from the white graveled circular driveway, was a cupid fountain that spouted water into a small pond.

Kelsey and Desmond arrived at dark, maneuvering outside of the compound until they were situated behind the home. They hid themselves within a copse of trees and watched Raul and his men smoke cigars and talk by the side of the pool. Three topless girls lounged lazily in the Jacuzzi nearby, laughing and sipping frozen drinks served to them by a poolside bartender.

Kelsey pointed the orbiter listening device towards Raul. This unit was able to pick up conversations nearly 300 feet away and they could hear them easily.

One of his men leaned forward, two guns resting on each hip like a cowboy. Kelsey recognized him from news photos. He was Raul's right-hand man in Colombia and his name was Pedro Agudelo. A nasty man responsible for a rash of kidnappings last year against the members of the Colombia National Police Force who dared to get in his way. Any person who could kidnap children and then simply dispose of them on the side of the street, dismembered for their families to find, was someone Kelsey one day hoped to hunt down herself. He reminded her of the animals from her dreams that killed all those little girls. She was pretty sure she wouldn't feel any remorse for getting rid of him, either. Kelsey leaned in to hear the conversation.

"There is a new cartel trying to horn in on our territory. It's run by a pair of brothers named Alberto and Jaime Silva. Their grandfather worked with Escobar. They think they're going to take over and run things the way he would have. They're small, but they've already infiltrated the northern part of the country, working with a new paramilitary group that defected from FARC. They're calling themselves 54 Cadres."

Raul nodded, smoking his cigar. He blew a smoke ring in the air. The girls giggled in the pool, pointing at it, but he ignored them. "How much they run so far?"

"Nearly one million this year alone. Moving the goods through Mexico to the United States."

"That's not so much yet."

"True, Raul, but the year isn't over."

"What does the DEA's Barranquilla Resident Office say? Haven't we paid them off enough this year? They were supposed to tell us of any new activity."

Pedro glanced at the other men. "They did, but while you were in the States the new head of the Colombia National Police came down on them. He fired nearly all of our men."

Raul stubbed out his cigar. "There will be others we can buy. Find their weaknesses and get to them." He turned to the man who hadn't spoken yet. A squat Columbian with a ridged forehead, protruding lips and a massive amount of body hair. "Marcus, you get Chico and Dee to go with you and talk to these brothers. Let them know exactly how we feel. See if they have any daughters…" He let that comment hang in the air.

Marcus nodded. "Of course, Raul. With pleasure."

Kelsey and Desmond listened for a while longer as the men talked more business, until Pedro finally changed the subject.

"Raul, we've been out to the monastery twice already, but I don't think they know anything. They're just three old monks from Tibet meditating out in the jungle in a tent. I can't imagine what they think they're doing here. Preaching to a bunch of monkeys if you ask me."

Raul fingered the key around his neck, musing. "Old Tibetan monks might hold secrets. Tomorrow morning, we'll pay them a little visit and they'll either tell me what I need to know or we'll get rid of them. Ah, we'll get rid of them anyway. They're so far from the city, they won't be discovered for weeks."

Talk turned to business and Kelsey and Desmond shrank back into the jungle.

"The monastery is only five miles away," Desmond said. "If we leave now, we could make it by morning, though I'd prefer not to go trekking through the jungle at night. Taking one of the vehicles would be a lot better, and faster. Unless you want to steal the map tonight while they're sleeping?"

Definitely not. Kelsey shook her head. "No, not here with armed guards swarming all over the property. If we get him on the way to the monastery, or there, we'd have a much better chance of success. Less people around, and then we'd be sure he'd have the map on him."

They crouched their way around the perimeter of the property towards the garage and watched silently as an armed guard roamed casually by, smoking a cigarette. At one point, he took out a silver flask and took a deep sip, then moved back around the house and out of sight.

A few dirty jeeps sat in the driveway along with two pick-up trucks and a beat-up Chevy. Two roads jutted off from the garage. One led back out through the compound and the other one went into the forest. The second one was rarely used, as moss and ferns crowded the once cleared path. This was the one they would take.

Desmond glanced back at the house. All the lights were still on and they could see the servants moving about inside. They could faintly make out Raul still by the pool. He had just taken off his clothes and gotten into the hot tub with the giggling girls.

Kelsey's muscles tensed she stared at Raul. She didn't want to wait. What she really wanted to do was storm into the house and shoot the bastard and everyone else with him. She stared at Desmond for second and realized it was a foolish, impulsive thought. He could get killed. *Wait, her first thought was to keep Desmond safe? What was that about?*

She didn't want to let that thought linger. "We might as well get some rest. I don't think we'll have a lot of it tomorrow." She turned and moved further into the jungle.

Desmond followed her and they hiked until they were far enough out that they could no longer see the lights from the house. Kelsey took out a small portable flashlight and watched as Desmond removed one of the palm-sized sleeping bag packets from his bag. He glanced up at Kelsey, a pained expression on his face. They could each have their own sleeping bag, but these were built for two and it would be so much better to conserve the other one in case they were outside for another night. There was no way of knowing how long they might be sleeping in the jungle.

Kelsey saw Desmond stare at the littered floor, knowing he must be thinking of the millions of insects which roamed through the rot. She remembered reading there were at least twenty-five million different types of insects in the Amazon-- ants, beetles, and 3,600 different species of spiders. Tarantulas, jumping spiders, wolf spiders. She'd come to realize quite quickly that he hated bugs. He was probably terrified, but hiding it for her. At least the sleeping bag would zip around them, protecting them with its sturdy outer layer from anything crawling on them while they slept.

She watched him open the packet, spread it out, and sighed, in frustration. *Oh, I really don't want to get in there with him.* It was one thing to have to sit next to him on a plane, or travel with him, but to be pressed against him in a sleeping bag and try to sleep? This was going to be unbearable.

He moved into the sleeping bag and looked up at her, since she hadn't moved.

"Kelsey, come on. Unless you want to waste another one, will you please get in before something crawls in here with me?"

With a groan she dropped her knapsack on the ground, shut the flashlight and shimmied into the sleeping bag, keeping her back to Desmond. He quickly zipped it up around them. How it was supposed to fit both of them comfortably confounded her. He was just too big. He tried to turn his back to her, but it was way too tight and with their backs pressing together their faces were plastered against the walls of the sleeping bag.

"Oh, for Christ's sake, just turn around, Desmond," she grumbled. "If you don't, I will."

Desmond flipped himself around and pulled himself close to her, gently laying his arms on top of hers. She couldn't help tensing. He was careful to keep most of his body away from her. Thankfully. She could feel him adjust his legs, putting his knees against the back of hers and then there seemed to be an enormous amount of room. *Oh my God, this is just awful.* Her stomach flip-flopped and it suddenly turned hot. She was sure it wasn't only because they lay on the floor of a rainforest and it was still eighty degrees outside.

She was glad they were both fully clothed.

"Hey, it's not so bad, Kelsey," he said, trying to sound light.

She couldn't say a word. He was too close to her and she was so damned heady from it. What was it about this man? She had to relax, but she was sure he felt her body taut as a wire. Thankfully, as time went on the sounds of the jungle lulled both of them to sleep. As she drifted off she felt his arms fall around her, and hold her close, with her head against the crook of his neck and his breath tickling her cheek.

That was the last thing she remembered until she started screaming at him a few hours later.

* * * * *

Desmond was flying. The city was so tiny below him. He could see the people walking on the sidewalks and the yellow taxis whizzing by, all as small as ants. As small as tiny spiders, scurrying to their destinations throughout the city. He swooped down, circling through it all, over cars and busses and over buildings. He flew through a wooded park, through

159

the trees and playgrounds and then soared up again into the sky, over the skyscrapers and into the clouds. His hair blew against his brow and his arms were spread out like wings. He couldn't stop grinning. He flew by a passing plane, so close he could see the pilots' surprised expressions as he waved at them. He banked up further into the clouds, fluffy white pockets of cotton which felt wet and cold on his cheeks.

He flew even higher and saw, off in the distance, the colors of an aurora borealis hovering on the horizon. He reveled in looking at them and flew contentedly for a while just basking in their rays.

He dreamed a lot of flying. He felt exhilarated when he flew, like he could do anything in the world.

The dream shifted and changed and he flew back to the park he had seen before, but Kelsey was now there, sitting on a bench. He glided down next to her. She was dressed in a black Tae Kwon Do uniform, her hair cascading down her back and her make-up picture perfect, just like she had appeared at Garters. She held a bouquet of red roses in her hand. Three kittens frolicked at her bare feet, batting each other playfully. She gently poked at them with her toes. Without any preamble, she put the roses aside, leaned in towards Desmond and kissed him. He wrapped her in his arms and pulled her against him, feeling her body in all the right places. Pressing his mouth to hers, he could hear her sigh, pleading with him and egging him on. She called his name...asked him a question...

"Desmond, what are you doing?"

The dream shifted again. Kelsey had turned around and her back was now to him. He started kissing her slender neck and her long hair tickled his face. She seemed so small and vulnerable in his arms and he wrapped them around her protectively. For some reason he felt she needed protection that only he could give. He ran his hands up and down her body, realizing she was naked. He couldn't get past how warm and soft she felt. He sensed himself getting aroused and pulled himself even closer to her. He felt her back against his chest and her perfect breasts as he fondled them. He couldn't get enough of her, like she was the very air he needed to breathe. She called his name again...

"Desmond, I swear if you don't let me go I'm going to beat the living crap out of you!"

Something wasn't right. She was upset? The dream changed. Kelsey yelled at him again. He felt himself shift, the scene blur and suddenly...

* * * * *

He opened his eyes, but it was pitch black and for a moment he wasn't sure where he was. All he knew was he had his arms wrapped around an unhappy young lady, his body pressed fully against hers, excited as hell, his hands grabbing her chest and his lips pressed wetly to the back of her neck.

With a startled cry, he released her. She flipped herself around, grabbed the zipper and opened it up, jumping out of the sleeping bag.

She kicked him hard in his side. "What the hell were you doing?" she barked.

What had he been doing? Good question. "I - I must have been dreaming. I'm so sorry."

"Dreaming? That's the stupidest excuse I've ever heard."

"No, Kelsey, I swear. I didn't know what I was doing."

A howler monkey sounded next to them, its cry piercingly close, and Kelsey jumped.

He pushed himself out of the sleeping bag and then crumpled it up, thinking frantically about how to fix this. Hell, there was nothing he could do. He had practically humped this girl as he slept. Probably had. Just perfect, Desmond.

Kelsey reached down and smacked her backpack a few times to brush off the bugs and then put it on, glaring at him. "Let's go. Unless you need time to calm yourself down enough to be able to walk."

"I'll be fine," he mumbled.

As they trudged through the jungle, he could imagine how angry Kelsey must be at him. He couldn't blame her. Face it, he had no control around her, but it made him smile, nonetheless.

The house came into view and they moved towards the garage. He glanced at his watch. 3:30 am. All the lights were out in the house, although up ahead he could see the faint glow from the front of the compound and hear the low hum of vehicles moving in and out of the facility. The drug trade never slept.

Slowly inching around to the front of an old Jeep, he leaned into the driver's seat. "The keys are in the ignition," he whispered, surprised.

Kelsey glared at him and then glanced around for the guard, who was slumped on a chair by the garage door, sleeping. The open, empty flask lay sideways on his stomach. His rifle was lying on the floor. She leaned in and put the car in neutral. Together they pushed the jeep towards the dirt road, its tires crunching on the gravelly driveway. Thankfully, the sounds of the jungle drowned most of it out. Once they got out of sight of the house, they jumped in. Desmond started the ignition and seconds later they were jostling down the back road towards the monastery.

Chapter 22

BACK TO TEDANALEE

The jeep bounced wildly as Desmond drove the jungle road, littered with downed trees and deep potholes. It was like driving in a pool of black soup. The front headlights barely broke through the darkness. Many times they had to stop to remove debris before continuing. It was an arduous task in the dark, with the ever present threat of meeting one of the paramilitary groups. Now and again, there was a gap in the trees, the full moon illuminating a stitch of jungle that appeared like a photo taken from another world.

Kelsey constantly monitored the GPS tracking system, trying to keep them on the right path. It was early in the morning and they thankfully passed no one, except masses of howler monkeys.

"It should be right up ahead, about a half a mile." She was still annoyed at Desmond, but what was she going to do about it? Absolutely nothing. She was stuck with him. At least he seemed embarrassed. *Good, I hope you choke on it.* She peered down the road. "There!" A side road jutted off and Desmond slowed down to make the turn. He drove the car into a copse of trees and left it there, hidden in the brush. They made their way to the temple, which was supposedly just a few hundred yards in.

What a monastery was doing in Colombia in the jungle was beyond her. It made no sense. There was no one here to enlighten unless they were expecting to edify the souls of those who ran Raul's drug ring – a doubtful idea. Otherwise, the closest village was easily twenty miles away.

They pushed past another group of trees and stopped at a wide clearing. "This is it?" She stared incredulously at the gher, lit only by the light of a full moon. The temple was no more than a group of three patchwork felt tents, the same kind they used in Tibet when they rebuilt the monasteries after the purges from various factions over the years. "Desmond, this makes no sense."

Nothing in Kelsey's teachings explained why a sect would open up a monastery, no matter how small, in such a location. Many of them were in remote locales, but they, at least, had a large brethren with them. This one supposedly only had three disciples, and elderly ones to boot.

"It looks like it's a Vajrayana sect," Desmond said, pointing at the small picture on the front of the tent of Mindroling Trichen, a spiritual leader of the Nyimapa division. He turned to her. "Just like they follow in Tibet. In fact, just like at the Bodhidharma Monastery, but these seem to be influenced by Theravadu as well."

She stared, baffled, as they moved towards the gher. Usually sects adhered to one discipline or another. She remembered bits and pieces of her times in Tibet, where it seemed the monks that taught her combined the various doctrines of different Buddhist theologies, mixing them all together at times. In all her studies back in the States, she never remembered seeing that type of teaching anywhere else. She had thought she must have misunderstood them because she had been just a kid, but here again that very ideology was before her.

As if they were expecting them, an old, wizened monk came out. A vivid sense of déjà vu hit Kelsey hard and she took a startled step back. This man reminded her exactly of the monks from the Bodhidharma monastery who had taught her for the two years she lived there.

He seemed to have emerged from the past, dressed in the traditional robes of monks from twenty-five centuries ago, though they were worn and filthy from his time in the jungle.

He wore the uttarasanga, the large, red, rectangular kashaya robe. It covered his left shoulder and left his thin right shoulder bare. Under the uttarasanga, he wore the antaravasaka wrapped around his waist like a sarong. This covered his body from his waist to his knees.

While it was warm in the jungle, the monk still had a folded sanghati, an extra robe, draped over his shoulder.

He stared straight into Kelsey's eyes, and she shivered.

"Don't be afraid, child." His voice, something about his voice. Out of the blue, a vision came unbidden to her mind.

"I see you've been studying your scriptures, child. I'm pleased to see this. You're a quick study." His kind brown eyes in his wizened old face smiled down at her. "Thank you, Bhante Shingen," Kelsey said, her nine year old visage staring at him adoringly. "I've been studying hard."

"I can tell, and yet, there are many distractions in this world that attempt to take you away from them," he said.

Kelsey's eyes widened. "It's true, Teacher. I'm trying not to let them sway me. Sometimes it's so hard. As if there are things out there pushing me away from your teachings, but I keep making myself come back."

"I know, Kelsey. We all have desires. It's our control of them that allows us to keep to the path. You're doing wonderfully. Just follow your heart and do the best that you can. That is all that anyone can ask of you."

Kelsey turned back to her books, ignoring the birds chirping outside the window and the gardens blooming. There would be time for that later, after she studied. She loved the

Tibetan culture. Loved studying the language and learning about the foundations of Buddhist tradition. She'd been with their school for a year already, ever since her parents had brought her to Tibet, and she took to the lessons eagerly. She was secretly proud, that because of her intellect, she'd been hand-picked from some of the other children to learn the noble truths, the more advanced meditation to take her to further enlightenment. She loved learning the various ceremonies and practices and could do the invocations and mantras in her sleep.

A bell sounded and another monk called to Bhante Shingen. "It's time. Bring the child."

That voice. Yes, that was the one.

"Come, Kelsey," Bhante Shingen said. "We'll do these lessons later. Let us go to the inner sanctuary. It's time to travel..."

Kelsey blinked. "I know you, don't I?"

The monk simply stared at her.

Desmond pushed past Kelsey. "Venerable sir, please, we must leave here with your brothers immediately. There are men coming who intend to do you great harm. They'll be here very soon and they won't leave without ending your path in this world."

The monk stared at Desmond intently. "We know what he comes for, young man, but the answer doesn't lie with us. It lies with her." He nodded towards Kelsey. "You do know me, child. I am Shojuharu. Do you remember calling me that once?"

She nodded her eyes wide in shock. "Shojuharu from the Bodhidharma Monastery?"

Desmond turned to the monk. "Wait, you're from that monastery? Did you know my brother, Connor Gisborne?"

166

The monk gazed at Desmond and nodded. "Come with me, both of you." He turned and moved into the gher and they followed quickly. The dawn's light had begun to break through the trees.

There was so much Kelsey wanted to talk to him about, but there just wasn't time right now. Raul was coming. "Please, Venerable Shojuharu, we really must go…" Her voice trailed off as she stared at the scene before her.

Two other elderly monks sat on yellowed bamboo mats on the dirt floor of the gher. A Buddhist statue with one fat candle burned next to them. On the floor before them, a small fire was lit with a pot of tea brewing on a metal rack situated atop it. The scent of spice and fruit wafted in the air. One of the monks began moving his hands in a rhythmical-like pattern, fluttering the fingers, over and over again. *Oh my, God, what is he doing?* Stunned, Kelsey took a shocked step back, bumping into Desmond.

"Why are you moving your fingers like that?" she asked, horrified. The past came back to haunt her the very moment the elder monk began his strange dance. Her strange dance. The dance she did when she was fleeing to Tedanalee. She found it suddenly hard to breathe and put her hand to her chest.

"He's praying, child," Shojuharu said quietly. "Just like you used to."

Kelsey stared at him. "Praying? What are you talking about?"

The monk stilled his hands. "She doesn't remember," he said, bitterly. "I told you this was all going to be for naught. We came here for nothing."

Shojuharu shook his head. "She does know, Takechiyo. She just doesn't remember yet from where she knows. She's protected herself from the knowledge, but don't forget, we

167

know for certain it's there, just hidden deep from her conscious mind. We know who she really is."

What were they talking about? What do they mean about who I really am? Names from the past tickled her mind. Takechiyo. Shojuharu. Her mind wandered. She was suddenly walking through the cold gray stone halls of the Bodhidharma Monastery, praying in front of a statue of the Buddha, carved from a single piece of white sandlewood. She had sat with the monks on colorful, fluffy pillows, reciting incantations, her fingers moving rhythmically in time, fluttering up and down, over and over, for hours upon hours until she simply disappeared.

Moving her hands? Disappearing? No, it couldn't be the same dance! Kelsey turned to the last monk whose eyes had never strayed from the teapot. She stepped over to him. She bent down to his eye level and placed a light hand on his slim arm. He shook slightly. "Please, Venerable sir, please look upon me." The monk glanced up from the flickering flames, his kind brown eyes emanating from a wrinkled face. Kelsey's breath caught in her throat.

She started crying and laughing at the same time as she stared at his beloved face. "Bantu Shingen? Teacher, is it really you?"

He reached up and grasped her hands with his gnarled ones, his fingers thin and cold, but his smile warm.

"Yes, Kelsey. We once thought we lost you at the very hands of the man who seeks us now, but we learned you didn't succumb. Your path wasn't to end at that time. Our enemy didn't win this time." He pulled her down to the floor. Then he glanced at Desmond. "You, too, Desmond."

Desmond started.

The monk smiled "Yes, we know who you are. Come join us, for you've been brought into this path as well. Your fate is connected to Kelsey in ways you can't imagine."

With a quick intake of breath, Desmond took a seat next to Kelsey and joined the other monks. Shojuharu sat down as well.

Kelsey remembered him now. "You were the Senior Elder who worked with my father. The one who gave him the map." She stared around her, incredulous. "What are you all doing here? You're in terrible danger. We need to leave and take you to safety." She tried to stand, but Bantu Shingen stayed her by gripping her wrist and shaking his head sadly.

Shojuharu stared at her. "Our time is now, child. We've come to the end of our paths and we know what awaits us. Don't fret, for we know we'll be reborn immediately."

"But there's still time here in this lifetime," Kelsey beseeched, thrusting off Bantu Shingen and standing back up. "You don't have to die a senseless death at the hands of this monster. Why did you come here in the first place?"

"We came, because it was foretold you'd be here. Those at the next level saw this, so let's not waste any more time and let us teach you one last lesson. We must break the chains which bind you. The chains which cloud your vision." He leaned over and struck the edge of a metal bowl in front of him. The gong echoed hollowly in the gher. Then he crossed his legs, closed his eyes, and rested his palms up on his knees. "Now please sit down with us. Close your eyes and start to breathe."

Was he out of his mind? Kelsey stared at him. "You want to meditate now?"

Shojuharu turned to her and opened his eyes. "Yes, now. We need to clear your head so you can take in what we must show you."

Kelsey wanted to scream in frustration. "There's no time! If we don't leave now, you're all going to die!"

Bantu Shingen spoke gently. "Kelsey, I taught you nearly every day for two years. Allow us to teach you now. Please, child. There's always time for teachings. Don't let the threat of what's coming cloud your mind."

Takechiyo turned to her as well, but he wasn't calm and gentle and she was taken aback. She had never seen an angry monk before. He threw his hands in the air. "Enough of this. You both coddle her as if she were still ten-years old." He turned to Kelsey and pointed at her. "Listen to me, little girl. Mara is the threat that's coming. We know this and you do as well, if you'd look deep in your mind and stop hiding in denial!"

She flinched at his words and her stomach clenched violently at the mention of Mara.

"Takechiyo, not yet. She isn't ready," Bantu Shingen admonished. "Kelsey, sit, please."

Shaking, and not knowing why, Kelsey sat down between Bantu Shingen and Desmond. A strange, horrible feeling crept into her gut, one she couldn't explain.

Shojuharu spoke up. "Now, quiet your minds. Forget the men who're coming, forget the past. Just concentrate right now on your breathing. Breathe in peace and pure light, breathe out the hate, the confusion, and all your earthly desires. Rejoice in the happiness you can bring inside yourself."

All was quiet for a few moments in the gher as the five of them concentrated on their breathing. Despite herself, Kelsey felt her mind turning inward as she became still. Her thoughts slowly silenced as she mentally shut off the terrors invading her life.

Shojuharu voice was a whisper. "Now start your dance, Kelsey. Just like you do in your dreams to take you to your special land. Just like we taught you all those years ago when you reflected with us in the sanctuary."

Fear suddenly laced her heart and she shook herself. "I can't. I'm – I'm afraid, Teacher." She glanced down, embarrassed. She'd never been afraid of anything, but this was too close to her. It was just too personal. And it wasn't even real!

Bantu Shingen leaned over and squeezed her hand "There's much to be afraid of, but this isn't it. You've always had a choice in everything you've done and your decisions have made you unique, Kelsey. Your path in this lifetime pulled you in so many different directions, but you've always chosen the right path. So, do the dance the way we taught you. It's the way through to the next level and I promise you don't need to be afraid of your dreams or where we're going or how we get there. Your dreams are no longer just dreams, Kelsey, but your reality. Now close your eyes. I promise, it will all come back to you and you'll begin to understand and to learn once more."

Kelsey glanced at Desmond, seeing how puzzled he was, but he sat like the monks, with his hands in his lap, simply waiting. *I can't believe I'm going to do this.* She took a deep, shuddery breath and turned back to the monks.

"Follow us," Shojuharu called softly.

All three monks closed their eyes and started fluttering their fingers.

"Move your fingers in the rhythmic dance and join us, Kelsey," Shojuharu called. "This is how we taught you to meditate and to move between the worlds. It is how you travel to your world of Tedanalee. Just breathe and dance."

Kelsey closed her eyes and bit her lip uncertainly, but then relaxed her mind. She began moving her fingers in the way she thought only she had made up. Up and down, up and down like a wave, one after another. It was so familiar and calming. Again and again they fluttered. She squinted and saw Desmond, his eyes closed, moving his fingers like the monks. She closed her lids and let the thoughts flow from her mind. One by one, she breathed them out and released them. The visions of surf crashing on the beach coming to the forefront of her mind. Then she watched them recede into the ocean. She let them come, let them surge and ebb, pushing the water further and further up the sand, breathing in and out, each surge of water a breath. Slowly the waves disappeared and her mind calmed until it stilled and became nothing but tabla rosa, all desires and earthly needs gone…

The air around them began to shimmer.

* * * * *

Kelsey stood on the edge of the stream, bending down to watch the strange pint-sized fish jump and flip around the rocks in the current. They made little splashing noises like tinkling glass. She glanced up, the sunny blue sky streaked this afternoon with ribbons of orange and pinks stretching across the horizon. A warm, jasmine-scented breeze blew her hair. It was tied back with a chain of green crystal jewels, attached to multi-colored strings which ran down her back. The wind brought with it the whinny of her fedelia. She turned, surprised to see Ishu resting on the ground next to a magnificent stallion-like creature she didn't recognize. Heads taller than Ishu, he had a thick mahogany brown mane and his muscles bulged with strength throughout his massive body. Kelsey watched as the stallion leaned over and nuzzled Ishu's neck affectionately. She strolled towards them, her green, gauzy shirt and silky pants flowing in the breeze.

"Kelsey?" She stopped in mid-step, shocked, and turned to the familiar voice. Desmond stood on the edge of the forest, looking like he was born for this world. A white cotton tunic covered his chest, and brown breeches stretched to his calves. His feet were encased in rawhide sandals. A dagger with a jewel-encrusted hilt was attached to a belt around his waist along with a large sword. He wore a bow and a sheath of

arrows across his back. Another ream of quivers were attached to his hip. As Desmond stared, he reached up and fingered his forehead, feeling the thin jeweled headband adorning his brow, keeping his unruly hair out of his eyes.

Kelsey studied the scene, so like her dreams, but now so different. Desmond was here. Here in Tedanalee with her.

That wasn't possible.

"Where are we? It seems somehow... familiar." He took a step forward and sniffed the air. He appeared amazed as he took in the forest with its strange scents. He glanced at the sky, a dumbstruck expression on his handsome face. He stared at the alien beauty and awe-inspiring colors of the aurora borealis swirling above his head. Beyond, the golden city of Tedanalee stood within the mountains. The massive sanctuary dominated the center of the city. Fashioned after an imperial palace, it was a grand mix of stone and wood, filled with gardens, shrines, and great halls. It was also where she had lived with the Emperor and Empress as a child. Even from this distance, she marveled at its eclectic mix of structural works with its multiple terraces, colorful walls and bell-shaped stupa tower. The main stupa, the highest point of the sanctuary, was covered in gold and glowed in the sunlight.

"We're in Tedanalee, though I'm not sure how you're here with me."

"Tedanalee?" He couldn't stop staring at the world around him. At her.

She nodded. "This is the secret fantasy land I've escaped to since I was ten-years old. But it's just a dream world. I must have fallen asleep back in the gher with the monks while we were meditating and conjured you."

She stepped over to Ishu and patted her creamy white mane. Ishu whinnied contentedly and nuzzled her cheek. Then she turned to the creature next to her, giving it an appreciative eye. He was a beauty. "Your steed's magnificent, Desmond."

"My steed?" Desmond moved over to stand by the massive animal. It turned its jet black eyes towards him and Desmond froze, his eyes wide with comprehension. "He is mine," he said, softly, amazed. It wasn't a question, but a statement.

"What's his name?" Kelsey asked.

"I don't know."

"You'll know. Look into his eyes and ask him."

Desmond stared at the creature and then smiled. "Dorje. His name is Dorje. That means indestructible one, doesn't it?" He reached out to the animal tentatively. The creature was nearly twenty-feet in length, but it was tame and Desmond ran his hand down his body. The fedelia whinnied in pleasure and stood, his mammoth wings snapping open like sails. Its power took Kelsey's breath away.

Desmond turned to Kelsey. "How do I know his name?"

"Because he told you. Because he's yours in this world. Each warrior is given his own fedelia. You're linked to each other."

A long horn sounded in the distance and they both looked towards the monastery.

"What are they calling for?" Desmond asked, stepping towards it.

"We're being summoned to the sanctuary. In this land, we're soldiers, here to protect the Emperor and Empress. Come on."

"The Emporer and Empress?" He squinted, confused.

But before she could explain further, the sky rent apart. The sound ripped through the land. Black holes opened up, tearing through the ribbons of color. A gale of wind threw them both violently back to the ground. The air was ionized, like it smelled before a coming storm.

Ishu reared up, baring her teeth and Dorje did the same, wrapping his wings around all of them so the whirlwind didn't whip them away.

174

"We have to get to the temple!" Kelsey cried, jumping on Ishu with a swift, practiced leap. The squall intensified as the blackness invaded the sky, quickly covering all the color.

"Kelsey, what's happening?" Desmond asked.

"The dark is coming! The Devil of all worlds. There's no time to talk, Desmond. Go to Dorje and jump on. We have to leave right now!"

Desmond ran to Dorje, unsure of what to do, but the creature leaned down and pushed him with its tremendous snout onto his back. Desmond leaned over and grabbed the mane and the animal launched itself to the sky. They flew fast, other riders racing to the temple with them as the blackness expanded like spidery streaks.

"Hurry, Desmond. We have to hurry!" Pain suddenly ripped through Kelsey's chest and she shrieked in agony.

The blackness opened up, sucking them in.

Ishu reared the way she had come, desperately fighting the pull, but it kept drawing her and Kelsey in further.

"Kelsey!" Desmond's stallion reared, too, fighting the pull and winning, while he gripped the mane desperately so he didn't fall off.

Dorje whipped his head around, grabbed Ishu's tail with his mouth and with a tremendous effort, wrenched them back.

The entire sky opened up, the blackness enveloping them all and they plummeted through the void.

Falling... falling... falling...

* * * * *

With a shriek, Kelsey pushed herself backwards, away from the monks until she was against the gher wall. She clutched herself. Desmond sweated and shook, his eyes both terrified and amazed, and Kelsey realized this had been no dream. He had actually been there with her--in Tedanalee.

Heaving, she turned to the monks. "What does this mean? How could he have been there with me? How do you even know about this place?" The questions flew from her, one after another, begging them to help her understand. "It's not even a real place. I made it up to protect myself after I was attacked."

Shojuharu was about to speak, but the sound of an approaching jeep sounded outside the gher.

He turned to Kelsey, urgently. "Whatever happens, you must promise to help. You must go back and protect them from the evil that's coming."

"Protect who?" Her eyes widened in understanding. "The Emperor and Empress? You can't be serious. They're not even real."

The doors of the jeep banged shut. Male voices spoke. "You think they're awake yet? It's early."

Shojuharu stared at the gher tent flaps, then turned back to Kelsey. "They're real, Kelsey. As real as any of us. The man who comes now has come to you before. Mara is influencing him. This man doesn't follow the path of Pancha Shila. He has no morals. He comes to aid the Devil in opening the worlds and destroying all the paths to every universal truth."

She leaned forward, desperately. "You believe Mara is influencing Raul? How? When did he come before? Please, you have to tell me."

"He came twelve years ago to your hut. He came to kill you."

She reeled back, but Shojuharu leaned forward and with surprising strength grasped her ankle. "Child, whatever happens to us, you must survive. You must continue to fight him. Do you understand? You must go back and find your Emperor and Empress and help them." He stared at Kelsey

176

and when she didn't respond, he grasped her ankle harder, his fingers digging in until it hurt. "Kelsey, do you understand what I'm saying? Mara is here in this world. You are the only one who has the power to stop him. Think, Child. Think back to who you are, who you were and who you've been. We mean nothing. Our paths are done. It's you who must survive. It's you who must save them. You who must reject the influences of your past. Promise me, Kelsey. For when you make a promise, you must maintain it. Do you understand?"

"Yes, yes! I promise!" she cried. *I'll promise you anything, but I don't know what you mean.*

Raul and his men stormed into the tent.

Chapter 23

THE MAP

Raul took in the scene. "Well, well, what do we have here? A little Buddhist tea party?" His gun trained on them, he stared at Kelsey and Desmond. His eyes widened. Those blue eyes. That hair. He took a look at Desmond, understanding flooding through him and he turned back to Kelsey. "You!" he spit out. "You were the couple from Garters. Get up. Now!"

Kelsey stood slowly, facing Raul. She glared at him in fury. "You've come to a place of worship. Put away your gun. These men are unarmed."

Marcus moved to Raul and whispered in his ear and Raul's eyes widened again, quickly becoming angry slits. "Are you sure it was her?" He took a menacing step towards Kelsey, swallowing hard, then spit on the floor. "You were the one who killed Ricardo. You were the one who killed all of them, weren't you, you little bitch?"

That's right, you disgusting pile of filth. She smiled at him and it was as if a light had been turned on for Raul. He nodded in understanding as a sigh escaped his throat. "You were the imp in Tibet whose parents we killed? Ahh, it all makes sense now. The killings, the robberies. It was you all along, wasn't it? You obviously lived through our time together. I thought we might have killed you."

Kelsey could see Desmond staring at her out of the corner of her eye, confused. Raul noticed it.

"Did she ever tell you what we did to her?" he teased. How we murdered her parents and then me and my men took turns on her? I remember your screams when we broke your arms and legs. Like little twigs they were. I remember shoving your face in the dirt when we played with you. I thought we killed you, but I guess I was wrong. We should have done a better job. It's a mistake I won't make again. I promise this time you'll enjoy it even more and now we have an audience who can watch as well." He sneered at Desmond.

Kelsey shook her head. "You're the one who's going to be killed, you worthless piece of shit." In a flash, she pulled her gun and fired. Marcus propelled himself in front of Raul, taking the bullet to his chest. He fell to the ground, his foot hitting the fire and scattering the wood, the embers flying into one of the gher's tent walls and erupting into flames.

Kelsey dove forward as gunshots erupted. Out of the corner of her eye, she saw Shojuharu and Shingen both fall to the floor in a shower of bullets. "No!" she screamed, turning to run to them, but Desmond's cry stopped her.

"Kelsey, the box!"

She twisted her neck, noticing Pedro with the map's box in his hands as he tried to escape the tent. Kelsey fired at him, hitting him in the leg. He collapsed, the box crashing to the ground and bouncing away from him.

Desmond fell on it, tackling it like a fumbled football and propelled himself backwards, while more gunfire and flames erupted around him.

Kelsey fired again, hitting another of Raul's guards in the chest. Raul backed out of the tent and she stumbled after him, firing constantly.

"Kelsey, let him go. We have the map."

From the floor, Pedro reached out and grabbed her leg. She fell and he climbed atop her and brandished a knife. The air shimmered around them and Kelsey noticed Takechiyo, his

179

bloody face lying on the dirt floor, fluttering his fingers ceaselessly. His eyes met hers, boring into her and she understood. The sound of multiple long horns riddled the air and the tent disappeared. For the briefest of moments, they were in Tedanalee, and then the real world flooded back.

It was enough. For a mere second, Pedro didn't know where he was, and with a terrified shriek, released his grip. Kelsey took the opportunity to land a hard punch to his face and pushed herself away from him. He tried to rise, but she put her gun to his temple and fired.

Without giving him a second glance, she crawled back to the monks, trying to lift them and save them from the flames consuming the tent, but she couldn't. Shingen and Shojuharu were already dead, so she crawled to Takechiyo. She sobbed and he grasped her hand.

"My path is done here. Go to Tibet. That's your destiny now." He gripped her harder. "And take your companion with you. He's been sent to help you and you'll need him. The choices and temptations you'll be faced with will be great. Do everything in your power to fight them."

Why does he keep talking in riddles? Please just tell me what I need to know. "Please, I don't understand what you're saying!"

The monk's gaze bore into hers and he whispered one word. Kelsey leaned down to hear it and then gasped. With a satisfied smile, Takechiyo slumped to the floor, the light in his eyes gone.

"No!" Kelsey shook his shoulders. "You can't die on me. What does that mean? Why did you say that?"

Desmond stepped to her side. The flames and smoke were intense and it was hard to see. "Kelsey, they're dead. We have to get out of here." He started hacking.

"No, he tried to tell me something. I have to understand." A coughing fit doubled her over as well. The flames

180

surrounded the tent and they were trapped in a wall of orange fire. One tent wall collapsed, raining embers on them.

"There's nothing more they can tell you. Now, come on!" Desmond grabbed her around her waist, pulled her away, and shoved her out of the burning gher.

They fell to the ground. Desmond drew his gun, but Raul and his jeep were gone. A bloody trail followed him from the tent to where his tire tracks remained.

As Kelsey and Desmond lay dazed on the forest floor, they watched the small monastery burn to the ground with the three elder monks and Raul's men inside.

Kelsey crawled over to the burning flames, angry tears streaking her ashen cheeks. Desmond inched over to her and placed a tentative, comforting hand on her shoulder and she turned to him, laying her head on his chest and cried.

After another minute, she pulled away and swiped at her eyes. "At least they saw the Clear Light before they died." She crawled onto her knees and began to recite the Sadhana Heartfelt prayers for the deceased monks. She thought back to all her teachings. It was the least she could do for them. They sacrificed themselves to give her a message and to bring her the truth, and they had died because of it.

With a strength and purity of intention, she spoke the invocations, remembering their mind of compassion to their philosophy, the understanding of the knowledge that they were going to die on their final path of their life. She remembered their devotion to the Buddha. She finished with a dedication prayer and then sat there quietly, watching the last of the flames burn themselves out.

Desmond stayed with her. After everything that had just happened--Tedanalee, Raul, some knowledge of what had been done to her in Tibet--he said nothing. Just leaned over and took her hand.

He comforts me somehow. Even now, without even saying a word. "They've achieved Dukkha," she said quietly. "Great inner peace and contentment. I just hope their ultimate sacrifice brings them enlightenment."

Desmond nodded. "Maybe they've reached Nirvana." He leaned over and picked up the box, turning to Kelsey. "We have it. Their deaths weren't for nothing. I don't know how, but they brought you to this spot, to this moment and they knew this was going to happen to them. It was possibly all a divine path and one you now follow as well. It sounds like you've actually been following it all along."

Like a damned puppet. She nodded, her eyes still filled with tears. Taking a deep, choked breath, she removed the chain from her neck and holding the key, leaned over and put it in the box's lock. It turned easily in her hands and she lifted the lid. An overwhelming sadness filled her and chills ran down her spine.

The map was there. The map her father had died for.

She ran her fingers across the yellowed scroll, knowing once her dad had held this very map in his hands. She picked it up and unfurled it. "It's time to avenge both our families."

Desmond touched her arm hesitantly. "Kelsey, what did Takechiyo say that made you so upset?"

She pursed her lips. "He said the word, 'Tanha."

He crinkled his brow. "Tanha? What is that?"

"It's not a what, but a who. She's a person from Hindu lore."

Desmond squinted, apparently trying to remember. "Wait, isn't Tanha the name of one of Mara's daughters?"

Kelsey nodded. "Yes. She was one of the demons who were sent to tempt Siddhartha while he meditated under the bohdi tree."

Desmond squinted. "Why would he say that?"

"I have no idea."

Then why was she shaking so badly?

* * * * *

They retrieved the jeep and drove all morning to a town on the outskirts of Bogota, where they abandoned the vehicle behind a local restaurant. They then caught a civilian bus that took them on a meandering journey to the city, booked a room at one of the larger hotel chains and after showering and grabbing a quick lunch, were in their room studying the map. They remained there all afternoon and straight until dinnertime as they tried to decipher its strange codes. After that it was another quick bite in the downstairs restaurant and then back to the map, where they memorized every aspect of it, trying to unlock its secrets.

Kelsey discovered she could read all the words inscribed on the margins. Words written in a language which seemingly no one else on earth, save for Ari, knew.

Kelsey pointed towards the northern end of the map, to a point at the peak of Mount Abora. "It says here, *"We hide from the world. Only those of pure consciousness may come forth."* And another spot on this side says, *"Here is the place where you choose your path, where judgment is made."*

"Do you know what any of this means?" Desmond asked.

Kelsey shook her head. She started typing again on her computer, as she had been all afternoon, in constant touch with Ari, Julia and Seung via Skype. She had taken a photo of the map and digitally sent it to them and now translated all the words inscribed on it. They were nearly done.

Ari's voice came through her computer speaker. "Kelsey, the words on this map are all centered in Buddhist doctrine and I don't believe they're random messages. There's an underlying theme about choices and karma, the force which drives samsara."

"The cycle of suffering and rebirth?" Desmond asked. "How do you see that?"

There was a pause on the line and they could see Ari's brows crease as he glanced at Desmond. *Easy brother.* Ari still hadn't made peace with the fact that Desmond was with Kelsey. His voice was tight as he spoke. "Because many of these written words are actually Vajrayaha's mantras to ward off negative karma. The monks at the Bodhidharma Monastery have combined various different theologies of Buddhism together, as if they are practicing under all one tenant. Possibly these very mantras have a direct link to Xanadu."

"Like what happened in the gher," Kelsey said. She had told them about the monks' prayers, the meditation and how she and Desmond had both traveled to her mystical land of Tedanalee.

Ari and the others had been stunned.

Ari had asked her to try to recreate the vision. She had sat on the floor, in the lotus position and started fluttering her hands, but nothing had happened. Desmond had tried to help her, too. They couldn't recreate the scene and bring her back to Tedanalee.

Seung spoke up. "I want to take this from another perspective. Have you ever thought that maybe Tedanalee is really Xanadu?"

Is he serious? "You think my world of Tedanalee is a symbol of Xanadu?" Kelsey asked.

"No," Seung said. "What if it actually IS Xanadu?"

Kelsey scoffed. "How can it be? That's a real place on this earth we're trying to find. Not a dream world." She knew once she said it, Seung would latch onto that idea with zeal.

She was right. His passion for philosophy was just heating up. "Kelsey, think about it. What if your dream world was always Xanadu, but you called it Tedanalee to protect it? What if Tedanalee is not a dream world at all and you actually travel there? What if you've been traveling there ever since you were a child?"

"So you're saying I can travel to a land, a fantasy land at that, without my physical body? That I've been going to the very world my parents had been seeking all along? Come on, Seung."

"Listen, the Buddhists believe the celestial body, the physical body, and the soul don't necessarily have to be connected. What if you're able to take your soul there whenever you want, leaving your physical body in this plane of existence? You did go somewhere for those six weeks when you were catatonic with the Goldmans."

"Catatonic?" Desmond stared at her questioningly and Kelsey stayed him with her hand.

"Yes, after my attack I obviously retreated deep into my mind to protect myself. What you're suggesting now is magic and I'm no magician."

Seung's face filled the screen. "Well, maybe you are, Kelsey."

Ari pushed him aside. "Whether magic was employed or not, or you simply had a shared meditative experience, according to this map, Tedanalee, or Xanadu is obviously centered around Mount Abora, the Bodhidharma Monastery, and right near where your parents had their hut. You have to go there."

Julia piped up. "I have you both booked on a flight tomorrow morning to China. You'll be meeting up with a tour group going to the Kungri Nako Monastery. It's one of the only monasteries still accepting visitors after the most recent shutdown by the Chinese militia, but it's only a day's walk to the Bodhidharma Monastery. Which is where you'll eventually need to go."

"Those monks obviously know more than anyone and I'll bet they know where Xanadu is and are protecting it somehow," Ari said. "Maybe from Mara himself. Maybe he's the blackness you keep seeing in your dreams. At the very least, you should be able to learn why they sent three monks to Colombia to meet up with you, knowing they would probably die there."

"Ari, one of them uttered the word, Tanha, to me before he died. He told me I was going to have to make some choices. What does that mean?"

There was silence over the line for a few moments. "Maybe she's the darkness that's coming," he said. "Maybe you need to protect this world from her. She was Mara's daughter, the Princess of Desire, right?"

"Yes," Kelsey said. "I felt so strange when he said her name. It gave me chills."

Desmond had been quiet, but couldn't hold back anymore. "You're all talking and acting as if Tedanalee is a real place. It can't be. Kelsey dreams about it. Dreams just aren't real. Even if it felt real when I was there." He rubbed his brow in confusion.

Seung piped up again. "Dreams can be real, Desmond. There are spiritualists who believe we all share a human consciousness and if you're capable of astral projecting, you can share your experiences with someone. It's like a combined astral projector and lucid dreamer in one consciousness. Humor me, Kelsey. What was Desmond doing in Tedanalee when you saw him?"

"Standing on the edge of the forest, looking around, and then he moved over to me and met his steed. He was right there with me, as if he belonged, right down to his clothing."

"It sounds like the monks were able to tap into your consciousness, brought you to your dream world and for some reason helped Desmond along via meditation," Ari said. "There's no question in my mind anymore that you need to get yourselves to Tibet and to the Bodhidharma Monastery. I'm certain they know exactly what's going on. And, you better get there before Raul does. I'm sure he won't have any problems buying entrance to the country if he's still alive." He let that comment hang out there.

She felt deep in her gut that he was already on his way. People like Raul seemed to have evil guardian angels watching out for them. She couldn't be so lucky to think he died in the attack at the gher. "He's not dead and I'm sure he's going to Tibet. I have his map. He's going to try to intercept us or he's going to make those monks tell him what he needs to know. With the map gone, he has nothing more to lose.   What about our guns? We can't get them into the country," Kelsey said.

"Mail them back here," Ari said. "Then you'll have to find a way to get some there. I may be able to make some calls to some contacts I have. You're going to need protection."

Seung chimed in. "You know, more important than the monks needing protection are the Emperor and Empress in Tedanalee, or if I'm correct, Xanadu. The monks believe they're in danger, from a blackness, from Mara himself, from his daughter. Who knows? I'll bet they're more than just royalty in that world and I'll bet you feel it, too, Kelsey. In your dreams you're always trying to protect them. This darkness that comes to you has been a constant threat for the past few years. Your visions of the blackness invading the sky sound like you're possibly even lucid dreaming while you're in your own world." He sucked in his breath, as if he realized something of great importance. His excitement came across the miles. "Let's take this a step further. What if you really travel to this land, and there are times you're there on your own, but other times the monks are astral projecting themselves into your dreams, teaching and educating you on the danger coming to the land?"

Kelsey almost laughed in disbelief. "Astral projecting *while* I'm dreaming and in Xanadu? So now they're also experts in mind control? All the way from Tibet, right to my bedroom in New York City? Come on. I've never heard of any type of shared dreaming like this. And to then add this other reality on top of it? And bringing Desmond along? It just isn't done, Seung. You're insinuating fantasy worlds and real magic actually exist."

"Well," Seung said, smugly. "This type of thing is obviously not done in our world, but who's to say our world is the only one? There are things you don't know, Kelsey, no matter how brilliant you are."

Touché.

It was late when they finally hung up the call. Kelsey had gone to the lobby and had the front desk mail her and Desmond's guns back to the states. Now she was back in their room. She rolled the map and put it in a small tube container.

There were two double beds and she fell onto one of them, watching Desmond slide into the other one. She grinned as he sank into the soft mattress, groaning in obvious pleasure. There was something to be said for clean sheets and a pillow to sleep on after traveling for days and hiking for miles in the middle of the jungle.

As she closed her eyes, and for the hundredth time, she tried to figure out what it meant for Desmond to have been with her in Tedanalee. If Seung were correct, then a shared consciousness did truly exist. If the latter were true, it meant that Tedanalee, her dream world, was a real place, and if it were, it was in terrible danger. She wondered how Desmond was handling everything. She opened her eyes.

Do I ask him? Indecision rocked her. Finally, she did. "Desmond, are you okay about all this?"

He took a moment before he answered. "I'd be lying if I said I wasn't having a hard time accepting it. I think of myself as pretty rational and I'm most comfortable in a world of facts, science, and rules." He sat up. "But, no one can convince me that what I had experienced wasn't real. I smelled the flowers in that land, I felt Dorje's fur. It had a familiarity to it that I can't explain. And you," he glanced at her. "You're different there, too."

"How?" she asked.

He blinked and swallowed. "Just different."

Just different. Geez, that wasn't much help. Still, part of her knew what he meant. Desmond was different there, too. He seemed to light up with an ethereal glow. Was she like that for him? *No, I don't want to think of him that way. To think maybe he has feelings for me.* He had just been excited to be in the land, just like he had been excited back in Garters. She had to remember that.

She glanced up at him, their eyes meeting, but then she pulled her gaze away and turned over, her back to him. Within minutes, she drifted off to sleep, the sounds of Tibetan long horns playing hauntingly in her mind.

Chapter 24

DEVAS

The plane bounced lightly as it hit a pocket of turbulence. Staring out of the windows of the first class cabin, the world was a brilliant canvas of white peaked mountains jutting to pinnacle heights across the Himalayan range and stretching for hundreds of miles in every direction.

Huge puffs of snow, appearing like smoke rising from the peaks, tufted up in great swirls, mixing with the clouds that streaked across the horizon. It made the entire landscape seem otherworldly and magical. It wasn't hard to imagine why multitudes of people took spiritual journeys to this land every year to find peace and contentment. A journey that had been repeated over and over for centuries in their attempts for enlightenment. It was a supernatural world which seeped into the very pores of your being as you gazed upon its beauty.

The Tibetans revered these mountains. According to Buddhist philosophy, mountains were sacred and should never be touched by human feet, and as a result, only a few mountains had been given clearance for expeditions by The Tibet Mountaineering Department. The Chinese made it even more difficult to travel throughout Tibet once they invaded the country. Even the Dalia Lama himself fled to India because of the constant threat of imprisonment by the Chinese.

Kelsey was lost in thought as she stared out at the snowcapped alps and glittery turquoise lakes. They glinted in the barren expanse. She loved it here and was more content and at peace in this land than she was anywhere else on the planet. Even with what was coming, with Raul here, this world tugged on her.

Her thoughts turned to her parents who had made their hut at the base of Mount Abora, tucked nearly a mile away from the Bodhidharma Monastery. Why hadn't the monks protested it? Had they known the Porters were there to help them? Or, more importantly, had the monks been using the Porters all along, knowing there was danger, but never exposing the risks to them?

That thought plagued Kelsey. To think the monks had put her family in a perilous situation, without ever telling them or giving them the knowledge they'd need to protect themselves. It went completely against the sacred truths. Even the Chinese militia hadn't known they were there. That was probably why her parents made their home where they did.

What if the reason the monks never explained the danger was because their presence was tantamount to the survival of something they were unable to care for? Was that allowable? Trading one life for another? If Buddhism regarded the mind and the body as two separate entities, then the "vessel" of the body on its own didn't matter. Maybe they felt if something were to happen to her parents, while protecting a sacred truth, their sacrifice would transcend them directly to Nirvana, straight to the Pure Land. It didn't matter either way. Her parents were innocent victims.

A bitter thought settled in her gut like a bad stomachache. What about her? Had she been expendable as well? If they had set her parents up, then what did they think would have happened to her? She was lucky to have even survived the attack. She should have been dead.

Unless of course, it had nothing to do with her parents at all, and everything to do with her. What if they'd been using her all along?

She had spent her whole life taking back control. Learning, training, working towards the day she would find Raul and his men and destroy them to avenge her family. It was the driving force of her life. She felt she'd been in charge of all of it, right down to her relationships with men and her friends and family. It hadn't been easy. She had desires and needs just like everyone else, but she chose to fight them and pursue her demons on her own terms. She had thought it was all her own choice. Now to think the monks had used her and directed her the entire time? To think she may have always been destined for this path because of what they had done to her. She still didn't understand how she knew about Xanadu, but now she was reasonably sure she did. She knew the language; she knew the meditation to bring her there; and the monks said they had taught it to her. Obviously, it had been during her time in Tibet. *Then why don't I remember it?*

She glanced at Desmond, sleeping in the seat next to her. A stray curl fell across his brow. A protective feeling rushed over her and she leaned towards him and gently pushed the lock aside. He stirred and she froze, but he didn't wake up. The monks said he was connected to her and that she needed him, but what did that mean? She didn't understand, and it disturbed her.

Her ears popped slightly as the plane descended and the pilot came on the speakers.

"We'll be starting our descent into the Lhasa Gonggar Airport. Please put away all your portable devices and bring your tray tables and seat backs up as we prepare for landing."

Kelsey collected her empty cups and snack tray and handed it to the stewardess as Desmond slowly woke up.

He rubbed both his hands up and down his face and turned to Kelsey. "What time is it?"

"It's early." She had come to a truce with him. After the deaths of the monks in Colombia, she realized she needed help. More importantly, she wanted it. When Desmond had been with her in Tedanalee, it felt natural and right. Maybe they had been cosmically pushed together because he followed his own path to redeem his family. She didn't know, but it made some sort of convoluted sense. Buddhism was about continuity and enlightenment. Until they both found their own inner peace, perhaps their paths would continue together until they could finally give up all earthly quests and achieve their own nirvana.

So, ignoring him was no longer an option. First, it would make things much easier if they were on speaking terms and second, she was just too tired to be angry at him constantly. Third, and the one she was still too embarrassed to admit, was that she cared for him. It didn't mean she wasn't still uncomfortable and embarrassed by what had happened, but for now she'd try to at least put it behind her until this was over. Then he could disappear from her life and she could finally move on.

The plane landed without incident. After they made their way through customs, they secured a taxi to the Qunghai-Tibetan Railway. The train ride would take them to a small village relatively close to the Kungri Nako Monastery where they could pretend to catch up with the tour. After that, it would be over a day's walk on foot from there to the Bodhidharma Monastery.

As they moved into the train's cabin, Chinese soldiers strolled by, asking for IDs. Kelsey and Desmond gave theirs, and after a few cursory nods, the soldiers moved on to another cabin.

"We're going to need to be careful, Kelsey. The Chinese hold no sympathy for the Tibetans, or Americans for that matter."

She nodded, knowing she and Desmond stood out like sore thumbs. "I know. It's worse in Lhasa. There are going to be manned checkpoints all over the city, with soldiers everywhere imposing curfews." She turned back to their small cabin, glancing at the sole bed and with a sigh, shook her head. It was just a small double sleeper berth, because Julia had booked them as a married couple for believability. It wasn't lost on her how the gods must continuously be laughing at her as they tried to thrust her and Desmond together. She glanced at him. He tried not to smile, but she could see the sides of his mouth twitching.

She placed their bags on the overhead rack. She kept the map on her person, rolled in a poster holder she had flung over her shoulder.

"We should grab something to eat in the dining carriage before the effects of the altitude kicks in," Desmond suggested.

"How high up are we traveling again? Four thousand feet?" Kelsey sat down and bounced on the bed. It squealed under her weight and she could feel the metal springs thrusting through the thin mattress covering. It was not going to be a comfortable night's sleep. Sighing, she glanced around, noticing there wasn't much more room in the cabin, either. As it was, Desmond was flush up against the door, just a few feet from her. Damn, the room at Garters had been bigger than this.

"We're going higher than that," Desmond said. "Over the Tangulla Pass, which has a maximum altitude of over 5,000 meters. It's funny, I read they make individuals sign a Health Declaration form because so many people get altitude sickness when they travel here."

I guess we better eat before one of us starts puking.

They passed the day talking quietly, eating boiled eggs and noodles and drinking tea while watching the breathtaking scenery streak past them. There were the typical paddy fields and low lying hills. Small, brightly-painted temples dotted the

194

skyline and were seen nestled into the mountains. Villagers and herders drove their sheep and goats across from one valley pass to another.

As they climbed into their bed that night, Kelsey couldn't fall asleep. The bed tilted to the center and although Desmond kept his back to her, he was flush against her and she found it distracting. To take her mind off of him, she closed her eyes and imagined herself in her magical land. She could take herself there so easily. One moment she was in the cabin, the feel of the train rumbling under her and the next she was thinking of lounging by the stream with Ishu, the creature resting contentedly on the soft grass. Little raccoon-like animals with large rabbit ears cooed and called next to her, sounding like bubbles popping on water.

God, she so wanted to really be there. It was nice to daydream about Tedanalee, but when she fell asleep and dreamed, or when the monks had meditated with her, it truly came to life. Just like when she was a child after the attack. She remembered walking through the village and through the colorful corridors of the sanctuary. She was in the care of the Emperor and Empress and they had accepted her as one of their own. She remembered getting Ishu as a gift from the Empress. The fedelia had been just a baby at the time, about as small as a puppy. Kelsey had taken care of her, learned with her and healed with her. Though she had only been there six weeks in real time, it felt longer. Ishu had grown quickly and before she had left Tedanalee, they'd learned how to fly together.

Kelsey remembered how hard it had been to come back to reality. Through the walls of her conscious mind, she could hear the Goldmans beseech her, but they always sounded so far away, as if there were behind a closed and cloudy window. She could see their shadows vaguely on the other side and hear their muffled voices, but it had been easier to just pretend they didn't exist. They weren't her parents and she hadn't wanted to return to a world without her mother and father. A world that held evil in it, like the men who'd hurt her.

But even in Tedanalee there was blackness. Sometimes it would seep across the sky like an inkblot on paper. Everyone in the court would stare out the windows, silently watching. Some with tears in their eyes. She remembered one time…

* * * * *

"What is it?" Kelsey asked. The little girl stood on a terrace, leaning on the outer balcony's stone wall and stared at the sky. It was daytime and green and yellow ribbons of color floated in and out of the clouds that day. There was also a blackness like a spider's web trickling across the sky.

The Empress placed a comforting hand on the ten year-old's shoulder. "It's a darkness that's trying to invade our world, but don't worry little one. We're fighting it."

"It feels funny," Kelsey said, touching her hand to her chest. "It hurts me here."

The Empress glanced at her husband. His face was calm, but Kelsey thought she saw fear in his eyes. That scared her, because he was the bravest man in the land.

The Emperor cupped Kelsey's chin in his large hands, moving her eyes away from the black streaks, and bent down to face her, his expression again strong and sure. "We are powerful beings, Kelsey. Our job is to destroy foes and to vanquish enemies and evildoers who come to this land. We will protect you, so listen to me. I want you to ignore this evil when it chooses to visit us. When you see it or feel it, I want you to push it away the same as you push bad thoughts back during meditation. Reject it and it will disappear and you'll no longer be in pain."

Kelsey glanced at the sky again and then closed her eyes. "Go away," she whispered. She peeked through her slit eyelids, but it was still there.

"Let's go inside and away from the darkness. It can't hurt you right now. It's just testing itself and trying to intimidate us. To see if it can sway us and make us fear. Let's ignore it and it'll have no power over us." The Emperor and Empress took her hands and guided her back inside the sanctuary.

Kelsey heard the laughter of children echoing down the corridors of the monastery. Yes, she'd go back inside and play with them and forget the darkness that was trying to scare her. She glanced once more behind her as she walked with her guardians. "You can't hurt me here," she whispered, and turned to disappear into the hallowed halls filled with golden Buddhist deities.

With that, the streaks faded from the horizon, to return another day.

* * * * *

She was always taught by the Emperor and Empress to ignore the blackness and they tried their best to distract her from it whenever it came. There was something about it that was so familiar to her. Familiar and terrifying at the same time.

Kelsey opened her eyes and with a quick glance at Desmond's back, she took the chance that he might already be asleep and decided to go back to Tedanalee on her own. She closed her eyes and started moving her fingers. Over and over the dance played. Over and over they fluttered like waves on the sand, making ripples, up and down, up and down. It felt so easy and natural. She concentrated on her breathing, forcing her breaths to coincide in time to the motions of her fingers. Over and over they played. There was a slight change in the air. She opened her eyes for a moment, but everything was blurred, and she closed them again, letting her fingers fly, on and on in their incessant dance. She concentrated on her inner self, becoming one with the motions, heard Desmond's soft snores coming from far away, felt her fingers flying ...

...and heard the distant, droning sounds of the long horns playing their haunting aums. Not calling the land to arms, but to announce the coming of the night. Kelsey glanced at the sky, the setting sun turning the land to dusk and the aurora borealis in deep reds and purples. Riders astride their steeds flew high on their missions to the temple, like little black birds dotting the sky.

Kelsey strolled across the grass and into the woods, the strange curling tree leaves, reaching out to her as if they wanted to caress her cheeks. Now and again, she took one of the leaves in her hand and stroked it. They trembled, as if they could feel her.

She took the path, worn from years of use, but rimmed with wildflowers, towards the little home in the forest. It blended in with the woods. If you didn't know it was there, you might have walked right by it, except for the strange animals that played in and out of the low bushes nestled against it. Thick sheets of ivy and fragrant flowers climbed the walls, framing the little one room hut. In her dreams, the Emperor and Empress had it built for her when she was a teenager and had given it to her as a gift. Her own little home and haven in this world. She felt safe here.

"Kelsey?"

Kelsey froze, turning towards the voice coming from just beyond the hut. The moon was bright and Desmond slipped through the trees. His eyes were wide in surprise. "I'm here again."

She stared around her and then back at Desmond. *"I must
have brought you."*

*He wore an open neck, short sleeved tunic, his muscular
chest barely contained by the shirt. Loose, earth brown pants
and leather sandals completed his clothing. Weapons were
strapped to his body in a warrior fashion, with a quiver of
arrows on his hip, a sword strapped across his back and a
dagger in a holster at his waist. His unruly hair was again
swept back from his brow by small strands of glittering beads,
held in place behind his ears.*

*Kelsey took a step towards him. "I was in our cabin on the
train and I thought I'd try to meditate and take myself here
like I did long ago. If I'm still dreaming or meditating, it's
possible I've astral projected you here and we're lucid
dreaming together, much like the monks did. Or else you're
not here at all and I just conjured you up. But it feels real."*

*He shook his head. "No, I'm definitely here and I'm most
certainly not lucid dreaming. I studied it in college, even
practiced it aggressively, and this isn't it. I can't make things
happen here if I simply wish it to, like in true lucid dream
states. This place is real, Kelsey, and each time I'm here it
seems more and more familiar, as if I'm just coming out of a
fog. I don't think on my own I could ever conjure a place of
this intricacy. The way the leaves of this plant curl up towards
my fingers when I touch them or those flowers by that hut. I
don't have that kind of imagination. I don't know how you did
it, but you've taken us both to Xanadu. You can really travel
here, Kelsey." He took a few steps towards her and held out
his hand. "Come with me. There's something I have to show
you."*

*Curious, she grasped his hand and for a moment he
stopped and just stared at it. He paused, swallowed hard, and
then turned and led her back into the forest.*

They moved together down another worn path, one she had traveled countless times, but when Desmond turned off the path a few feet later and moved aside a purple bush of lilac-like flowers, she gasped in surprise. The lights of the colored ribbons and the bright moon helped her see something that had not been there before. She would swear to it.

A high stone wall now stood before her, twenty-feet in height and covered with ivy. Its curling leaves stretched in tendrils all around it. Kelsey quickly moved forward, walking around the wall and noticing that an identical one stretched to the other side, creating a courtyard. In parts where the ivy hadn't grown, depictions of the Buddha and other deities were etched in the rock face.

"I've never seen this place and I've traveled these woods countless times," Kelsey said. "It must have been veiled. How do you know about it?"

"It's where I woke up," Desmond said. He moved towards the wall and pushed aside a strand of ivy, revealing a hidden door. He opened it and they walked inside.

Kelsey was dumbfounded.

He ducked under a low-hanging tree branch and turned to her. "Look."

She sucked in her breath, her mouth dropping open in astonishment.

"It's the Shitenno." She stared at four impressive stone sculptures in the center of the garden, each bound to a square flat pillar and each looking out in a different direction.

"I recognized immediately what these were," Desmond said. "They're devas, used to protect the world from evil spirits. I awoke right in the center of them, right on that slate square over there."

Kelsey kneeled in front of the one closest to her, placing her hands gently on its base and then stood, running her hands up it appreciatively. "Look at the armor he's wearing.

This one is Tamonten, I believe. He's the most powerful of the four of them."

Desmond nodded. "It is him. There's a huge statue of him at the Longmen Grottoes, that ancient sculptural site in China. I studied him in school. He's supposedly the richest of the devas, having been awarded with great wealth after practicing austerity for nearly one thousand years."

Kelsey stared at Tamonten's left hand, noting the deva held a pagoda-shaped treasure house in his palm and, in his right hand, he held a spear. "They actually call him The Black Warrior, because he's the protector of holy places."

Desmond stared at her appreciatively. "You've studied your Buddhist history well."

"Desmond, was he protecting you?"

He shrugged. "I don't know, but they're protecting something. Maybe this area is a portal to this world?"

"Or, maybe it's just another concealed place, like Xanadu was concealed. A place hiding in a hidden world."

A dungchen horn with its droning, deep bass aum sounded. A breeze picked up, bringing the whinny of Ishu. "Come on, Desmond, let's leave this temple. There's nothing we can do here right now. This world is protecting itself from something coming which could affect its very survival. I feel it in my very being. It pulls at me." She glanced around, noticing a final deva in the corner of the garden. This one seemed out of place. A Trayastrimsa deva from the peaks of Sumeru, the tallest mountain in the world. Something about him tickled her brain...

Desmond pulled her from her thoughts. "The last time we were here, the blackness that invaded the sky..."

Kelsey nodded. "Yes, and now I think I know what it is."

Desmond reached for her arm, turning her to face him. "It's Raul, isn't it? You think he's coming to this world?"

201

Kelsey grimaced. "I do, but I don't know how he can get here." The horn sounded again. "Come on, we have to leave." She'd come back another time to examine the statue of the Trayastrimsa deva.

She went to grasp Desmond's hand when suddenly the entire world tilted. She screamed for Desmond, who fell backwards between the devas, and suddenly she was pulled with him, falling backwards, too. Falling...falling... falling...

* * * * *

Kelsey felt someone shaking her. She opened her eyes and Desmond leaned over her, his face inches from hers. The bed coils shrieked violently, but he didn't notice. His eyes were wild and excited. "We were there, Kelsey! We were there! You did it again!"

He jumped out of bed, breathing fast and nearly hit the wall. He turned to her. "Do you know what this means? You can go there whenever you want. You have the ability to travel to Xanadu – you must always have had the ability. And you can take people with you."

Kelsey sat up, and then stared at her fingers. She fluttered them, closed her eyes, but nothing happened. "But how?"

"You did it by meditating somehow. You must always be recreating what the monks did at the gher. You've obviously been doing it since you were a child."

Kelsey shook her head. "I never learned how to meditate like that. Moving my fingers was just a thing I did to calm myself down."

"You just didn't know," he said. "You went to school at the monastery when you lived there, right?"

She nodded. "Of course, but I was only eight-years old when I started and went there for just two years. I'd only just begun to learn the rudiments of The Noble Eightfold Path.

They taught me to breathe, to calm my mind. It was just the very basics of meditation."

"They had to have taught you more. Try to remember."

Kelsey squinted. "I learned Tibetan, the philosophy of Buddhism and the history, but I never learned Kalachakra, the highest level of the Buddhist tantra anuttarayoga. Supposedly, I was gifted, and they let me try some of the more complicated techniques as the years went on, but the ability to leave my celestial body and travel worlds and realities? Like to the mystical world of Shambala? Come on, I'm no Buddha!"

Desmond shook his head. "This place certainly seems like Shambala, doesn't it? A mythical world where all the beings are enlightened? It's so perfect there."

"Well, if you're going to play a mythical lands game, it also seems like Shangri-La, too," Kelsey said. "A paradise with immortal beings and strange animals, immersed in a green valley. My world of Tedanalee and both these other mythical lands all take place in the Himalayas."

"Just like Xanadu," Desmond said, his voice awed. "What if they're all the same place? What if they always have been?"

Kelsey stared at him and Desmond suddenly started laughing. "By the way, did you say tantra annuttarayoga? I wouldn't imagine they'd teach you that. You were just a child."

She sighed, exasperated. "What is it with people? Tantra is not always about having mind-blowing out of body sexual experiences and having great superpowers. It's about continuity, the everlasting continuum through all our lifetimes. It's about connections and when even our most subtle mind seems to turn off, it really never will. It just continues on and becomes the basis for attaining enlightenment. I wonder…?"

"What?" Desmond asked.

Kelsey bit her lip. "The devas we saw in the dream, the advanced meditation, the mixing of all the theologies. Xanadu and Tedanalee. Why are they all connected to me?"

Desmond shrugged and stared out the window at the dark night, uninterrupted by any lights or moon. "I don't know Kelsey, but I'll bet the monks at the Bodhidharma Monastery do."

Desmond crawled back into bed and lay down on the squeaky mattress. They talked some more about the second and third levels of tantra and the methods for becoming a Buddha. When they finally fell asleep, they both faced each other. At one point in the night, Kelsey rolled closer to Desmond until she was against his chest, her head in the crook of his neck. Unconsciously, he wrapped his arms around her and they both returned to dreamless sleeps.

Chapter 25

IT'S YOU

It was early morning as the train rolled to a stop in the small, remote village of Bugkambra. Kelsey and Desmond grabbed their things and stepped onto the platform, taking in the sounds and scenery.

The village was set in a deep valley, surrounded by snow-capped mountains. Children herded goats and sheep and a bleating cacophony heralded their passage. It was cold and their breath smoked in the air in front of them. The villagers were already setting up their market stalls, filled with the staples of the area: turnips, potatoes and Chinese cabbage. There were other stalls filled with barley and wheat, mutton, yak and other dried meats, along with buckets of live fish, caught that very morning from the large lakes and rivers that ran throughout the town and residing mountains. It would have been scenic and tranquil, except for the sound of a Chinese Army convoy driving by, the inordinate amount of soldiers patrolling the streets, and the Tibetans staring at them in abject fear. As they moved through the town, the villagers gave them a wide berth.

While some of the residents wore western clothing, most donned their native attire. The women were dressed in their shubas--long robes with wide sleeves that cinched up at the waist so their skirts only hung to their knees, even in the winter cold. They kept their hair long or wound in complicated braids and many wore large, felted conical-shaped hats. The colors of their clothing were exotic with deep oranges, blues and reds.

The men wore their hair the same as the women, though some shaved their heads. Many of the men wore sheepskin drawers under their herdskin coats and high leather boots to ward off the cold.

As Kelsey and Desmond stopped at a stall, they were approached by a Chinese soldier who asked for their papers.

They handed over their passports and their itinerary. "We're trying to get to the Kungri Mako Monastery to meet our tour." Kelsey's Mandarin was flawless. "We were detained in Europe because of bad weather."

He pursed his lips, eyeing them. Kelsey knew how the Chinese felt about followers of Tibetan Buddhism. It was a constant battle between religious beliefs and China trying to maintain their sovereignty over the area.

He handed them back their papers. "Go to the constable and there you'll find a guide."

Thanking him, they moved on, passing an elderly lady with pleated braids who carried a metal and wood prayer wheel in her hands. Her eyes widened when she saw them and she quickly scurried away.

Desmond hefted his backpack, his breath coming fast as he dealt with the lack of oxygen in this place called The Roof of the World. "The influence of the Chinese is appallingly apparent here. I didn't think they'd be enforcing this far into the mountains. With the unrest happening in the country, it's no wonder the people are scared."

"And they won't help us, either," Kelsey said. "They probably fear the Chinese might think they're aligning themselves with us."

A little boy ran by chasing a mongrel dog and a man pulled a yak across the street. A group of women, carrying bags of goods for the market stopped in mid-stride to stare at them. No one smiled.

Kelsey paused by a small stall that was filled with wild plants, but the elderly merchant had a myriad of Zongzi for purchase as well. She pointed at one of the pyramid-shaped bamboo wrapped leaves and asked the proprietor what was inside them.

He stared at her, then at the Chinese policeman glancing at him from the end of the stall. For a moment it seemed as if he were going to ignore her, but after seeing her bag full of yuan and jiao, he seemed not to want to lose the sale.

"Those are sticky rice filled with sweet bean paste and these have pork with mushrooms and egg." He spoke in Tibetan and didn't offer any more information.

"I'll have one of each, good sir," she said, handing him too much money.

Without giving her change, he pocketed the coins, handed her the food in a piece of paper and turned away.

Kelsey didn't say anything, just bowed slightly and left the stall. She leaned towards Desmond. "He didn't want to take my money."

Desmond leaned close to her, whispering in her ear. "Probably because now he'll have to pay half of it to that policeman. I'd be surprised he doesn't take the entire sale from him. Come on."

They continued to pass stalls with intricate rugs and others filled with jewelry made of Naga Shell and Lapis beads, along with a multitude of turquoise bracelets and necklaces. She expected the merchants to come to her to haggle, but they avoided her. From what she could see, they were the only foreigners in the immediate area.

The constable's building was ahead. But before they even made it near the front door, a local policeman came out and stopped them from going further. Dressed in gray camouflage, his hand on the butt of his gun, he blocked them so they couldn't enter the building. He spoke English. "You should return home. There's no climbing here today." His gaze skittered across the road, settling on a group of Chinese military policeman entering a local store.

Desmond glanced at Kelsey and she moved forward, speaking Tibetan. She craned her head to look up to the man, who was much taller than she. He was tall for a Tibetan, even towering over Desmond. *"Sir, we're going to the Kungri Mako Monastery and hired a guide to take us. We missed our tour and our travel planner told us to meet him here."* Julia had secured a mountaineer escort to take them to the monastery, where they would sneak away to travel onward to the Bodhidharma Temple.

The policeman glared at Kelsey. "So, you speak the native language?" he said, replying in English. "You're the second group of people to come here who missed this tour. That's your own fault. Foreigners aren't allowed to roam freely around Tibet and no guide has come here to take you." His gaze again settled on a soldier walking down the street. He turned to stare at them. "Not to mention all foreign tourists have recently been instructed to leave the area, or don't you even heed the advice of your own embassy?" He crossed his arms.

Kelsey moved closer to him, staring into his eyes. *He's angry, but also scared.* "Who was the first person to miss the tour?" Realization dawned on her. "Did a man come here recently? Yesterday? Did he threaten you?"

The policeman averted his eyes and wouldn't look at her.

Desmond slowly put his backpack on the ground. Then he lowered himself to the dirt, his palms, elbows, toes, knees and forehead placed on the ground. *Oh my god, that's brilliant, Desmond.* Kelsey quickly threw down her own backpack and did the same.

The policeman started, surprised at the exalted show of respect they gave him.

Desmond looked up. "The man that came, was he dark? Latino with two large scars running down both his cheeks?" He ran his own fingers down the front of his face, like tears falling from his eyes. "Did he say he was going to the Kungri Monastery, too?"

The policeman swallowed hard and gripped the butt of his gun. "No, he said he wanted to go to the Bodhidharma Monastery. I told him no one visits that most sacred of temples. He said he made a mistake. That it was the Kungri Mako monastery he meant to say, but I didn't believe him and told him to go back to where he came from. You know this man?" He glared at them and clenched his jaw.

Desmond nodded. "His name is Raul Salazar and he lied to you. He means to go to the Bodhidharma Temple and harm those at the monastery. My partner," he turned to Kelsey. "Grew up with them as a child."

The policeman turned his stare to Kelsey. "You were never planning to travel to Kungri Mako, were you?" His eyes were angry slits. "You're after this man?"

She nodded. Initially, she had thought the policeman was young, a new addition to the force, but quickly realized he was actually in his mid-thirties. *Does he know about me?* "Sir, did you work here twelve years ago?"

The policeman squinted. "I was hired by the original constable when I was twenty-two. That would be thirteen years ago."

Kelsey took a chance. "There an attack on an American family around that time. They were living near the monastery. Do you remember anything about it? I read that it had gotten quite a lot of attention."

For a moment the policeman's eyes widened in surprise and then clouded. He pursed his lips and nodded. "I do. It was one of the most violent incidents with Americans in this area in a long while. What do you know of it?"

"I know quite a bit, sir. The man I'm seeking committed the crimes against that family."

The policeman shook his head, remembering. "It was awful what had been done to the American couple and their little girl. I was the guide who took her parent's friends to their camp."

"So you were there," Kelsey said, quietly.

He nodded. "I helped the family pry that poor child from her dead mother's arms. Oh, what had been done to them. The last time I saw the little one was when they put her broken body in the ambulance to take her to the hospital. They say she was never the same." He closed his eyes a moment, creasing his brow and put his hand to his forehead. "The vision of her when we found her still haunts me." His eyes teared and he brushed them away fiercely, obviously embarrassed.

A powerful feeling overtook her and she gently took the man's arm. "Constable, I'm that little girl. I'm Kelsey Porter."

As if struck, the man reeled back. "By the gods," he breathed, staring her up and down. He peered into her eyes, recognition dawning on him. "It is you. Those blue eyes. I always wondered what became of you." He glanced down sheepishly. "My wife and I planted a bohdi tree in your memory. It sits in our garden and sometimes on a full moon we go and pray for you."

Kelsey smiled, touched by his compassion. He was obviously a devout Buddhist. She could use that. "I could have succumbed after what happened to me, but I didn't and I allowed the teachings of the Buddha to drive me. I didn't allow the negativity of my past to cloud my mind. I persevered with a single-mindedness to live and beat my demons."

The policeman looked at her shrewdly now. "You speak philosophy, but you still seek the devil who did this to you and your family?"

Kelsey stared at him, knowingly. "Yes, I do. I know I'll never be truly enlightened unless I give up my earthly desires and the objects which influence me, but I can't, sir. I don't crave personal fame or riches, but I do crave the need to drain the life force of the being who hurt me and my family and who intends to hurt the monks at the monastery. For that, I may never be enlightened. I've accepted my lot. It's something I'm willing to sacrifice if it means saving others from the same fate."

The policeman nodded in understanding. "Anyone who seeks to protect, like myself, knows at some path in our lives, choices must be made which could hinder our ability for retribution. The very things which will cause us negative karma." Again he glanced down the street at the military personnel. They had left the stall and strolled towards the train station, their hands filled with bags of food. He turned to Kelsey. "There are bad influences in the world everywhere and I believe at the end of my path, my spirits will know how far I went to protect innocent souls. I know death is inevitable, but I do feel people must have a chance to live the life others might have wished to end prematurely. I have to think that means something and hope it gives me the enlightenment I need when I enter the third and fourth bardos."

Desmond rose and extended a hand to Kelsey. They stepped forward. "Constable, when exactly was the man here?"

"I saw him last night."

"Was he injured?" Kelsey asked.

The policeman nodded again and pointed to his left arm. "He had a bloody sling wrapped around his shoulder, but he could move it. When he tried to gain a guide to the monastery and then started his lies, I sent him back to the train station."

"And he just left?" Kelsey asked, incredulously.

"He had to. A Chinese government official had the military take him to the station, but I don't think he actually left, because in the middle of the night last evening, two yaks and four sheep were slaughtered only a farm away from here. Maybe a group of drunk Chinese military did it, but I don't think so. Only a man with no soul would do something so heinous to a small farmer and his family by taking away their sustenance. I know in my heart it was this man. In fact, I sent one of my own deputies up to the Kungri Nako Monastery to protect them in case he made it there. My deputy should be there by now." He turned back to his office. "Come with me. I'll get you a guide. He can take you as far as that temple, but not on to the Bodhidharma Monastery. We don't want to attract any more attention to it than we need to. You'll be able to get there yourselves after another day's walk." He was about to turn away, but then stopped. "Your assault was the first in a series of violent attacks during my time here. A few years later there was an ambush at the monastery as well. I've heard there were other incidents at other monasteries around the globe. Each time those from the Bodhidharma Monastery left to seek new ministries, they were targeted. Do you think it was the same man who attacked all of them?"

Kelsey nodded. "I do."

He pursed his lips and moved into the hut. "Then we must find him and I must help you." He glanced at them. "Do you have weapons with you?"

Kelsey shook her head no. "But we know how to use them if we did."

The constable thought about it and nodded. "Give me an hour."

Kelsey and Desmond strolled towards a quaint little park outside of the police station and sat on a bench next to the river. Some local men fishing glanced at them curiously now and again as they sat there talking.

It was a picturesque spot, quiet and peaceful. Snow-capped mountains ridged the valley and they could see sheep and yak grazing on the sparse grasslands in the distant fields. Their breath streamed in the cool air as they sipped the warm buttered tea the constable had offered them and ate their zongzi from the market.

"I had no idea the extent of what happened to you, Kelsey," Desmond said. "I wondered where you were when your parents were killed and had thought for some reason you weren't there. That maybe you had been safe with the monks, or someplace in America and it was the reason you were still alive and seemingly okay." He sighed, seeing her pained expression. "I'm sorry. We don't have to talk about this. I know how personal it is."

It's going to come out anyway. You could probably look it up in old archives somewhere. "I'm sure you could get the story from the Constable with a few glasses of Lhasa beer. If anything, it'll explain a lot about me." She told him about the attack, leaving out very few details, and then about what happened to her afterwards with the Goldmans.

He was stunned, disgusted and horrified. "I'm having a hard time trying to imagine what the two days after your attack had been like. It must have been horrible."

"It was a long time ago, Desmond. It's okay."

He shook his head. "No, it's not okay. Here you went through this horrific crime, are spending your life avenging your parents murder and I have acted like a sex crazed ass. I forced you to sleep with me at Garters, because I thought you were something you're not. You did try to explain it to me and I wasn't listening because… well, because I was caught up and wanted to get laid." He stared at his feet, his face beet red in embarrassment. "I have no idea how you've been able to work with me."

She grunted. "It hasn't been easy." She felt her heart softening. *Don't tell him how you feel. It will just complicate things. Stay in control.*

They were quiet for a bit, sipping their tea. Finally, Desmond spoke. "Do you remember when the Goldmans came to get you?

"To be honest, I don't remember much of anything during that time. After Raul and his men finished with me, I remember nothing but pain as I lay there in the dirt. I couldn't even move or cry, until I felt my mother's hand on my shoulder. She must have crawled to me at some point. She took me in her arms and held me until I felt her body grow cold. It's the last conscious memory I have of my time in Tibet. They say I was catatonic when they found me. For six weeks I couldn't do anything in this world, but when I was in Tedanalee, I healed. I do remember hearing people trying to talk to me every now and then and calling my name, but they always sounded very far away." Kelsey glanced up at the clouds floating lazily in the sky. "I would be in the monastery, playing with my pets and I'd hear something faint and otherworldy. Funny, right? I was in another world, but I would think something was otherworldly there. Anyway, I remember glancing out the window and noticing a hazy shadow behind a cloud. Sometimes it scared me and I would tell the Empress, who in those days was my constant companion. She'd watch the shadow for a long time and then talk to me about it…"

* * * * *

"Kelsey, please come back to us," the gentle voice called.

Kelsey turned to the window of her quarters, staring out at the clouds floating next to the colorful ribbons streaking across the sky. The rug was soft under her as she sat, stroking the back of a little creature. She giggled as it whipped and wriggled up her arm and nuzzled her cheek.

The voice called again. "Please, Kelsey. Honey, let me help you."

The Empress kneeled down next to Kelsey and stroked her hair, pushing aside a wayward strand which had escaped from her jeweled headband. "Would you like to go see who's calling for you? She sounds very nice."

Kelsey turned to the window. The voice was still there, but it was so soft, like a whisper on the wind.

Kelsey clutched her pet in her arms protectively and started shuddering. A tear rolled down her cheek and she shook her head no. "It's not my mother."

The Empress shook her head, sadly. "No, it's not."

"Then, I don't want to go. Please don't make me."

The Empress took her in her arms and held her tight. "We would never make you leave. You don't have to decide now. There will always be another time. When you're ready to let go, they'll still be there waiting for you."

"Who is it?" Kelsey asked, her curiosity getting the best of her.

"Someone who cares for you deeply."

"But you care for me," Kelsey said. "I want to stay here with you and the Emperor and the others. I feel safe here."

The Empress glanced at her maidservant and the two exchanged knowing looks. "You can stay as long as you like. But remember, even if you do go to see who's at the window, and decide to go with them, we'll never leave you. We'll always be here for you, no matter where you are. You can always come back to us, forever and ever. Do you understand?"

Kelsey nodded and then turned her back away from the window and the soft, beckoning voice faded away.

* * * * *

"It doesn't take a masters in psychology to know I didn't want to know who it was. I wasn't ready to return to this reality."

"So they took care of you."

Kelsey nodded. "I spent the first few days in Tedanalee in bed sobbing and mourning my parents. But the Emperor and Empress and their court saved me. They came and comforted me, talked to me, fed me, children played with me and showed me so many wonderful and incredible things. I had no pain in that world, so I was physically fit and was free to move around and soon, with all the fantastical animals and the amazing scenery, I was transfixed. When they brought Ishu to me as a gift, I truly came alive there. She was just a baby, the size of a small puppy. I could hold her in my arms and together we grew. With her, I mentally healed while my body slowly healed in this reality."

"Who are the Emperor and Empress? What are they? Are they people?"

Up until a day ago I thought they were just figments of my imagination. She shrugged helplessly. "I don't know. I never associated them as part of our world. None of them were. They were just dream people. It's funny, I called them the Emperor and Empress when I met them because they seemed so regal and lived at the monastery, which was like a big imperial palace, but now I realize no one else in the land referred to them that way." She squinted. "Now I'm wondering what they really are. In fact, what all of them there

216

are." She was quiet for a moment. "What I do know is as I got older, I realized that while they did protect me when I was little, they were the ones who also needed protection. Everyone there seemed to be a warrior or a fighter of sorts and now I wonder why Why did I fit into that role as I got older?"

Desmond was silent for a moment. "Why do you think they protected you in the first place?"

What is he talking about? She cocked her head, confused. "What do you mean?"

"I mean, why you specifically? Not that I'm discounting the horror you experienced, but why you out of all the other children in the world who suffer hideously?"

She was speechless. She'd never thought of this before.

"Well, there has to be a reason." He paused for a moment. "You told me I was also a warrior in Tedanalee, there to protect against this blackness. Is that blackness Raul?"

He could be. I hate not knowing something. Kelsey squinted, frustrated. "I just don't know."

They watched a flock of geese fly gracefully across the water's surface, settling on the far shore.

"So the first time you ever went to Tedanalee was after your attack?"

"Now I don't think so. I actually used to have dreams about it before the attack and would draw all these crazy little animals and scenes from that world. Ari's parents figured it was all in my imagination and I had created this safe, fantasy world, this retreat, so I could cope and heal. I realize the monks must have taken me there at an earlier point, but I just didn't remember when."

"And all your friends know about this place now? And Ari's obviously known about it since the beginning, right?"

"He's the one who suggested it existed to my parents in the first place."

Desmond paused for a moment. "You two are close."

"Of course. He's my brother."

Desmond squinted. "Well, he's obviously not really your brother."

What is he getting at? "Of course, he isn't biologically." She bit into the last of her zongzi.

Desmond kicked the ground with the toe of his boot, not meeting her eyes. "He just seems to have a bit more of an interest in you than a normal brother would, if you catch my meaning."

He actually sounds jealous. Oh, stop it, Kelsey! She licked her lips, wiping her mouth with her sleeve. "Yeah, I catch it, but you're wrong. He's my best friend in the world and I trust him with my life. Still, it doesn't stop him from being a huge pain in the ass and overprotective at times, as you well know."

Desmond peered at her out of the corner of his eye. "So, nothing has ever happened with him?"

"Oh, Desmond, come on. Are you serious?"

He eyeballed her and she rolled her eyes. "No, nothing has ever happened!"

He smiled slightly. "Well, I guess I tested his limits."

You have no idea. "It's a good thing you were quick in his office. He's an excellent baseball player. He was going for your head."

Someone called out and they turned. "Hello? Are you Kelsey Porter?" A young man ran up to them and thrust out his hand. "I am Tenpa Dondrup. My uncle is Constable Dondrup. He called me to help guide you up the mountains." His accented English was clear and he shook both their hands enthusiastically. He was jumpy and couldn't seem to stand still and his clothes bounced on his slim frame in his excitement. He glanced behind him, his eyes gleaming. "All clear, no soldiers coming to get us!" he laughed. He had a wide smile and was eager to help them. "I can take you as far as the Chemi Pass and the Kungri Nako Monastery, but then I have to get back to town. I work for a group of Chinese officials and don't want to raise any flags if I'm gone too long. It'll only be a day's walk or so from there for you both, and a difficult one, but you look like you can handle it."

"We understand and thank you," Kelsey said.

Tenpa turned and they ran to keep up with him as he jumped into his jeep. There Desmond and Kelsey found two pistols and extra ammunition the Constable had procured for them.

They drove through the low grasslands for an hour. Tenpa told them about his time growing up in the village, then every piece of gossip over the past ten years and then finished up with a round of old Tibetan jokes. He spoke the entire time, his words a rapid current, right up until they hit the first low-lying mountains of the Himalayas. They drove until the jeep couldn't climb any further over the rocky terrain and then abandoned it at the base of a valley, making their first leg of their journey up the mountain on foot.

The trail was easy to follow, worn from thousands upon thousands of people who trod the slope. "This is the route to the Kungri Nako Monastery, which is a very popular tourist destination. The Bodhidharma Monastery is much more remote and doesn't accept visitors. I'm curious. Why do you want to go there?"

"I went to school there when I was a child."

He stared at her, his eyebrows raised in confusion. "Really? An American? It is not on the tourist maps and they keep pretty much to themselves." He leaned towards them conspiratorially. "They're a very secret sect, you know. Even the Chinese leave it alone."

Kelsey leaned towards him too, smiling. "My parents liked secrets. They were adventure seekers, in search of the mystical land of Xanadu."

Tenpa's eyes widened. "They think that place is real? You have a saying in America I like... If they believe that, I have a bridge to sell them!" He started laughing uproariously at his joke and Kelsey and Desmond couldn't help joining him.

They stopped midday for a light lunch that the Constable's wife had packed for them. She had gladly thrown something together so she could see the infamous Kelsey Porter, grasp her face in both her hands and give her a huge kiss and hug. Kelsey had been touched.

As they munched on momo dumplings, cold noodles and balep korkun, a flatbread used to scoop up the noodles, Tenpa kept them entertained with stories of old Tibetan folktales, but soon enough they were back on the path, following the way of the pilgrims from centuries ago.

It was a beautiful and scenic walk through the Himalayas, but arduous as they hiked to the temple.

Something's not right. It's too quiet. "I would have thought we would have seen some other pilgrims on this trail," Kelsey mused.

Tenpa pursed his lips. "Yes, it's strange we haven't seen anyone, not even a tour group. Possibly it's the cold weather? Those not from the mountains have a harder time with our climate." He let that thought hang in the air, but none of them believed it for a second. The usual chatty Tenpa quieted and picked up his pace. By mid-afternoon, they rounded the most strenuous part of the mountain and came upon the monastery. The architecture was a perfect representation of the early Tibetan temples. The temple was boxlike with covered walkways surrounding it and had a large stone staircase leading to the front door. Like many of the others, it was elevated, facing south with a flat roof to conserve the heat and multiple windows to let in the sunlight.

The temple was silent and no one came to greet them.

Kelsey placed her foot on the first step and her heart clenched. *Oh no.* She saw a sticky red pool drying in the sun. She touched it with the tip of her finger and then brought it to her nose, sniffing.

"It's blood." *The bastard had been here. They were too late.*

Desmond took out his gun and she quickly did the same. Tenpa stared at them, his eyes wide with fear.

"That man is here, isn't he? The one my uncle told me about?" He grabbed a thick branch from the ground for protection.

Desmond brought his finger to his lips and quickly mounted the steps, Kelsey by his side. Together they pushed through the door, their guns drawn.

Devastation met their eyes.

The bodies of monks and multiple tourists were scattered across the floor, fallen where they had been killed. Some had congregated in a pile against one of the back doors. A man in a camouflage uniform, the police officer Constable Dondrup must have sent, was splayed out, a gunshot wound to the back of his head.

Kelsey moved into the room quickly, her gaze darting to each one, bending down and checking pulses, desperate to see if anyone was alive.

She kneeled next to a young Caucasian man who wore an Oxford University sweatshirt and a gaping wound to his temple. He held the hand of a young blond woman lying face up, blood pooled under her head. Her eyes were wide and unseeing.

Tenpa came into the room, cried out and vomited on the floor.

Desmond turned to him. "Go outside and keep watch so no one enters."

His hands shook as he wiped his mouth. His voice shook. "But the man who did this? He may still be here."

Desmond shook his head. "I don't think he's here any longer. The blood is hours old."

Tenpa nodded, tears forming. He took his branch and left the room.

Desmond looked at Kelsey. "He has an automatic weapon with him. It's the only way he could have killed this many people."

Kelsey's rage filled her vision. She wanted to destroy this horror of a man who had so little value in human life. She moved purposely into the temple, past the portraits of past Dalai Lamas, Buddhist statues, and into a great assembly hall. It was empty.

A muffled cry made her turn towards a small hallway that jutted off the conventicle. Lit by a skylight, she and Desmond moved down it and stopped at the door to one of the attached apartments. The muffled cry came again. Desmond kicked open the door, his gun raised, and propelled himself into the room.

Three monks were bound and gagged. They rushed to them, cutting their bindings.

Kelsey spoke to them in Tibetan. "Venerable ones, what's happened here?"

She glanced around. The room had once been a small library, but now was in shambles, as if someone had been in a rage and taken it out on the old scrolls and books, looking and searching for something they couldn't find. Broken prayer wheels, candles, parchment paper and dripping ink wells spread across the floor.

A younger monk with a red gash on his forehead and a split lip spoke for the others. "A man came to us this morning, telling us he wanted the secrets of Xanadu and that we were to give him the maps to get there. We told him we knew nothing about that land, but he didn't believe us. He flew into a violent rage and killed our brethren and the pilgrims who sought sanctuary here. He destroyed our temple." He bowed his head.

Kelsey leaned down and took his hands. "But you lived, Venerable One. Your path wasn't to end today. I promise you, we'll find this man. I promise you he'll spend his ending days in Naraka for what he's done. I personally guarantee it."

Kelsey helped the monks to their feet and together she and Desmond searched the temple for any other survivors. There were none. Raul had killed them all. They found an empty automatic rifle lying discarded next to one of the victims.

"Sir, how long has he been gone?" Desmond asked one of the monks. They were congregated in the outdoor garden.

"At least five hours. He left by mid-afternoon, but we don't know where he went. Possibly back to the village? If so, they're in danger and you must go and warn them."

That's not where he's going. I'd bet my life on it. Kelsey shook her head. "No, there's nothing in the village he seeks. He'll be going to the Bodhidharma Monastery."

There was a collective sigh among the monks. "They'll be safe, then."

Safe? No one was safe from that man.

As if reading her thoughts, the monk answered her. "The monastery is built like a fortress and difficult to get to. Any approaching visitor can be seen for miles and they have a group of Shaolin Monks on the grounds, protecting them."

"Monks skilled in Kung Fu," Kelsey mused.

The monk nodded. "They will be safe. Even the Chinese military leave them alone."

Too bad they didn't have those Shaolin Monks when I lived here.

Tenpa came into the room. His fists were clenched and his face was a mask of fear and outrage. "Yes, they are left alone because of the secrets, right? Everyone knows that particular monastery is hiding something."

The monks said nothing.

Tenpa shook angrily. "Are these secrets worth dying for, Venerable Ones? That monastery is cloistered for a reason. The oldest Tibetan tales talk of hidden worlds and ancient ones who sought the protection of the order. If you know something, you must tell these people so they can help. Look at those who've died for this. Pilgrims who only came to you for enlightenment and still you say nothing to help them!"

Again the monks were silent.

They know. "You know what they're guarding, don't you?" she whispered. "You've been bidden to protect it. Please, tell me you know about the land of Xanadu."

The monks nodded. "We know all about it, Kelsey, as do you."

She sucked in her breath. "And you know my name." It wasn't a question.

The oldest monk stepped forward. "You're the chosen one, Kelsey. The very one who holds the secrets to what's coming and the only one who can stop it."

Me? Kelsey stared at them, helplessly. "But, how?"

"Go to the monastery, child, and you'll learn. They're waiting for you."

* * * * *

Within the hour, Kelsey and Desmond were on their way, leaving Tenpa to return to the village, report to his uncle what happened, and bring the police and government officials out to the monastery and their victims. There was no time to waste. It was a long walk to the Bodhidharma Monastery and they had to hope Raul wouldn't be able to get inside the temple before they arrived.

They'd forsaken the fire this cold evening so Raul wouldn't be able to make out their campsite, and set up the tent hidden in a crevice within the brush on the side of the mountain face. They hoped to get just a few hours of rest before they moved on again.

Kelsey took the last bit of Constable Dondrup's food. She couldn't keep her mind off the scene Raul had left behind of the monks and pilgrims, strewn about like discarded garbage. Just like her parents--killed and discarded as if their lives meant nothing. These monks knew Xanadu had to remain hidden from Raul and had kept its secrets. Like those in Colombia, they must have known their path in this world was over and Kelsey hoped they would move right through to nirvana. That their sacrifices meant something.

She felt Desmond place a comforting hand on her shoulder.

"Are you okay?" He crouched before her and took her hands in his. He sat in shadow, the light from the moon their only illumination as it penetrated the small plastic windows of the tent. His hands were wonderfully warm.

She stared at his fingers as he rubbed her hands together. She was cold. Slowly, pinpricks of feeling moved into them, but she couldn't stop shivering.

"Come here," he said, moving closer to her.

Kelsey eyeballed him. "You're not going to take advantage of me again, are you?" *Oh if I weren't so cold.*

Desmond rolled his eyes, huffing. "Yes, I'm going to take advantage of you in the middle of the mountains with a crazed armed lunatic on the loose in twenty-five degree weather. That's exactly the way I'd like my second time with you to be, since the first time was just so incredibly wonderful and fantastic."

Touché, Desmond. She stared at him as he held her hands tight, but didn't move. *What was wrong with her? Why couldn't she let this go?*

Desmond shook his head. "Look, Kelsey, I just don't want either of us to freeze to death, okay? You're shivering, it's freezing out here and for the last time, what happened in Colombia was an accident. I was dreaming."

She grunted. "Yes, but in my world, dreams are reality."

"While that may be true, let's try not to be so literal. I promise to be a total gentleman, and if I'm not, you're free to kick me again."

Kelsey considered this for a moment, but then a second set of shivers shook her and she crawled into Desmond's arms. He wrapped the sleeping bag around them both and they huddled together. She had to admit it felt good in his arms, but sleep didn't come easily. It was at least a half hour before they were both warm enough to nod off.

Before dawn's light, they awoke and struck the tent.

* * * * *

Neither of them saw the man watching them, hidden within the trees on the overhang above their tent.

Watching and scratching at the two long scars that streaked down both his cheeks.

Chapter 26

THE TEMPTRESSES

Raul faded back into the woods, his rage so intense he shook with each step. Those stupid monks at the monastery had told him nothing. Nothing! They had died for it, along with the pitiful pilgrims who'd sought enlightenment. Bunch of stupid fools. Now he wanted to kill the two he hunted.

He picked up a rock and threw it against a dead tree, wishing it was the bitch's face. He blamed her for everything and he wanted nothing more than to go to her tent and destroy both her and her boyfriend, slit their throats and beat them until they were unrecognizable. But he couldn't yet. He needed them to find Xanadu. That damned map was of no use to him anymore. It was her. She was going there and he was damned if he wasn't going there with her. To lose after all these years? It was unfathomable to him.

As the frigid wind whipped his face, shivers overtook him. He threw his pistol on the ground and wrapped his jacket tighter around his body, but it didn't help. He closed his eyes, and tried to breathe deeply and ignore the wind and cold, focusing only on the prize at the end.

He shivered again and he bit his lip, tasting blood.

"Here, let me help you."

Raul whipped his head around at the sultry voice. Incredibly, the bitch was in front of him and stark naked! He grabbed for his gun, but she moved forward lightning fast. She grasped his wrist with one hand and clutched his shoulder, pushing him to his knees with her other hand. Her grip was like a vice.

Raul tried to fight her, but realized he couldn't move. Focusing, he saw it wasn't the girl at all. There were similarities, though. She had the same long, dark hair and an incredible body, but this one was more voluptuous and taller. Her skin was darker too--a rich, olive tone. She wore a tear drop-shaped ruby bindi between her brows.

"Who are you? What the fuck do you want?" He stared at her lithe, delicate hands, realizing how warm they were on his shoulders. Warmer than a normal woman's should have been. He stared at her perfect breasts and the soft curves of her body. He also realized he'd stopped shivering.

The woman smiled seductively. She reminded him of an Indian goddess. "We're here to help you, Raul."

"We?" He was suddenly lightheaded and felt himself getting aroused.

She smiled at him. "My sister and I will make all your troubles disappear."

A second raven-haired beauty came towards him, gliding across the bare rock and dressed only in a sheer sari. He could see every outline of her exquisite body. She leaned over him and kissed him deeply, warmth radiating off her skin as if she had a fire burning within her. She began to sing. He felt himself disappear into the melody as if he'd been drugged.

Without a fight, he let the women lower him to the ground. Desire and longing flooded him and, though part of him feared these strange women being in a place no woman should be, there was nothing he could do as the temptresses slowly removed his clothing. His mind was no longer his own. Only his lusting thoughts propelled him forward. He would do anything for them, his free will sacrificed.

The first beauty caressed his manhood and kissed his torso. The other nymph spread her body out next to him and quietly hummed a haunting tune in his ear.

He nodded. "Anything," he breathed. "I will do anything you ask."

And his soul was lost.

Chapter 27

BACK TO XANADU

The morning was still. Even the rustling of the wind through the barren landscape of red rock sounded forlorn and silent. The tumult of the river far below was a faint gurgle, and a flock of birds, startled by their footsteps through the dry, sparse grass, erupted above them in a flutter of furious wings. As the dawn's light burst over the horizon, illuminating the snow-capped mountains with streaks of pink and gold, it did, indeed, seem they were alone at the top of the world. Pilgrims on a spiritual journey, seeking the enlightenment that only came with deep reflection and thought.

Kelsey and Desmond moved quickly across the worn trail, Kelsey in the lead, both their guns now worn on their sides. After the horror Raul had left behind at the Kungri Nako Monastery, they knew it was only a matter of time before they saw him again. Raul had come to Tibet for answers and if he didn't get them, he was prepared to kill.

"Kelsey, do you believe now that Tedanalee is Xanadu?"

Yes, she did. She thought about that as her footfalls crunched the dead growth. "It's the same place." Her breath streamed in the air.

Desmond prodded her. "Is it a real location on this earth or a dream world? Or, a different reality entirely?"

"What do you think?"

He stopped and stared at her. "I don't know."

Kelsey shrugged. "Me, either. But I've finally accepted they are one and the same. As to what it is exactly? I just don't know."

By midafternoon they reached the summit of one of the lower mountains and the valley stretched out before them for miles in every direction. Directly across the valley, the Bodhidharma Monastery showed itself majestically. It was built within the rocks itself, surrounded by the mountains. A massive structure, with tall, stone walls encircling it, it reminded one of a huge, impenetrable fortress. How it had withstood all the attacks and purges over the violent years was a mystery.

Kelsey stared across the expanse. "How my father ever got them to accept him is still a mystery to me. It's the most secret order in the world. No pilgrims are allowed to come and only a few local children are allowed to enter for schooling. To accept a foreigner, an American no less, under the political circumstances of the times, continues to amaze me."

"If they're protecting something and its very survival was in jeopardy, possibly they needed his help," Desmond said. "Of course, then there's Shojuharu, who said it was you all along, Kelsey. You were the one who needed to help them. It's just such an odd thing to expect of such a young child if it were true."

They made their way north, following the trail, down into the valley and then back up the summit towards the dark windows that faced them. It reminded them of eyeballs, windows to the soul, looking down upon them.

Any sentry would see there were visitors approaching and would be prepared.

Thirty minutes later, they neared the outer gate. A sense of déjà vu hit Kelsey as she ran her hands over the large tarnished bell on the outer wall. The familiarity was nearly painful. "I used to ring this very chime each morning when I came for classes. My father and I would leave at dawn and walk the mile to school." She looked over the valley, pointing. "You see that glen over there? That copse of trees that seems to rise up higher than the others? There's a small stream at its base and is rimmed with large, flat stones. We'd sit on them each morning and eat the tsampa my mother would pack for us, and then for the rest of the day my father would work with the monks and I'd take my studies with them."

She picked up the mallet hanging from a worn rope attached to the wall and struck the bell. Its gong resonated across the plaza. Just like in her youth, the doors slowly opened and she and Desmond crossed the threshold and stepped back into time.

* * * * *

A group of elder monks stood silently before them. Kelsey took a long, hard look. Yes, she remembered them. Slowly, names to faces came unbidden to her mind. Jampa, Kechok, Metok.

A Shaolin Monk, holding a long spear, quickly shut the gates behind them, but not before shifting his gaze back and forth across the valley. Another Shaolin Monk moved next to him, a butterfly sword in both his hands.

"Good Sirs, there's a man coming," Kelsey ventured.

The monk holding the spear jerked his head in her direction, speaking in Tibetan. His eyes were sharp and intelligent. "We know. Come with me. There's no time to waste." The Shaolin Monk ushered them swiftly past the elder monks, who stared at Kelsey with such pained expressions she became scared. *Had Raul already been there?*

"Are they afraid of the man who comes, Master?" she asked, running to keep up with him. Desmond kept pace at her side.

232

"They're afraid of the man, of you, of all of it. This path's time is running out. The worlds are colliding and they're terrified of he who hunts you. For he's coming for you right now, Kelsey. To stop you from what needs to be done." He froze in his tracks and turned to her. "We know he's the same one who murdered your parents and hurt you. He'll never see samsara for what will seem an eternity. This man is destined to reside in the hell planes with his master until eventually the karma which sustained his existence is exhausted."

"I understand, Master."

He shook his head. "No, you don't. You only know what you see on the surface. Not what's below and outside of your own personal existence on this plane. At least, not yet." He eyed her and she shivered. "This is the same man who's ripping apart your Tedanalee."

"Tedanalee? How do you know about that? And how is he destroying it?" The monk put up his hands, stopping her from asking more questions.

"The elder monks have been following you ever since you left Tibet. Your hatred of Raul gave him power and enabled him to poison this world. Your dvesha, your very hatred, has kept his path alive and brought us to this moment. Mara has used that to his advantage repeatedly. " He turned and continued rapidly down a garden path on the outer pavilion, leaving Kelsey stunned and running to keep up.

They passed through a multitude of dead gardens filled with hundreds of empty flower pots. She remembered sitting with the monks in this very garden as they told her the tales of Siddhartha. How she and the children would listen to the stories told by Bhante Shingen for hours on end about how Siddhartha persevered against the Buddhist devil and won. Kelsey followed the warrior monk down a cobbled path, passing painted pictures of the Buddha that adorned the building's outer walls.

They entered the temple and through the complex, moving through an ornate inner sanctuary and into the back rooms. The monk ushered them inside one of the apartments and announced their presence. "They're here."

Without a further glance at them, he turned and left, leaving Kelsey and Desmond to stare around them in awe. They had entered a world that had not changed in a thousand years. The room was a small temple with red walls painted with colorful mandalas, the Tibetan calendar and the rules for the monks. Prayer wheels rested on tables against the wall and a large golden statue of the Buddha stood at the far end of the room. Butter lamps held in wall sconces adorned the walls, their yellow light flickering and making shadows from an unknown breeze. The smell of incense wafted in the air.

Kelsey heard a haunting chant echoing through the room, floating down the corridors from another part of the monastery. Her gut clenched for reasons she didn't understand. Its sound was so ominous and profound that she felt, for a moment, she'd been transported to another world. She closed her eyes, letting the melodies flow around her. Something about it pulled at her in a way that made her uncomfortable. She felt herself getting lost in the music. The name "Arati" flitted in her mind and then disappeared. *Who is Arati? Oh yes, she was another of Mara's daughters, wasn't she? Why did she just think of her?*

A light cough brought her back and gave her the power to reject the sound. She turned in its direction. Three men stood at the far end of the room, the eldest, in traditional dress, stepped forward.

"That music you heard. Does it mean something to you?"

Kelsey nodded. "It's familiar to me, but it makes me uncomfortable."

The monk stared at her shrewdly. "As it should. It's the chant 'Om vajrapani hung', said to protect the secret teachings. We taught you it under deep meditation many years ago. It's a very old prayer song, though you may have heard it even before that."

She squinted. *I don't remember you teaching it to me. Why don't I remember?*

"You'll understand soon enough. I'm the Abbott of Abora, Dakpa Bakula. On any other day, I'd greet you as welcome visitors and have tea with you, but there's no time. You have too much to learn. Both of you. Come."

He ushered them to the floor and the other two monks sat next to them, reminding Kelsey of the scene in Colombia.

"There's so much you still don't know, Kelsey. We'll meditate and all will be explained. Hands on your laps."

Desmond spoke up. "How will I see? I don't understand."

Dakpa crossed his legs. "We'll be there with you, taking both of you into the depths of our memories."

Desmond's eyes widened in understanding. "So you do astral project. You've been manipulating yourselves into Kelsey's dreams all these years, haven't you?"

The Abbott shook his head. "Not manipulating, but observing and instructing. Teaching her things she already knew. Her own samsara, her own rebirth, influenced her path in this life, not us."

"My own rebirth?" Kelsey asked skeptically. "You believe my past life is affecting this one?"

The Abbott nodded. "Of course it has, as it does with all of us, but you've made choices in this world, Kelsey. Choices that have angered your father."

"My father? Benjamin Porter died twelve years ago, Abbott. You should know that."

The Abbott measured his words. "Your earthly father in this lifetime is dead, but your spiritual father is still alive. Now come. This is the fastest way to show you what you need to know."

Kelsey grasped the Abbott's arm, her voice desperate. "Wait, the Shaolin Monk who brought us to this room told me I poisoned Tedanalee. How did I do this? I never would have intentionally done anything if I'd known."

The Abbott gave her a small, sad smile. "It's not your fault. You didn't know you were doing this. Had you remained in Tibet with us, you may have been able to continue your teachings uninterrupted and protected, but fate didn't hand that path to you, nor to us. We all come with pasts, Kelsey, and your will has always fought yours, and fought hard. Your spiritual family is now coming for you, because they don't want you to be successful and reach the enlightenment you're capable of attaining. You're like Siddhartha, but where your spiritual sisters came simply to sway the Buddha, in this reality they come to end your path, to destroy your samsara, and the samsara of all others."

"Who's coming for me?"

"Mara himself."

Kelsey sucked in her breath. "Mara? The Buddhist Devil? The bringer of death and the enemy of all truth? You believe he's part of my spiritual family? That's ridiculous."

The Abbott narrowed his eyes. "It is anything, but ridiculous. He's your first father."

Anger laced her heart. "And which of his lovely daughters do you believe me to be?"

"It's not important, Kelsey."

She grabbed his arm again, her voice rising. "It is important! Which one do you believe I'm reincarnated from? Raga, Tanha, or Arati?

Another monk spoke up. "Tanha. You're the spiritual image of his daughter, Tanha."

The biggest slut of them all? The one who sleeps with any man she can find? Was that what Takechiyo was trying to tell her? Kelsey turned to him, so filled with fury she shook. "You all think I'm the Temptress Desire? How can you say this to me? She is the personification of evil. I am nothing like her!"

The Abbott stared at her. "Even beings from the Hell planes can change and move to other domains once their negative karma is used up, Kelsey. They don't have to remain there for eternity. The truth is, you are Tanha. Please, think upon your life. Your beauty and your brilliance. How one smile from you makes men fall at your feet. How strong you are and your ease with killing. Have you never thought about your spiritual self before this life? Why you are the way you are? But you have a voice and a soul. A soul that has been rejecting your father for centuries. And now he's angry."

"How angry?" she asked, spitting out the words.

The Abbott pursed his lips. "Extremely. For hundreds of your past lifetimes, he's ended your path prematurely as soon as he realized you were again rejecting his orders to return to his side. He's murdered you countless times in this reality as an infant and as a child. At times your destiny allowed you to make it to your teenage years. This is the first lifetime you've ever lived to the age of twenty-two. He tried to kill you in this incarnation already at the age of ten, but we intervened and your Emperor and Empress saved you from that fate."

Kelsey stared at him, shocked. "You knew this? You knew he was going to come for me?"

"No, when we first met you, all we saw was your essence, your soul and your past lifetimes. We saw the torture of the deaths you've endured for centuries. The ones you relive in your nightmares.

"When Raul showed up and threatened us, it was then we first thought he might be a minion of Mara. Of course, once he attacked us and then your family, it all became clear. No matter who else died, Mara was always after you personally. He didn't want you to grow up and pursue enlightenment, for it would go against the very fabric of his existence. He wants to end the entire cycle of rebirth and if you live, Kelsey, you could stop him from destroying the very thing your karma is bidding you to protect."

"You're talking about Xanadu, aren't you?" she asked.

The Abbott nodded. "But while Mara didn't succeed in killing you, he set up a chain of events in this world which were devastating. He hurt you badly and took your destiny in a different direction. It drove you to become the woman you are today, but it came at a high price."

"You're talking about the Three Poisons, aren't you?" Kelsey asked. "I didn't know."

The Abbott shook his head. "Nor would you. We never got the chance to tell you. Your hatred of Raul is a fundamental and deeply-rooted emotion in you. In a normal person it can exist and affect only their own karma and their own path in this life. But you're different. Tanha is a part of you and because of that you have immense capabilities. You have the power and ability to bring Raul to Xanadu, bridging a gateway to Mara's world which should remain closed."

She stared at him, incredulous. "But how?"

"We'll show you."

A monk lit another set of incense sticks and soon the room was filled with the aroma of jasmine flowers. The Abbott leaned towards Kelsey. "This scent will help clear your mind and spirit, leaving you ready to receive whatever the atmosphere gives you. Don't fight it. I know you've heard a lot, but remember who you are in this human lifetime, not who you once were. As humans, in this plane of existence, there is always a choice and we are always seeking enlightenment. Accept what we show you." He clanged a small chime and then sat back, speaking quietly. "Relax your mind. Breathe in and out. Let the events of the recent days flow from you. Breathe in light, breathe out hatred." This went on for a mere two minutes. "Now, move your fingers in the pattern we taught you, Kelsey. The pattern that brings you to your inner world."

Without even thinking about it, Kelsey started moving her fingers and the other monks followed, beginning to chant.

Kelsey and Desmond continued to breathe, continued to move their fingers in the same rhythmic pattern, waiting to see what would happen. It happened fast. The air started to shimmer and one moment Kelsey was in the inner sanctuary, and the next, she was…

…gone.

* * * * *

A nine-year old Kelsey sat on the edge of the garden in the back of the Bodhidharma Monastery, playing with a green and pink caterpillar slowly inching up her hand. She stared at it, pretending she wasn't listening to the monks arguing. They seldom quarreled, but for some reason they were concerned, and it was about her.

"She's too young, Abbott. We can't entrust this entire world to the hands of a mere child. Furthermore, you know where she comes from."

The Abbott stared across the garden at Kelsey and she pretended not to notice. "Her lineage plays a huge part in this. She is who she is and nothing we do can change that. But we can instruct her and guide her along this path to continually make the right choices. The child is strong of heart and mind. She's pure and noble. Furthermore, her mental transformations enable her to travel the celestial worlds quicker and faster than any others before her. Before even you, Tashi."

Tashi stared at Kelsey. "The danger is already here and must be addressed immediately. Raul and his men came again yesterday and threatened our brethren. He's going to threaten her, eventually. You know his quest is to find the land of myth, just like all the other glory seekers, but this one's different. There's the chance he's being influenced by Mara himself. You know that."

The Abbott nodded and pursed his lips. "Tashi, there is no one else here who can do what must be done. We must trust in the Americans. The Porters are good people. They're here to help us and will keep the secrets. But the child needs to be taught. There's the chance she can help them and we don't have the luxury of years to find someone of her caliber to train."

Tashi appealed to him. "Please, tell them to send the child back to America and let the parents bear the burden. Let's teach them instead. This journey is not for a little girl. She isn't strong enough, no matter what her spiritual lineage is. In this reality, she's but a vulnerable human child. Completely defenseless to what is possibly coming."

The Abbott shook his head. "She isn't defenseless. She has powers she doesn't understand and we'll do everything we can to protect her. If something happens, we'll do what must be done. I wish there was another way, but the choice is made."
He called over to Kelsey. "Child, come."

Kelsey raced over. "Yes, Abbott?"

"Are you enjoying your studies?"

Kelsey nodded.

"And enjoying the meditations?"

Again, Kelsey nodded enthusiastically.

The monk smiled. "It's time we learned how far you can go, little one. How would you like to travel to another world?"

Kelsey's eyes widened in surprise and she jumped up and down, clapping her hands.

The Abbott turned to Tashi. "Go get the other brothers and meet us in the inner sanctuary. It's time."

A chime sounded...

* * * * *

Kelsey opened her eyes and saw Desmond shaking his head, bewildered. She realized the monks had allowed him to see a shared memory. He looked at her quizzically, and she just imagined how he tried to rationalize her being both that child and the temptress Tanha.

Kelsey turned to the monks. "So you picked me to learn about Xanadu because you believed I was the reincarnation of Mara's daughter, Tanha? Why not kill me right then and there? How did you allow me to walk your hallways and teach me your disciplines? How could you even conceive of bringing me to Xanadu? It opens a direct gateway to Mara if I chose a different path."

"We chose you because you were the most brilliant student we'd ever encountered and because you had a soul, Kelsey. We could see your past lives and see how you've grown with each rebirth. You have been rejecting the sway of your father each and every lifetime. You've continually evolved, have chosen a better path and grown in each and every existence and we knew we could use it to our advantage."

Kelsey laughed, scorn edging her voice. "There's nothing in the scriptures saying Tanha ever rejected her father. You're reaching, Abbott."

"Scriptures don't always tell the true story, as you well know. Our sect is different than others. Most Buddhists believe in one ideology, but we have the knowledge and belief that they are all combined. And, as you know, monks have the unique ability to discern who are the reincarnations of past monks, and with that gift we can see the souls of others as well. When you first came to the monastery, there was utter shock and instant recognition of who you really were. Your abilities astounded us. You learned Tibetan in only months, memorized all the teachings, prayers and mantras within a year. People were drawn to you, even our own brothers who took vows of celibacy. They needed to be isolated from you, because even at your young age you pulled at them, swayed them and occupied their minds during meditation. Even Desmond. He joins you on this quest, not simply because you can help him find the murderer of his family, but because you entice him. And yet, while Tanha's influence consistently pushes you towards him, your own personal will continually rejects the attraction you obviously feel."

Kelsey felt the blood rushing to her face. "It's not true."

The Abbott waved his hand dismissively. "Of course it is, but you constantly fight with yourself not to give in. Tanha never would have curbed any opportunity for sensual satisfaction. She would have used him for her own needs without a care to how he felt and then she would have discarded him and found another to satisfy her lust. But you fight the attraction between the two of you because your inner soul is trying to reject her influence and subsequently, by rejecting her influence, you're ultimately challenging Mara and his authority over this plane of existence. You're unique in this world and we couldn't simply let you go without trying to help you."

"Help me? You used me and pushed my family towards something dangerous."

"Kelsey, you would have existed in this world whether we intervened or not. Would you rather have been helpless, once more without protection, when Mara sought you out to kill you? If we didn't intervene, you would have died on the floor of the hut with your dead mother's arms wrapped around you. Why not intervene and guide you? Help take you to the next level if that was your fate? Help you attain your true path?"

The monk clanged the chime. "What we just experienced was a shared memory. Now we'll go even further inside, to a deeper memory. Close your eyes, let your fingers flow and let us take you all the way back."

The monks started chanting again, the sound so impassioned and haunting it took Kelsey's breath away. Her mind was a mass of emotions, but she shut them down. Closing her eyes, she let her fingers fly on their own accord, up and down, up and down. It all was coming back to her. Things she had forgotten, things she thought she'd simply conjured as childhood fantasies. Feelings she had kept hidden and repressed. Everything felt as if the pieces from a missing puzzle were all finally joining together. She was Tanha, but other identities started to come back to her in flashes of insight. Names and faces so familiar to her. The dead girls from her dreams. They weren't symbols of her, they *were* her. She was Lilly, Sarah, Nadia and Sanzida. She was Leah, Tanisha, Qian and Fatima. She was a baby on her mother's breast. A toddler chasing a butterfly. A teenager on her first date. Then, the horrors came. Illnesses, murders and accidents. Each life cut short. Lifetimes after lifetime flashed in her mind until she was finally just Kelsey, here and now. The air around her became heavy and when the sound of a Tibetan long horn sounded, Kelsey's heart soared. It was the call of the dungchen, its droning wail resonating in her mind…yes, there was hope…but also so much more…

* * * * *

The three monks stood on the edge of the hill, watching Shingen and Kelsey on the small hill. Desmond stood behind them.

The pair held hands as they overlooked the valley below. Beyond them, across the vale, rose the city of Xanadu, glowing like a giant golden nugget. The garden glen they stood within was filled with flowers and hundreds of butterfly-like

243

creatures, with wispy, fluttery wings edged with cascading tendrils that looked like streamers during a holiday parade.

Kelsey laughed as they circled her head and gently tickled her chin. She clapped her hands and like a flock of birds, they took to the sky. She chased after them, running across the soft grass. Her feet were bare, her long hair untamed and cascading down her back. Kelsey glanced up, squealing with delight at the spectacle above her. "Look at the sky, Bantu Shingen!" Ribbons of pinks and yellows swirled overhead, moving lazily like a lava lamp. She cocked her head, her face curious. "Do you hear something? Like a thousand voices whispering?" She turned suddenly serious, her hands on her hips and her eyes squinting mischievously. "Where'd you take me, Teacher? This isn't like our other meditations. Did you put me to sleep and I'm dreaming?"

The monk with the kind eyes smiled down at her. "No, you're not dreaming. We've gone beyond mere meditation, Kelsey. We've traveled deep into your inner mind and have opened your psyche to a secret land we shall call Tedanalee. A wondrous land the monks have been bidden to protect."

"Protect? But, why? Is it in danger?"

"It is, child. We protect this place, because it's a world sacred to the very fabric of all human existence. This place is the basis of our religion. It's the place where death and rebirth come together. All of eternity meets in this plane when they die, determining their next samsara, their next rebirth on who and what they wish to be when they come back.

"Come with me and let me introduce you to it. There are people here, bodhisattvas and arhats, who would very much like to meet you." With that, he took the child's hand and together they walked down the small hill into the valley, on their way towards the monastery at the heart of Tedanalee -- of Xanadu.

244

The three monks and Desmond watched them move into the forest.

"How am I here with you, seeing this?" Desmond asked. He glanced at his clothing, noticing he wore the same clothes he had worn into the monastery. He peered around, secretly wishing to see Dorje.

The Abbott turned to him knowingly. "Your fedelia isn't here, Desmond. He's not even born yet. You're not actually in Xanadu right now, but deep within Kelsey's memory. Her first memory of Xanadu. We called it Tedanalee to keep it safe until she was older. And yes, we have astral projected you into it."

"I recognize that little girl. I… think I've seen her before."

The monk remained quiet.

One of the butterfly-like creatures floated towards Desmond and he raised his hand to the pink and green animal. It passed through his palm.

"We're not really here," Desmond remarked. It was true. He couldn't smell the scents of the hundreds of flowers filling the glen. He couldn't touch this world. "You've been using Kelsey all along, haven't you?" He felt his words flowing from him as if they were a powerful emotion, filling his mind along with the minds of the monks with him.

The Abbott nodded. "She'll know when she awakens that we used her, but it was for a noble cause. With each rebirth, her will has been in a constant struggle between the good and the evil which permeates it."

"And even so you wanted her?" Desmond asked. "Knowing where she came from?"

"If she can ignore the temptations of Mara just as Siddhartha did, she can succeed. The Emperor and Empress, who are really arhats, saw this potential in her and deemed

her soul worth fighting for. It's why they agreed to take her in and help her heal."

"And if the Emperor and Empress decided not to take her?"

The Abbott pursed his lips. "Then she would most likely have died in this lifetime to be reborn again. But now there's hope. Hope to conquer the beings coming from the lower levels to invade this world. Beings sent here by her own spiritual father, Mara."

"So what is this world?" Desmond asked. "Nirvana?"

The Abbott shook his head. "No, not Nirvana. It's one of the four bardos. The third one. The place where souls are reborn and vortices chosen. When people die, they come to this plane and decide what their next path is, what their next lifetime is going to be."

Desmond thought about that. "So it's a resting place?"

"Of sorts," the monk replied.

"And what would happen if Mara comes to this plane and attacks it?" Desmond asked.

The Abbott stared at him, his expression pained. "If this interval of existence is destroyed, no one will ever be able to choose their correct incarnation. They will all travel straight to the other five worlds, all of which are inferior to the physical world."

Desmond nodded in understanding, horror seeping into his thoughts. "I learned this," he whispered. "So, if this bardo is destroyed, you're saying no one will ever be able to create new Karma and all chances of spiritual growth or redemption, any chance of enlightenment for anyone, is destroyed with it?"

The Abbott nodded. "Yes. Dharmata, the essence of all things as they are, vanish not in the light of wisdom, but into nothingness. The Lord of Death will have won for eternity. There would be no physical rebirth for anyone, ever again. The human plane of existence will cease to exist and we will roam within the other five domains, the animal, the god, the hell planes, but never the human plane again. In essence, if Mara destroys this world, human beings as a species will simply disappear."

* * * * *

The chanting stopped and Kelsey opened her eyes, aware of everything. Her mind had been opened and she remembered all that had happened to her. Remembered her first visit to Tedanalee--to Xanadu. Remembered the daily trips the monks made with her to this world while they meditated. Remembered meeting the Emperor and Empress for the first time. The awed stares from the members of the court. She remembered everything with perfect clarity.

And now she was furious. She turned to the Abbott, livid. "Do you have any idea what it's been like for me to think at the very edge of my existence, there's a secret land I've visited in my dreams? One I thought was so real I suspected I was losing my mind? And then to think I was damaged because I kept dreaming about the hideous deaths of one girl after another? I believed a part of me was mentally ill and lived with this belief for twelve years. You never thought to tell me the truth and reveal what you were doing with me?"

The Abbott shook his head. "And what would you have done had you known the true nature of Xanadu or your spiritual path? Would you have believed it? Would it have changed anything?"

"It would have changed everything! I don't even know what these people are. Who are the Emperor and Empress, really? Enough deceit – tell me who they are!"

"They are spiritual practitioners called Arahants or Arhats. In different sects of Buddhism, they represent different things, but they are ultimately the protectors of the bardos who have chosen to dedicate themselves to defending the existence of the human realm rather than traveling to Nirvana. Much like bodhisattvas."

Liar. "They're not Arahants. Every text tells you Arahants don't feel things and these people do. The Emperor and Empress have strong emotions. They have cravings and desires just like the rest of us. They cared for me and were loving and kind. Again, you're reaching to make it sound convenient and fit the lies you tell."

"Kelsey, not everything in Buddhism is an absolute, nor is one sect of Buddhism the complete truth. The differences in Mahayana and Theravada regarding Arhats are as different as they are in the other sects as well. What people believe is dependent on which doctrine one chooses to follow, but here we follow them all and here we know the truths as they exist."

"Everything about you has been deceitful." She was so angry, she gripped her hands into fists until her knuckles were white. "And what about me being Tanha? You didn't see fit to share that bit of knowledge with me?"

"Better not to know so you could cope after your ordeal."

Kelsey turned on him. "My ordeal? How can you speak of it so blithely? You knew my family was in danger and you did nothing. Abbott, you let Raul murder my parents. You might as well have killed them yourself, because you knew he was coming for a year and you did nothing to protect any of us. You knew he was after me."

The Abbott shook his head. "That isn't true. We did try, but we were too late to help them." He rang the chime again, and relit the incense. "But we were in time to help you. Come, let us show you and you'll understand."

And back into time they went again…

Chapter 28

THE SCENE OF THE CRIME

The Abbott and the monks once more stood with Desmond, watching a vision unfold from the depths of Kelsey's memory. The scene before them was horrific and Desmond unconsciously moved forward to help, but the Abbott stayed him with his hand. "There's nothing you can do in this recollection of events, Desmond. This happened a long time ago. Kelsey is a figment of her past here. You can only help her by learning and watching. Each time we bring you back with her, your mind is opened a little bit more. Science is the basis for our beliefs and your brain has the capacity to change itself when it learns new functions and roles."

"You're talking neuroplasticity," Desmond said. "It's being written about now in scientific circles of how meditation can literally change the way your brain is wired."

"Scientists have fancy words for it, but it's all the same in the end. Just watch and you'll see that we've always been here to help her."

With a deep resolve, Desmond turned back to the tableau, determined to see what needed to be seen, but it was difficult.

He stood with the monks to the side of the hut. Kelsey's father, Benjamin, lay in a crumpled heap, his blood pooled on the ground beneath him. Her mother, Margaret, was on her knees, clutching her abdomen. Her face was a picture of agony.

Kelsey lay on the ground in the middle of it all, her naked body battered and bloody. She wasn't even crying, but wide-eyed in shock. Desmond saw her try to rise, yet couldn't. Both her arms and one of her legs were broken. A strangled, miserable cry escaped his throat.

He watched Margaret begin to crawl towards her daughter, holding onto her eviscerated stomach as she dragged herself forward, inch by inch. Her blood streaked and pooled behind her. When she finally got to her child, she bent down with a smile so radiant it could light up the sun, as if she'd not a care in the world, but there only to bring happiness and comfort to her daughter. She wrapped her arms around Kelsey and together they lay there for hours, until Margaret passed away, though in Desmond's timeline it seemed mere minutes.

"Now watch," the Abbott said.

Out of the woods a congregation of battered and bloody monks raced into the clearing. They stood next to Kelsey and her family, their faces torn by sorrow.

"We're too late!" one of the monks yelled, throwing himself to the ground and sobbing. A cut stretched from his forehead and down his cheek. The blood streaked down his robe.

Bantu Shingen limped forward and kneeled next to Kelsey and Margaret. His eyes brimmed with tears, mixing with the blood and dirt staining his face. Raul and his men had raided the monastery. The monks had fought hard, but at a price. After they'd taken care of their brethren, they realized the threat must have moved to the Porters. They scrambled to their hut, but it was a mile hike through rough terrain and they were all injured. They hadn't arrived in time.

Shingen placed his hand on Kelsey's heart and looked at the others, hope in his eyes. "She's still alive. He didn't kill her."

Shojuharu stepped forward, nodding. "And now they have the map. They think it's all they'll need. We're fortunate they don't know the truth and the extent of our diversion. Come, there's no more time. We must take her to Xanadu. The Arahants will protect her."

Bantu Shingen stared up at him, horrified. "Take her to Xanadu now? She's critically wounded and needs medical care here in this world, Shojuharu. We can't just leave her lying in the dirt. She's not some princess of the Underworld, but a mere human child!"

Another monk stepped forward, placing his hand gently on Shingen's arm. "And how do you propose we get her to the local hospital, Shingen? Carry her the two day journey on our shoulders? Mara's minions slaughtered our horses and destroyed our vehicles and even if we somehow were able to get her there by walking ourselves, she'd probably die along the journey. Mara will have won again. Look at her. If we take her to Xanadu now we can put her body on this plane in stasis. By taking her to Xanadu, we can slow down her physical process here and give her people time to come for her. She'll be uninjured in Xanadu and it will give the Arahants the ability to work with her."

Shingen shook his head, uncomprehendingly. "But who will come for her now that her parents are gone?"

Shojuharu's eyes alighted on the transmitter in the corner of the hut and moved over to it. "Benjamin told me often he speaks regularly to his good friends, the Goldmans. He showed me how this works when I visited him a few months back." He picked up the receiver, punched in a number listed on the side and after a few more seconds, started speaking. Eventually, he hung up the phone and moved quickly back to the group.

"Help is coming, but it will take time. Let's do what we can for her now until they arrive. Let's do what we can for all of us."

After covering Kelsey with blankets to keep her warm, the ten battered and weary men encircled her and her mother, sat down, crossed their legs and began to move their fingers in the age old dance. They began to chant. Their voices echoed across the valley until soon the very air began to shimmer in front of them. On and on they chanted, until they suddenly stopped. It appeared as if they all had stilled, as if they had become frozen in time. If a person had come upon the scene, he would have been confused. Ten silent and unmoving monks encircling a horrific murder scene. But if he could see behind their eyes. See where they went...

* * * * *

Desmond watched, alone, from the edge of the glen as a new scene unfolded before him...

Bantu Shingen held Kelsey tightly while she sobbed hysterically for her mother. He watched the sky, waiting for a response to their call. It was early evening in Xanadu, the heavens darkening and thick with deep purple and blue green ribbons, but still light enough to see the army of winged creatures flying to meet them. Like a flock of birds, they streaked in a brilliant pattern, edging closer until they surrounded them in the glen where they stood. Creatures of mammoth size spread and shook their glorious wings in a tremendous roar, as their soldiers jumped to their sides.

A man and woman leaped off their magnificent steeds and marched towards them. They were regal and ageless, their beauty only marred by the ancient expressions in their eyes.

The woman moved forward. She was slight and her amethyst-colored robes flowed around her as she walked. Her jet-black hair cascaded down her back and was pinned with diamonds and other precious gems--as if they were nothing more than mere trinkets. The monks bowed low, but she only had eyes for Kelsey. Her expression held a mixture of emotions ranging from horror and fear, to awe and reverence. She turned to her companion, nodding, and he stared back at her.

"Are you sure?" he asked.

She beckoned him forward with her hand. "Can't you see it? Feel it? She's back again."

The man moved forward and stood before Shingen, staring down at the sobbing child. Tall by human standards, massive and strong, he dwarfed the monk.

"Kelsey," he said. "Look at me."

Startled, she glanced up with her red-rimmed eyes and stared into his face. The man flinched ever so slightly.

The little girl hiccupped. "Are you... an... Emperor?"

The man nodded. "If that's what you wish to call me."

Kelsey started crying again, and buried her face back into Shingen's chest.

The man glanced at his partner. "It's her, and her powers have grown. It's very clear her path changed again. She continues to fight against her urges and she's stronger than ever before. Mara failed this time."

Shojuharu found his voice, and bowed before them. "She's severely injured in our physical realm. We brought her here to you in hopes to save her."

The female Arahant turned to the monk. "We know what happened, Shojuharu. Give her to us and we'll care for her. It's her soul that needs saving this time."

The man stepped forward, and gently took Kelsey from Shingen. She was like a doll in his arms. In one swift motion, he returned to his steed and jumped on while his mate flew to her own mare. With a call, the Arahants and their army took to the sky, flying back to the monastery at the heart of Xanadu.

The monks watched until they had disappeared from view and then Shingen turned to Shojuharu. "I hope this was the right thing to do. We've removed her from her reality and here she'll remain. She may not be strong enough to come back. For that matter, what if she chooses to stay?"

"Our world will beckon to her, Shingen. She'll come back when she's ready." Shojuharu nodded, convincing himself. "And when she does, we'll continue to teach her and protect her, no matter where she is. In the meantime, we must fight the blackness until we can't fight it any longer."

Shingen shook his head, his voice bitter. "You mean until Kelsey fights it for us."

"Only time will tell, brother. We've made a vow to protect her and our order protects Xanadu. We're on our own mental continuum to keep that promise." He stared out across the glen at the city of Xanadu. The lights in the temple's windows sparkled in the night sky. "Come. There's nothing else for us to do there until she returns to our world. What will be, will be."

With that, they closed their eyes and disappeared.

* * * * *

Kelsey opened her eyes. "You brought me to Xanadu."

The Abbott shook his head. "Not I, child. Shojuharu and Shingen and the other monks took you. They only wanted to protect you. The reason we never said anything is because we didn't want to call Raul's attention to you. He had thought he killed you and he was now spending his life seeking out the monks at all the other monasteries to decipher the map. For the moment, you were safe in his ignorance of your true fate."

"So you believe he's Mara's minion, brought here to murder me? To finish what he started?"

The Abbott nodded. "I do. Raul searched for members of our sect throughout the world in his efforts to destroy Xanadu at the wishes of his master. We scattered, trying to protect the secret, but he kept finding us and attacking us. We never contacted you directly for fear he was watching, so instead, we kept our distance. But we still needed to teach you so we astral projected ourselves into your dreams to continue your lessons. It was the only way to bring you deeper into your inner self and take you to Xanadu where you could grow and learn and become an integral part of that world. To help you see the true Clear Light and way of the path, yet protect you at the same time. If your own spiritual father tried to kill you hundreds of times before for rejecting his ways, we had to find another way to let you live and grow without his constant influence. We wanted to keep you hidden without calling more attention to you. To spare you the horror of reliving your attack again."

Kelsey shook her head. "I think it's more than that. You knew I would hate this man. Maybe you thought I would bring Raul there and that I would do something to hurt Xanadu."

The other monks bowed their heads. "We knew your hatred of Raul would be one of the defining things in this lifetime and if we said you needed to protect this world from him, it would possibly hurt your path in this life. Sometimes knowledge isn't always the best thing to have. By telling you all this history too early, we believed it would influence you and sway your destiny. We just didn't want to stop your spiritual growth."

Kelsey stood up, incredulous. "Stop my spiritual growth? Sway my destiny? Are you actually still worried about my samsara? Trust me, I'm definitely not ascending to any higher level in this lifetime, Abbott. Do you have any idea what horrors I've committed redeeming myself and my family? I'm lucky I don't come back as a roach scavenging for food in the depths of the New York City subway system or living in the Arbuda Naraka hell plane, naked in a frozen wasteland with oozing blisters covering my body for the next hundred thousand years."

Desmond spoke up. "Kelsey, please."

She turned on him. "No, Desmond. I've been a pawn my entire life for these people, because they think I'm the descendant of an evil temptress who happens to be the daughter to the Buddhist equivalent of Satan. My parents died for those beliefs and I've killed many people because of it. My samsara is already set."

"Kelsey, we were only trying to save your soul," the Abbott said.

I'm disgusted by all of you. "You shouldn't have spent any time worrying about it. I've created my own fate. You were worried about my karma? Well, let me tell you something. I've killed nearly every person who was part of that night. I murdered them, stole from them, did everything Buddhism finds reprehensible and I haven't lost one single night's sleep about it. In fact, I enjoyed every moment of it."

"That's Tanha's influence on you."

Kelsey pounded her chest. "No! That's my influence on me! You want to talk about the three poisons and how they lead to evil and suffering? Well, Raul had greed, had hatred and was ignorant. I'm not. But there was no way I wasn't going to avenge my family. And yet you still think I'm needed in Xanadu to fight some sort of battle that's coming down? You think I should fight alongside bodhisattvas and arahants after what I've done? You live and breathe this world, travel to it, protect it, yet, do you even know what exactly is supposed to be coming there to threaten them? Is it Mara?"

"It could be Mara or his minions, or something else entirely," the Abbott said. "But I can guarantee you it's something evil that is going to try to destroy that realm."

She crossed her arms, her voice suddenly very cold. "Maybe the evil is me. You ever think of that, Abbott?"

"Kelsey, it isn't you. I promise you that."

She cocked her head. "But you don't know for sure now, do you?" She stared around at the other monks. "Do any of you know for sure? Maybe my spiritual father's influence has been stronger in this lifetime. Maybe I came once to tempt Siddhartha, and now I'm coming again to help destroy all that's left of humanity once and for all. Maybe it was our evil master plan all along."

"Kelsey, come on. Stop it," Desmond said.

She stared at the monks, but no one said anything.

"You don't know what to say, do you, because none of you have an answer? I'm done here." She turned towards the door.

The Abbott appealed to her. "Kelsey, please! You can't just leave those in Xanadu unprotected when you have the power to save them."

She shook her head in amazement. "And just what do you expect me to do? I'm only one person. A human person, Abbott. Nothing more, nothing less. And for that matter, they are dream people to me. They're not even in this reality."

"But they are real and you must help us. It's your duty. It's the least you can do."

She glared at him. "The least I can do? My duty? Listen to me. You may have been bidden to protect Xanadu, but all of you had a responsibility to protect me as well. That was your duty and you failed miserably. Instead, you let Raul and his men kill my parents, let him abuse me and left me in ignorance for many, many years. Those are your own poisons you'll have to bear."

She turned to leave the room, and then glanced back, her eyebrows raised questioningly. "Desmond, are you coming with me or not?"

He jumped up and followed her. "Where we going, Kelsey?"

She turned to him, ignoring the monks behind her, her voice low. "I figure we're going to go find Xanadu."

He leaned towards her. "You know how to get there?"

She nodded. "Apparently, I've known all along. The map is going to bring us right to one of the portals. Right to where a set of devas might be. We'll figure it out as we go along. Come on, we have a long walk ahead of us."

Chapter 29

BACK TO WHERE IT ALL BEGAN

Desmond and Kelsey moved through the worn trail, their guns drawn and ready. Raul could be anywhere, waiting to make his move, but they didn't think he'd shoot Kelsey. He didn't know how to get to Xanadu and he needed her, if only for a little while. Desmond, on the other hand, was expendable.

The trail was barely visible through the undergrowth, but even after all these years, Kelsey knew it well. She'd traveled this path daily for nearly two years.

They circled a stand of rocks and slid down a slight ravine. At its base, with the mountains stretching magnificently above them, was a clearing and within the clearing was the remains of a small building.

I can't believe I'm back here. Mom and Dad, I miss you so much. Kelsey stood there for a long time, just staring at the pitiful structure. The sadness nearly overwhelmed her. The hut's walls had caved in and in the twelve years since, the forest had reclaimed much of it, but she could still tell it had once been a home. With a deep resolve, she walked towards it and stepped inside.

She turned to the first room, kicking aside decaying tree branches and dead leaves and stared at a small object resting within the springs of an old, rusty bed. The bedding was nothing more than strips of cloth, the decrepit mattress riddled with holes from burrowing animals and insects. Kelsey bent down and picked up the object, turning it in her hands. A sigh escaped her.

"What is it?" Desmond asked, moving to her side.

She held it up. "A doll Bantu Shingen had given me." The wooden face was a blank, rotting surface as the paint had ebbed away over the years. The clothing was nothing more than a strand of string and the rest of the wood frame was warped and wet. She laid it back on the bed and moved out into the rest of the home.

Kelsey stood in the middle room, the sky open above them and stared at the ground. Desmond recognized where he was. They stood right in the very spot where Kelsey and her parents had been attacked. The blood stains were long gone, but he was sure nothing could get rid of the stains in her heart.

Kelsey holstered her gun. She took out the map and opened it up. "You see this line written on this margin?"

Desmond nodded. "What does it say?"

"It says 'the path starts from where the mind is opened'. I think it means there's always a portal or a way in once you know where to look."

Desmond thought about that. "Kelsey, when we were under the monks influence, they said the map was a diversion. What if nothing on this map is real?"

She pursed her lips. "It's possible, but then why make this map the burning goal of my father? Why reward him with this, unless…" She paused and squinted, as if in pain. *Oh God, no.*

Desmond gently touched her arm in understanding. "Unless the map truly meant nothing and they toyed him with it to keep you in Tibet." He let that thought hang in the air. It felt too true. Horribly true. "And, it also offered a layer of protection for the monks if the map got into the wrong hands."

Kelsey rubbed her temples. *Everything to protect them. The monks, the beings in Xanadu.* "Where was my protection, Desmond? Where was the protection for my parents?" She stared at the map again. "Maybe there's more to this. Maybe the true path to Xanadu is anywhere the mind is opened. Maybe people themselves are the portals. In Colombia, the monks took us to Xanadu. Here, the monks from the monastery brought us."

"But you took us as well on the train, Kelsey."

"Yes, I did."

"Then I guess you're a portal, too."

She shook the map angrily. "So this means nothing? My parents died for nothing?"

A gunshot startled them both and with a grunt, Desmond fell.

Kelsey dropped the map and reached for him, but more gunfire erupted. She threw herself to the ground and her holster snapped and broke off. Her weapon tumbled away from her.

Raul loped into the clearing. A bloody gauze wrapped his arm and another fluttered uselessly on his leg. His pants were unzipped and his shirt was unbuttoned. He wore no jacket, though the temperature was close to freezing. In his state, he didn't seem to mind. He trained his gun on Kelsey as he lurched forwards.

She turned to Desmond. His leg bled profusely.

"I've got her! I've got her!" Raul screamed to no one in particular. He raised his pistol.

Kelsey closed her eyes and started moving her fingers... she had just seconds.

"Kelsey, there's no time. Get away from here!" Desmond yelled, watching Raul jerk his finger, a maniacal smile trained on his face. At the very moment he was about to fire, the air around them shimmered and Raul glanced up, the shot going wild.

They disappeared.

Chapter 30

THE BATTLE

Kelsey fell to the ground with a jolt, the grass doing nothing to soften the blow. As she lay there, momentarily stunned, she heard multiple long horns wailing fiercely in the distance.

"Kelsey!" Desmond burst from the forest and into the clearing. "We're here. You've brought us here again." He was no longer bleeding, but whole and healthy.

Kelsey glanced up, fear flooding her heart. "If I've brought you, then I could have brought him, too. Where is he?" She flew to her feet, her sword drawn.

Desmond glanced at the sky, horrified. "Oh, my God. Look!"

The heavens were filled with black, spidery streaks. The lines pierced through the aurora borealis ribbons, etching themselves like patches of blood oozing across the sky.

The horns sounded again, calling the land to arms.

Kelsey put her hands to either side of her mouth. "Ishu! To me! To me!" In a flurry of wings, Ishu descended into the glen alighting next to Kelsey and she jumped on. The creature whinnied and reared back to take off, itching to fly.

"Desmond, call Dorje, now!"

Desmond glanced up, but Dorje already flew across the expanse. The air shook with the thunderous fluttering of his massive wings as he landed next to them, whipping them about. Desmond jumped onto him and they took to the air, flying towards the monastery, along with the other riders.

An ominous noise like a million pieces of glass shattering sounded as part of the sky broke away from the spidery streaks and opened. A gaping hole, like a cavernous mouth, widened. Thousands of daggers shot out of it, piercing the warriors and their steeds and sent them plummeting to the ground.

Kelsey and Desmond reared back and away from the void. "Evade them, Desmond! Fly away from the opening."

Kelsey glanced into the void that lay beyond the open wound in the sky, knowing now what lurked within. A hell plane she herself had once come from and had tried desperately to escape. A physical pain stabbed in her chest, but she ignored it, knowing now what it was. Her only goal was to get to the temple.

They flew directly into the inner court where hundreds of warriors and their steeds surrounded the pavilion. The Arahants, her Emperor and Empress, rushed to the front of the group, their eyes searching and seeking. They found Kelsey and she ran to them, embracing them in a fierce hug.

"I'm so sorry. It was me all along. Me bringing them here to Xanadu."

The Emperor shook his head, vehemently in denial. "Listen to me. We knew he would have come eventually. This is the path this lifetime has led us and we must end this cycle of death here and now." The Emperor stared at the sky and drew his sword. "They come! To arms!"

Another terrible rendering sounded, like a metal car being ripped in half. Thousands of monster demons on winged beasts streaked through the gaping hole, like ants pouring from an anthill. Kelsey recognized Raul, with his head sitting atop a hideously deformed mount, a maniacal smile plastered on his face. While the other riders took to the sky, their fedelias, fearless as they met the demon creatures head on,

Kelsey stood her ground, watching and waiting for Raul to come meet her. The shrieks and cries of the battle echoed throughout the land. She now knew who all these people were in Xanadu. They were all protectors of humanity, and so was she. Trained for this very moment.

Come to me. Raul flew towards her, his sword slicing through the air. Kelsey met him, ducking his blow, and rearing back, spun her body around to slash her sword right through his neck. His head rolled off his body and fell to the ground where he exploded into ashes.

With no time to think, she turned to Desmond who battled a beast with the head of a falcon and the body of a grotesque, naked woman. Kelsey ran towards it and plunged her weapon into the demon's side, its banshee-like death shrieks painful to her ears. The air was filled with screams. More and more hideous beasts poured out of the void and flew towards the pavilion.

"Kelsey!" The Empress ran to her. She bled from a scalp wound. "You must shut the gap." One of the monsters grabbed the Empress, its talons pushing her towards its yawning, reptilian mouth. An arrow flew through the air and the monster dropped in a crumpled heap as the Empress freed herself from its embrace.

Kelsey turned to see from where the arrow had flown. She saw Desmond, his face set in an expression she'd never seen before. Deadly serious, his eyes blazed with intensity. His body radiated power, and confidence oozed from him. Again and again, he drew his arrows, setting them towards his targets, his aim true.

"Desmond?"

"I'll cover you, Kelsey. Close the gap." He shot another arrow and another minion fell to the ground.

Kelsey turned towards the front of the pavilion, desperately searching the sky for a way to shut the hole, but she didn't know how. More monsters tumbled through the opening. More than they could possibly handle. There weren't enough warriors to fight them all off. Shrieks from the other fighters chilled her soul as she saw countless men and women falling from their fedelias to land in sickening, growing heaps on the ground.

She had one idea, desperately hoping it would work. *I've got to get control.* She scanned the pavilion, searching for Desmond. Sprinting to him, she grabbed his hand. "Come with me!" She pulled him to the temple's side wall, where for the moment, they were hidden.

"Kelsey, what are we doing? We have to fight."

"I'm ending this right now. He wants to kill me? Then let the coward come get me himself instead of sending his minions. Now, hold onto my wrists and don't let go. I need your karmic powers. Fate has linked us together somehow and I need to use that."

As Desmond gripped her wrists, Kelsey closed her eyes, ignoring the assault going on around her. She closed her ears to the cries of death that riddled the land, closed out all of it and brought her thoughts deep. "Come with me, Desmond," she whispered. She started moving her fingers. Up and down, up and down. The sounds of the battle slowly faded away as the power of the meditation took over. Down through the centuries she plummeted, living life after short life in mere seconds, down and down until she was finally at the base of her father's feet, staring at him and telling him she was leaving.

* * * * *

ELYSE SALPETER

The Kamaloka Palace in the Naraka Hell Plane

Dancers moved throughout the hall, gyrating to music being played by minstrels, but pain seeped through their strained smiles as they swayed to the melodies. Each step made them wince as the feel of knives pierced their skin with each footfall. More than one glanced down now and again to see if the floor was covered with their blood.

As the musicians stroked their violins and blew into their flutes, blisters continuously erupted on their fingers and lips. A mixture of blood and pus oozed down their hands and faces and onto their instruments, collecting in pools on the floor. Still they played on, never stopping.

The Master's slaves moved through the room, each with their own burdens to bear. Some blindly scuffled along the floor with rags, cleaning up the bloody secretions of the minstrels, while others carried heavy loads of food on their crippled shoulders, only to move them from one table to another, over and over for centuries on end. Still others cared for their master's pet kravyadas, ruru animals, who tore at them and ripped at their flesh.

Mara's minions, those deemed close enough to mingle with their master, sat on couches and coupled with those around them, but their lovemaking was frenzied and unsatisfying, never reaching any plateau of satisfaction. Each being in this hell plane, in Naraka, had their own burden to bear, each their own punishment.

Mara lounged on a red velvet throne, one leg thrown over the gold plaited arm as he patted the hair of a slave at his feet--a timid, naked girl, who shivered uncontrollably from the ice pillow she lay upon.

Tanha approached him, stepping casually over a screaming man who writhed on the ground, while a guard

266

pierced his body with fiery spears. She gave her father a scornful look, ready to start the argument again.

Mara stared at his oldest daughter with a mixture of anger and amused disbelief. "This again? What do you mean, you want to leave? And where do you intend to go?"

Tanha eyed him, her thick black hair cascading in waves down her back. She radiated such desire that the minions kept glancing in her direction because of her pull on their very being. Their want and need for her tore at them.

"I told you this already, Father. I want to go live in the human realm."

Mara laughed derisively, and the sound echoed throughout the hall. The dancers ceased swaying for a moment.

"Continue!" Mara ordered, while guards whipped the girls into obedience, their struggled dance resuming again. He turned back to Tanha. "You think by moving to the human domain you'll be free of me? No matter what you do, you can't ever leave me, Daughter. I'll always be here. I'm alive in every single man in existence, as are you. You're 'Desire', the kilesa, which defiles every man's body. You can never escape that. It's who you are, what your essence is and no matter where you reside, it's a part of you."

Tanha frowned. "Even humans don't remain in our domains forever, Father. Once their negative karma is used up they can move on to the other levels. Why can't I? There must be more than this. I'm more than just a sexual vessel. I feel it."

Mara shook his head in disgust. "Why would you want more than the perfection of who you are and what you have here? I let you rule the Desire kingdom and you wish to throw it away as if it means nothing? Look around at the life of luxury you lead. Any desire you have, any need and craving and it's yours. You want for nothing here. I'm telling you this,

Tanha, if you leave you'll never have the peace and enlightenment you seek. Your very being won't allow it. Every man who sees you will fall at your feet. They will crave and desire you, not even knowing why. No human will ever be true to you, because they'll only be influenced by who and what you are. Your essence stains your soul and no matter what you do, or how many lifetimes you try to live, you will never be able to escape your lineage."

Tanha removed a strand of exquisite black and pink pearls twisted in her hair and laid her father's gift at his feet.

Mara glared at her. "You leave and I promise I'll destroy you in every lifetime you try to lead. Don't challenge me, Daughter."

Tanha turned to her beautiful sisters sitting intertwined on the divan next to her while naked slaves brushed their hair and massaged essential oils onto their already silky skin.

"Will you join me, sisters?"

Their expressions were patronizing. "We know who and what we are, Tanha. Accept it."

Tanha shook her head and turned back to her father.

"Well? What's your decision?" he asked.

With a smirk, Tanha turned on her heel and left the hell kingdom behind her, the furious bellows of her father resonating through all the thirty-one realms.

* * * * *

Desmond yelled, releasing Kelsey's burning wrists. He stared at her, seeing her for the first time. Who she really was.

Rising, Kelsey stared into Desmond's eyes. "I know who and what I am and know what I can do." She moved back into the pavilion, power radiating from her skin. She turned her face to the sky. "Come and get me, Father!" Her voice boomed across the battlefield, magnified a thousand fold.

A thunderous roar rocked the heavens as an immense beast tore through the opening. Riding a winged, multi-horned elephant, and he, having a thousand arms, Mara streaked across the land towards Kelsey.

Yes, I know you well, Father. She ran to the clearing, her sword drawn to meet him head on.

Other demons tried to attack her and their own master struck them down with his arrows. "Leave her! She's mine!"

Desmond darted in front of her, but Kelsey pushed him back. "No! Get back. This is my fight."

At the very moment Mara was about to strike his daughter down with the thousands of weapons he held in his arms, the brightest of lights shot out from the cavernous hole. Kelsey froze. A voice echoed to her.

"Child, be like Siddhartha. Call on the Earth Goddess."

Yes, the Earth Goddess! Kelsey raised her hands to the sky and screamed, "Phra Mae Thoranee, I beseech to you! I bear your witness!"

The Earth Goddess sprung from the firmament, towering over the land. She released her enormous mane of hair. A torrent of water flowed from her body, flooding the planes and drowning the monsters fighting below.

Mara laughed, scornfully. "A pretty little trick, but it won't help. You can bear as much witness as you want, Tanha, but you're no Siddhartha."

Another voice echoed across the land, coming from the very air she breathed. *"It's never too late, child. Awaken to the truth. He can't touch you any longer. He can't hurt you or hold sway over you. He has no more hold on your soul. Awake my child and you'll be released. Just like me."*

Siddhartha... Her mind opened, understanding of all things flooded her brain and her essence. With an unnatural calm, Kelsey turned to her triumphant father, watching as he made to strike her down, but he suddenly hesitated. The look in her eyes told him all he needed to know.

"No!" he shrieked. "I won't succumb!" Mara drew his arrows, prepared to fire, but Kelsey dropped her sword.

Desmond ran to her, shaking her. "Kelsey, protect yourself! He's going to kill you!" He drew his sword and faced Mara.

Kelsey shook her head, a strange, wistful smile on her face. "Don't fight, Desmond. Be like Siddhartha." She called out, her voice echoing, resonating throughout the land to her warriors. "Drop your weapons! We don't need to fight any longer. Remember who and what we are. We are protectors of this land who have forsaken all to protect this realm. Awaken! Be like Siddhartha and we will be released from fear. He can't touch us if we believe!"

With a belief and faith so powerful no other words needed to be spoken, the thousands of warriors of Xanadu instantly dropped their weapons, letting the demons attack them. Desmond dropped his own sword and with a desperate look at Kelsey, stood silently next to her.

Mara mocked her. "It won't work, Tanha. You're no Buddha. You have sent everyone to their deaths and killed humanity." With that he sent a thousand arrows into the heart of his child.

As each of them touched her, they transformed into flowers.

"No!" Mara screamed. Hundreds upon hundreds of fiery gashes and slash marks began shredding his body, as if each fired arrow had been a knife point piercing his own skin. Smoke and fire poured from his mouth.

Throughout the land, the demon's victorious shrieks were replaced with horrendous cries of pain as one by one they transformed first into flames, and then into flowers.

His body dripping with blood and gore, Mara leaned forwards and grabbed Kelsey. Holding her in his pincer-like grip, she only smiled at him, her expression peaceful. "It's over, Father. I don't fear you any longer. You have no hold over me, or anyone else in this realm. I'm finally free of you. Go back to your domain. You have no power here."

With a hideous howl that echoed across the valley, Mara exploded into a million bloody shards, his own soul shooting back towards the gap, along with all the thousands of other beasts he'd brought with him.

In mere seconds, the battle was over. The remaining members of Xanadu stood by silently watching the last of the demons disappear. The spidery streaks of blackness evaporated from the heavens as the gap closed, leaving colorful ribbons of pinks and greens rippling gently across the sky.

And the entire land was perfumed with rose scented petals.

Epilogue

ONE MONTH LATER

They strolled hand in hand through the ancient stone courtyard. The walkway was strewn with flowers and had magnificent views of the Piazza San Marco and its vast lagoon. The hotel was decadent and stunning with its two 15th century buildings linked together via a floral-scented passageway.

It had been a wonderful day. They visited castles and museums, had dinner at a lovely little bistro and an after dinner Bellini at the infamous Henry's Bar. After a short boat ride back from St. Marks, where they stared at the stars in the night sky, they finally arrived at their exquisitely decorated hotel suite.

Kelsey stood on the balcony that looked out at the open lagoon. She felt Desmond behind her and her stomach tingled in anticipation. He'd been so chaste with her the entire trip, trying hard to make sure he did everything just right.

After the battle in Xanadu, she awoke in the monastery. She explained to the monks what had transpired and then became a fixture at Desmond's side. The monks had bandaged his leg and a doctor from town was on the way to treat him. Neither of them asked what had become of Raul and the monks never shared that bit of information with them.

Kelsey was revered now by the monks, by the arahants in Xanadu and by all the members of the court. Her sacrifice over the centuries and the defeat of her father had made her a true Buddha, but she wanted none of it, only wishing to finally live a full life on the human plane and take whatever the fates had in store for her--just like everyone else. For the first time in her eternity, her destiny was her own to live. Mara could no longer touch her.

Desmond's voice was soft as he caressed her cheek. "This is how it should have happened with us the first time." He leaned in and kissed her softly on the lips. The first time he had kissed her since the Garter's fiasco in Miami.

She sighed contentedly and wrapped her arms around his neck.

For the hundredth time, she wondered at her good fortune. Her life had finally come full circle. She had avenged the deaths of her parents, she had saved humanity… but more importantly, she had saved her own soul. She knew who she once was and who she was now and she no longer felt torn. Now she could just be who she wanted to be and she was content to let her feelings and desires lead her, no longer conflicted. It was the most free she had ever been.

Desmond whispered in her ear. *"Ti Fasalati titidalaah tam, wihalatkla."* He flinched and his eyes widened in surprise.

A flush rushed to Kelsey's cheeks. "You're falling in love with me? How did you know how to say that?"

"I… I don't know, Kelsey. It just… came to me." He gently ran his lips against her neck and then with a swift motion, picked her up, and laid her on the bed.

"Ti titidalaah aha, titlashaphah," she breathed. (I love you too, my Light.)

As he covered her mouth with his, neither of them noticed the air begin to shimmer around them or the sound of a lone dungchen as it tolled its haunting wail through the open window.

The End